DANGEROUS TO KNOW

Colin Grainger's ex-wife Moira left him not because she no longer loved him, but because she was fed up with scraping a living in poky bedsits. Now a high-flying policewoman, happily involved with a fellow officer, she still sees Colin from time to time. Colin calls Moira because he has unwittingly stumbled across a major fraud on the internet, and he is convinced he knows the perpetrator, Charlie Radcliffe. Moira promises to make some off the record enquiries ... two days later she is dead – and Colin's investigation is drawing him ever deeper into a dark world of terror.

DANGEROUS TO KNOW

DANGEROUS
TO KNOW

by

Jane Adams

Magna Large Print Books
Long Preston, North Yorkshire,
BD23 4ND, England.

British Library Cataloguing in Publication Data.

Adams, Jane
    Dangerous to know.

    A catalogue record of this book is
    available from the British Library

    ISBN   0-7505-2248-8

First published in Great Britain 2004 by Allison & Busby Ltd.

Copyright © 2004 by Jane Adams

Cover illustration © The Old Tin Dog

The right of Jane Adams to be identified as the author of this work has been asserted by her in accordance with the Copyright, Designs and Patents Act, 1988

Published in Large Print 2004 by arrangement with Allison & Busby Ltd.

Magna Large Print is an imprint of Library Magna Books Ltd.

Printed and bound in Great Britain by
T.J. (International) Ltd., Cornwall, PL28 8RW

Prologue

It was a good day for a funeral. Grey, glowering skies dipped towards a bruised horizon and intermittent rain drizzled on the gathering.

He'd never been to a burial service before. His previous brush with funerary ritual had been cremations, the coffin lowered on a catafalque or drawn softly through a veil of curtains and the process that followed somehow less real for being less visible. And for this to be *her* funeral made it doubly hard. The memories flooded his eyes and turned to tears that he hid as best he could, keeping his head bowed against the light rain and his gaze fixed upon that yawning black chasm into which the coffin – and a good chunk of Colin himself – would soon be lowered.

Across from him stood Moira's parents, mother weeping, father staring stonily at the distant horizon, his eyes as grey and bruised as the heavy clouds. Beside them stood John Moore and, Colin noted, he even had his arm around Moira's mother, offering the comfort that Colin still felt should have been his to offer. John, new lover, friend, the third chief mourner in this tableau while Colin, who had shared Moira's life for almost seven years. Who'd loved her, could still taste her lips, catch the clean scent of her hair against his pillow on waking. Know the feel of her skin beneath his fingers just as he had when she had slept beside him. He was cast aside.

He could hear her laughter now, her voice in the rising wind, so clear and composed he almost looked around to find her there. The thought of all of that now dead and gone, rotting already in the brass-handled coffin, was more than he could bear. That, and his gentle but hurtful exclusion. His presence acknowledged briefly, but then ignored.

There were no flowers, by request of the family. Donations only to some Police charity or another, but Colin held a single, yellow rose in his cold, sweat skinned hand. Moira had hated the long stemmed florists roses, scentless and overbred and Colin had searched far and wide in the wintry, unready gardens of his neighbours, to find a single late but fragrant bloom. He felt chilled to the bone and the wind and rain had nothing to do with it. Guilt curled its fingers around his heart and was squeezing the life from it, killing him, just as surely as his actions had killed Moira.

He looked up, suddenly aware that the crowd about the grave had started to disperse. Civilian and uniform, pausing to shake the hands of grieving parents, say their words of brief condolence, walk slowly away from the dead place and back onto the living streets. John Moore met his gaze, Colin startled momentarily out of his own despair by the bleak, dry grief that showed in the other's eyes. For a brief instant, John gathered Moira's mother into his arms, kissed her gently on the cheek, then shook hands with the father, checking that they would be taken home and promising to join them for the wake as soon as he could. Colin, standing on the other side of the open grave, received from them the briefest of looks, the smallest of understanding smiles before they moved away. He devoured that smile, grateful even of the crumbs from the grieving table. Then he leaned forward and gently, carefully placed the single rose upon the coffin before he walked away.

John Moore caught up with him a few steps later.

'You're not off the hook, you know.'

'Oh, and what hook might that be?'

'Don't play bloody games with me, Colin Grainger. You know what I think of you. You had a hand in this. I'll bet my bloody career on it.'

Colin turned to stare at him. 'You think I'd harm a hair on her head?' he demanded.

'Hell, man, you loved her as much as I did. And I *did* love her, even you have to acknowledge that. *You'd* hurt her, would you? Put her in harm's way? No,' he answered himself, looking at the circles beneath John's eyes and the puffy flesh of an otherwise handsome face. 'You wouldn't deliberately do that and neither would I.'

'Far as the force is concerned, she died in the line of duty,' John Moore said heavily. 'But you know more about what she was doing than you're letting on, Colin Grainger. And I'll get it out of you. Bloody last thing I do, I will.'

'Pity you weren't close enough for her to confide in you,' Colin blasted back at him. 'Have a sharing relationship did you, John, or should I say, Inspector? Call you "sir" in bed did she?' He began to turn away, but Moore's fist made contact with his jaw and Colin went down, grabbing at Moore's arm as he fell. Moments later, the pair of them were brawling in mud that was slick and deep from days of intermittent rain.

Strong hands pulled them apart. Colleagues of John and Moira's. Voices telling them to pack it in, what the hell did they think they were playing at? Colin stared through the caked mud and the lock of sandy hair that had flopped down into his eyes. Two men held John Moore's arms, but, Colin sensed, the man's anger had been

10

spent now. He probably felt as ashamed of himself as Colin now did. They'd come here to mourn their loss not to take it out on each other. Whatever they felt, this was not the way to express it.

'Look, I'm sorry,' Colin managed. He shrugged off the hands that held him and stood, slightly out of breath, not knowing what to do or what to say. 'I think I'd better go,' he managed finally.

'Good idea,' someone approved. 'Get lost Grainger. You've no place here anyway.'

'I loved her,' Colin said quietly. He took a few steps away and then turned back. John Moore had been released, he stood quietly, watching Colin's departure. 'I loved her,' Colin shouted back at him. 'I bloody loved her more than you'll ever know.'

Then he walked away with John's gaze heavy on his back, the weeping clouds bathing his face in tears.

1

Barely a week before the funeral everything had been so absurdly normal. There had been no warning of disaster, no sense of dread or even the mildest apprehension. Colin had been going about his normal

11

business. Living life as he had done for all his adult years. Delving into the slightly less legal zones of his usual activities, it was true, but no harm intended and no harm done.

Colin Grainger knew there was no such thing as security and it always amazed him, the stuff that people were prepared to store on the hard drive of their computers. On occasion he'd found credit card numbers, passwords and intimate details of extra-marital affairs. And the number of folk who kept journals, laying out their most confidential thoughts for the whole world to see ... or at any rate, people like Colin with the skill and the savvy to crawl in through the often minimal defences and poke about inside.

Good job he was honest!

Colin never actually used the knowledge he acquired, or at least, he didn't use it for actual gain. It was more of, what could you call it? A hobby, Colin supposed, and he didn't see any harm in occasionally sharing odd aspects of his hobby with other interested parties.

Which was exactly what he was up to now. The little piccies he'd found last week had gone down very well at the club and he was on a promise to deliver more.

Mr Don Tyler was a regular source for Colin. The man was local, Colin knew that by the info he'd picked up on Mr Tyler's hard drive. He didn't even have the most basic of firewalls on his system – making Colin's work almost insultingly easy – and he kept his machine up and running twenty-four seven. Mr Tyler was an avid photographer. He had files of landscape, pets, abstracts – some of which had Colin so frustrated he felt like leaving a message, demanding to know what the hell the images were of – but better still, from Colin's point of view, Donald Tyler was into glamour shots. Nothing too risky, just bikini clad and topless, the odd artistic nude, but mainly good, though amateur, bedroom pictures, stored in files under the models' names.

Colin wondered what Tyler would think, should he ever suspect how easy it was for an outsider to access his machine and read his life, all from the comparative comfort of their own little flat. Colin Grainger was a hacker, and a successful one. Not that anyone would know that. He did it for pleasure, not for profit, and for the sense of power and achievement it afforded him when the rest of his life could sometimes seem a little drab.

There were two new names on Don Tyler's computer. Laura and Denise. Colin made a mental note to take a look next time round but, he saw, glancing at the readout in the corner of his screen, that time was ticking. He'd better get what he came for and call it a night.

He opened the folder marked, Alice. Alice was evidently a favourite of Tyler's, new images appearing every few days and Colin was not disappointed. Quickly, he dragged the images across to his own drive, converted them to JPEG format and saved them onto floppy disk. He grinned happily. Mark, at the club, he'd be pleased no end. Mark, like Donald Tyler, was a big fan of this woman. Colin had just grabbed the last picture when his connection went down. He swore. He kept telling himself that he must get broadband, ditch the dial up connection with its two hour time out and get himself a nice fast link. Truth was, it took Colin all his time to keep up with his existing phone bills and besides, Colin only rented his little bedsit (he liked to think of it as a bijou apartment) and knew his landlord would reject the idea of cable anyway.

Colin sighed heavily, was about to reconnect when the alarm went off. The old fashioned clock, topped off with brushed metal bells, clanged aggressively and fell noisily off the table.

He glanced at his watch. 'Damn!' Late again. The alarm never did keep time. Colin bent to pick it up, then dashed into the hall, grabbed his coat and crashed down the single flight of stairs to the communal front door. He'd have to run to make it.

Hillford, this time of night, was pretty

empty and the Hampton area, in which Colin's flat was situated, was quieter still. Mostly student bedsits and cheap hotels, it would liven up when the clubs had been open for an hour or two. Eight thirty on a Thursday evening was that kind of in between time when people settled in front of the telly before deciding if or where to venture out.

Colin ran up the steep hill on Cranmer Street and sharp left onto Hillyard. Cutting through the little alleyway between the houses and the allotments and climbing the gate, taking a short cut through the gardens and behind the industrial estate, hoping to gain a few minutes. Another climb, this time over the wall at the back of the Crown Public House and then a quick jog down Milligan Road and in through the back entrance of Skunk's Nightclub.

Colin was two minutes late as he shoved his jacket in the locker and caught the Skunk's t-shirt Mark chucked over to him. 'You're cutting it a bit fine.'

Colin grinned, too out of breath to say much, then, 'Made it, didn't I?'

'You want to watch it, Col, the big boss man's due a visit and you know what a stickler he is for timekeeping.' He crossed over to Colin's locker and sniffed delicately. '*And* for personal hygiene. Phwoar, Colin, forget to shower, did you?'

Colin lifted an arm and inhaled exaggeratedly, then coughed. Mark threw a can of body spray in his direction, grinning as Colin applied it liberally under his arms and across his chest. 'Get them, did you,' he asked, glancing round to make sure no one overheard.

'Here,' Colin threw the can of spray back to its owner and dug in his pocket for the disk. 'Sweet little Alice, all new and uncensored.'

'Right on.' He took the disk from Colin's hand and held it at arm's length, gazing admiringly as though he could see the pictures of 'sweet' Alice by interrogating the black plastic. 'Good on you, mate.' He shoved it in his locker and slammed the door. 'Let's get on with it then,' he added, rubbing his hands together. 'Office has some mug shots for you to look at. Undesirables they want throwing out if they show their faces.' He threw a massive arm round Colin's shoulders, almost crushing the breath from him. Mark Harris was the kind of man a bouncer was expected to be. Big and brash, with a shaved head and a chest that stretched his shirt almost to bursting. He wore a collection of large and loud gold rings on his heavy black fists. Colin, by contrast, was a mere scrap of a man. Five six tall and built for flight rather than fight, but he could hold his own beside any of the others, talking his way out of situations others used their fists over and possessed of the kind of light touch with the public that the management were officially trying to promote. He also had an almost photographic memory for faces, a database recall for misdeeds and an instinct for potential trouble that Mark and the others in the team had learnt to rely upon.

Had anyone asked what Colin did for a living, he'd have described himself as a computer technician, or maybe, vaguely, something in the data recovery business – both statements true, after a fashion; he even had business cards and letterheads to prove it. He earned a bit of extra money repairing crashed machines and recovering lost work for the large student community in Hillford – it always amazed Colin just how frequently these otherwise intelligent people failed to back up or protect their work.

In truth, however, it was the three nights a week grind at Skunk's and the bar work that filled his Monday and Tuesday lunchtimes, that kept his rent more or less up to date and paid his phone bill.

He made his way up to the front office to look at the mug shots they had for him. Local police and other clubs had set up an alert system to warn of trouble-makers and dealers. After scanning the photographs they took up station by the front doors, Mark on one side, and Pryce, a big white bruiser with a broken nose and hair the colour of a ginger cat on the other. Colin hovered beside the queue, looking for pretty girls dressed in next to nothing he could hand out free passes to, encourage them to come back. Pretty girls were what got the boys inside and the boys were the ones who spent the money and money was what Skunk's was all about. What its owner, Charlie Radcliffe was all about.

A grin broke across Colin's face as he thought about Radcliffe, owner of Skunk's and another nightclub in Hillford and a small, private – very private – very exclusive casino on the fringes of town. Purely by accident, or fortunate, God given synchronicity, Colin's computer escapades had recently brought him an unexpected bonus as regards Charlie Radcliffe and there was one person he couldn't wait to let in on his discovery.

2

The same night Colin had been downloading his soft porn from Tyler's computer, Moira had been in trouble and Colin had been the cause of it.

'Just an observation, Detective Sergeant

Barker,' Weaver put a painful emphasis on her newly acquired rank that caused Moira to wince inwardly, but she stood her ground as he continued. 'I suggest you get yourself a more reliable informant.' He turned on his heel and began to walk away Moira almost relaxed, then caught herself just in time as DCI Weaver about faced, *Columbo* style and announced, 'One more thing, Constable Barker.' He paused, ensuring that he had the attention of anyone within earshot. 'One more thing. I hope you're aware that you've blown the entire overtime budget for this quarter on your ridiculous wild goose chase.'

He turned again and Moira braced herself for him to return, but once, it seemed, was enough. Weaver crashed out through the swing doors and on up the stairs to his office.

Moira exhaled, suddenly aware that she'd been holding her breath. She reached out and grabbed the back of the nearest chair, slumping into it as DI John Moore dumped a plastic cup of scummy coffee on the desk in front of her and then perched beside it, one streamlined buttock resting on the corner of the rickety table.

'I don't need to ask who it was, do I?'

'Who what was?' Moira asked stubbornly.

'Your lame-brained, so-called informant.'

'My sources are my business,' she told him

archly, then glanced uneasily in his direction. 'I'm really sorry, sir,' she added. 'It seemed sound at the time. I...'

Moore shook his head. 'He's a waste of skin, Moira. When did Colin Grainger ever put two and two together and *not* make bloody fifteen?'

'I never said it was Colin.'

'You didn't need to say it was Colin. Moira, if I'd been here instead of that idiot Morantz, I'd never have authorised this, you know that, don't you?'

Moira nodded guiltily.

'Oh, I get it ... you waited till Morantz was the duty officer. Well, thanks a bundle, Moira.'

'It wasn't like that,' she told him hotly. Truthfully, she didn't know what it *had* been like, but yes, she had played on Morantz's sense of one up-manship with regard to John Moore. Morantz would give her hell later, Moira knew. 'Anyway, at least *you* won't have to take the flack for setting up the sting, and if it had come off it would have been the biggest haul of drugs in the past five years.'

'Colin doesn't know his hash from his elbow, Moira.' He sighed deeply, the attempt at humour less than half-hearted. 'Take my advice and get rid, love,' he leant in close so no one else could hear. 'You've a good future, *if* you leave the wasters and the

20

baggage behind and Colin Grainger isn't owed any of your favours if you ask me.'

'I didn't ask you,' she told him angrily, then her shoulders sagged and it was all she could do not to cry.

'Look,' he said reasonably. 'You're not the first and you won't be the last, we've all acted on tips that didn't come off. Including Weaver, so don't let it get to you. Take the flak, keep your head down for a bit and it'll be forgotten in a month. Just get rid of Colin.'

He got up, the desk rocking as he left his perch, coffee slopping onto its scratched surface. 'Weaver wants to see me,' he told her, patting her on the shoulder in a comradely, paternalistic fashion. 'Write your report and get off home. I'll give you a call later,' he added in an undertone.

Moira nodded, fighting the impulse to sneak a look around her, check that no one else had heard. While there was no actual regulation against her dating John Moore, he was a superior officer and Moira was still green enough for a few eyebrows to be raised at her rather rapid promotion.

She watched John as he stalked out through the big glass doors. He was a tall man and walked with an unconscious swagger; long strides and a bit of a swing to the shoulders. Nice, muscular shoulders, Moira found herself thinking. A good looking man with wavy, dark hair and grey blue eyes, used to attention, though, Moira had noted, rarely taking advantage of it. Unlike others in the department, Morantz, for example, John Moore had no love 'em and leave 'em reputation. Discreet at work, attentive when they were out together, Moira had high hopes that he could be 'the one' and she sure as hell felt she'd been single long enough.

Moira took a tissue from her pocket and mopped up the coffee John had spilled. Peered doubtfully at the rest and then dropped the cup and contents into the bin. Write your report, John had said, then get off home. Moira glanced wearily at her watch. Five in the morning. Great. She loved her job, knew, despite today's *faux pas*, that she was good at it, but sometimes the unsociable hours could be a killer.

Knowing she couldn't put it off any longer, she reached into the desk drawer and withdrew the report forms and a chewed black biro, wondering how she was going to explain that this dead cert drugs delivery had turned out to be nothing more than a lorry load of knocked off veg for the local Chinese takeaway.

3

Two hours later, seven o'clock that morning, had found Moira banging on Colin's door. She was tired, pissed off and it had begun to rain. Peering through the letterbox, she spied Colin trotting down the communal stairs, a big smile on his face and his sandy hair flopping heavily over one eye.

'Well?' he demanded as she pushed through the half open door and marched up the stairs. 'How did it go?' He ran after her, tugging at her sleeve like an impatient child.

Pausing outside his door, Moira pulled her sleeve away. 'You're a Wally, Colin Grainger,' she told him angrily, 'and I'm even more of one for taking notice of any-bloody-thing you have to say.'

He ushered her inside. 'What happened then?'

Moira shook her head. 'No drugs, Colin, no big bust, no... You know what the big secret was? A cartload of out of date fruit and veg that should have gone to the night shelter. Instead, someone at the supermarket must have decided it was worth a bit of profit, sidetracked it in the direction of Wong's Palace, or whatever the hell the place is called.'

'Up on the Priestley Road?' Colin wanted to know. 'I was up there the other night. Good spare ribs.'

'Colin...'

'Well, it's still a crime, isn't it?' he asked hopefully. 'I mean, the local supermarkets have this deal. Anything not sold on the sell by date, it goes to charity. I call that a crime, taking from...'

'Sure, Col, but it's hardly what we thought it was, is it ... what you thought it was,' she corrected. 'It wasn't what I took to my boss, wasn't what you gave to me, was it, Colin?'

Exasperated, she threw herself into Colin's one easy chair. He perched nervously on the end of the bed, watching her.

'I'm sorry, love,' he told her softly. 'But in fairness, Moira, I just told you what I'd overheard at the club and you were the one who...'

'Put two and two together and made fifteen,' she admitted wearily.

'Excuse me?'

She shook her head. 'Just something John said.'

'Oh. John.' He stared down at his feet. Following his gaze, Moira noticed that his socks had holes in them. Colin's socks always seemed to have holes.

'My fault,' she said reluctantly. 'You're right, I did the conclusion jumping that time

24

and you're right too, it's still a crime, just not the one we ... *I* thought it was going to be.'

Colin's smile returned and he looked up at her, that same puppy dog adoration back in his eyes that at one time had had her melting beyond reason. She wanted to tell him to take the look off his face and grow up, but found she couldn't, not even after all this time. 'Oh, Col,' she whispered, 'you don't change a bit, do you?'

He grinned happily and shook his head. 'No, why bother. Perfect just the way I am.' He got up and came over to where she sat, moving behind the chair, his hands resting on her shoulders and long, strong fingers moving to massage the tension from her neck. Moira knew she ought to tell him to stop, but Colin always had given the best neck massage of anyone she'd ever met.

'You get in much trouble over it?' he asked.

She shook her head, just slightly, not wanting to disturb his ministrations. 'Don't know. John thinks it'll ease over soon enough.'

His fingers paused for a second or two. 'Ah, well, John would know,' he said.

'Don't, Colin.'

'Don't what? Look, Mo, I know what he thinks of me and to be honest, you know, from his perspective, I can understand why. But I wouldn't want to be like him. Mr

25

Handsome, Mr Efficient, Mr Got-my-ex-wife.'

Moira jerked her head away. 'Can't let it go, can you?'

'You blame me? Best thing that happened in my life, you were ... still are. I've a right not to be happy because I don't have you any more.'

'And whose fault's that?' she demanded acidly.

'Oh, mine,' Colin agreed. 'Absolutely mine, if you look at it that way. Mo, I know I couldn't give you what you wanted and when you said you needed a divorce I made things as easy as I ever could for you, but you can't expect me to like it. You and Mr Perfect Man.'

'He's not like that. Look, you and John should get together sometime. You'd like him. Honestly.'

'John Moore thinks I'm a waste of space, not to say a superfluous use of DNA. Hardly the ideal drinking companion, Mo.' His hands started moving again, the fingers probing just at the edge of pain as he eased the tension from over-tightened muscles. 'Anyway,' he told her. 'I've got something else for you, Moira, something really big this time.'

Moira jerked away again and sat forward, twisting around to look at him. 'No, Colin. Not *this* time. I've made up my mind, nothing more from you, ever. None of your overheard conversations, or your little conspiracies or...'

He was shaking his head. 'This isn't like that. I've got proof of something this time, Mo.' He crossed to the computer in the corner of the room. 'At least look,' he said placatingly. 'You think it's useless, well, that's your call and I promise I'll not bother you with anything again.' He grinned again. 'Well, not that way anyway.'

Moira let out an exasperated sigh. When he smiled like that he looked so young, so boyish, like the student she'd fallen in love with way back when they'd both been nineteen and celebrating the end of first year exams. Sometimes, it seemed to Moira, she'd gone on and aged ten years when Colin had just stayed where he was. Looking the same, living a life that was no more responsible or stable than it had been in their University days. Still that same smile and unfocused near genius mind that collected bits and pieces of knowledge like other people collected stamps – and found about as much use for them.

Reluctantly, she pushed out of the chair and went over to the computer desk. 'What is it then?' she asked. 'But get this, Colin. Last time, OK?'

'OK,' he shrugged. 'Look, I won't bother you with the technical stuff, but well, this came into my possession a few days ago. Look,' he carried on swiftly, before she had the chance to ask about the 'technical stuff' and exactly how legal it might be. 'First off I thought he was just keeping two sets of accounts, you know, defrauding the old tax man, but then I'm finding other things and...'

He opened a file and sat back to allow Moira to see the numbers scrolling up the screen. She looked at them, then at him, her expression blank and uncomprehending. 'What am I seeing? Looks like a club or pub or something, orders for beer and stuff.'

'Well, yes, it is, but there's a second lot of figures and look, you put them side by side, you see the figures tally, but who the payments are made to, that's what changes. Look.'

Moira looked again, her tired brain at first refusing to see the significance, then abruptly, she noted one or two of the names, and a shock of recognition passed through her.

'Colin, who is it? I mean whose accounts are these?'

Colin's grin was triumphant. 'Told you I was onto something, didn't I?'

'I never said that.'

'OK, so if I told you that these were Charlie Radcliffe's books, you wouldn't give a damn. You'd let me wipe the disk and...'

'Radcliffe! How the hell did you get hold of... No!' She warded him off with a raised hand. 'I don't want to know. Col, for God's sake, if port scanning isn't illegal it's damn close and hacking into someone else's PC certainly is.'

'Thought you didn't want to know how,' he said mischievously 'Come on, Mo, you're impressed. I know you are.'

'What else do you have?' she struggled to keep the tension from her voice. Radcliffe was a big fish in Hillford. Big fish, suspect fish, Teflon coated sort of fish.

'Oh, letters, memos. Copies of emails,' Colin said casually.

'Show me.'

He showed her how to open the files and sat back, watching with an air of tangible satisfaction as Moira scanned through.

Names she recognised. Places, snippets of information that made a kind of sense, that fitted with something she knew John had spent months working on.

'Colin,' Moira said as casually as she could. 'Copy this for me, then get rid of it on your machine.'

'Am I onto something?' Despite his earlier assertions, he sounded genuinely surprised.

She hesitated. The truth was, she wasn't sure. 'I don't know. And none of this would be admissible anyway, not having procured it the way you did.' She glared at him in what she hoped was a sufficiently stern and forbidding way. The fact that Colin laughed told her she hadn't succeeded. She tried a different tack. 'Look, Col, I'm tired, I've been up since six yesterday morning and I want my bed. Make me a copy and then get rid. I promise, I'll let you know if anything comes of it.'

'You could always stay here,' he said, then. 'No, OK, no need to give me the gorgon look. I'll copy what I have.'

He hesitated for a moment, hand poised over a scatter of disks strewn across his desk. 'Look, Mo,' he said, his expression suddenly very serious. 'In case this *is* something, I'm going to hide it for you. You've still got that old DOS machine I set up?'

Moira nodded. She had a passion for the old fashioned computer games they had both played in their teens and the likes of *Pac Man* and *Spiffy Space Guy* were impossible to play on fast machines, even if she set up a DOS window. Colin had cobbled together a slow, antiquated system with a 486 processor and DOS command lines so she could indulge herself.

'OK,' he said sliding a floppy disk into the drive. 'Anyone accesses this in the usual way, all they'll see are a few pictures.'

'What kind of pictures?'

'Does it matter? OK, OK, she's called Alice and I got them for Mark. This is just a copy.'

30

'God Colin, you pervert. So what do I do?'

'Look, there's a lot of info here. So I'm zipping it. You remember how to unzip a file?'

Moira rolled her eyes. 'How long did I live with you?'

'Right, but first you'll need to access it and for that you'll need a command line. Want me to write it down for you?'

Moira shook her head. 'I'll remember,' she told him. 'Where will you put it?'

'The zipped up info goes in the boot sector. There's about 38k unused Inaccessible in the normal run of things, but put the command line in and...' He demonstrated, 'voila!'

'Um, clever,' Moira allowed. She stood up, holding out her hand for the disk. 'Thanks Col, but I really have got to go. I'm dog tired.'

He patted the bed and raised an eyebrow. Just for a second or two, she seemed to hesitate, then she shook her head, bent to drop a light kiss onto his forehead and, gathering her bag from beside the chair, she said goodbye.

Two days later, Colin was awoken by the police hammering on his door. Moira's body had been found in a back alley, her head caved in by a single, heavy blow. The last entry in her diary had been her early morning appointment with him.

4

When Colin returned home after the funeral he had tried to sleep, but failed as miserably as he had on the previous five days. He arrived at work looking bruised and haggard.

'You OK?' With surprising gentleness, Mark placed a massive hand on Colin's shoulder.

'Yeah. Guess so.' Colin flopped down on the changing room bench and stayed there, staring at the floor.

'Go home, man. You're in no fit state...'

'What would I do at home?' Colin asked bitterly. He looked up and gazed, hollow eyed, at Mark. 'I've spent the past week, near enough, sitting in my flat, staring at the wall. I can't take any more of that.'

Mark nodded. 'I can't tell you how sorry...' he began.

Colin waved him into silence and eased himself back to his feet. 'Don't,' he said. 'I know, but, please. I just can't...'

Mark nodded and Colin turned away, slid the key into his locker and found his work clothes. None of it seemed real. Not the funeral, not the night-club, not the hollow feeling in his chest. He stripped off his own shirt, exchanging it for the bright red garment emblazoned with the Skunk's logo, then took a deep breath. 'OK,' he said. 'Let's see what the free drinks have dragged in tonight.'

Charlie Radcliffe's surprise inspection visits were normally signalled well in advance and this one had been no exception. Management had expected a visit for several days. He arrived, complete with entourage, just after ten, when the club was filling up and the atmosphere just starting to build. Colin reckoned that Skunk's never really took off until eleven, but a Friday night like this one, usually proved the exception to that. The rain had stopped, skies cleared and people had come out early.

Colin wasn't on the door when Radcliffe arrived, he was mingling with the growing crowd, chatting to the regulars, passing back information about likely troublemakers, or little knots of revellers getting too drunk too fast who were likely to be a pain in the backside come chucking out time.

Skunk's had a heavy policy on drug use. It went on, they all knew that and the buzz amongst management was all about 'harm minimisation'. Colin gathered this was the latest official jargon. It had become a condition of employment the year before that all the doormen took a basic First Aid course and kept it up to date. Radcliffe's club had been the first in the area to provide free bottled water and a chill out zone. He wanted maximum profits and minimum hassle and, Colin noted, so far he was getting both. Users who lacked subtlety and dealers stupid enough to be spotted by Skunk's employees got short shrift. Charlie Radcliffe wanted his place clean of everything but cut price alcohol.

Colin spotted him a few minutes after he arrived. Radcliffe was chatting to the manager and Colin was suddenly aware that he was the subject of their joint scrutiny. He looked away, handing out water, keeping busy, exchanging pleasantries and watching Radcliffe watching him via the reflections on the mirrored walls.

Radcliffe was smiling, so too was the manager, Mickey Pryce, a toad of a man, in Colin's opinion. Colin wondered what they had to grin about. He thought of Moira, not that she had wandered far from the centre of his thoughts all evening. He thought about the info he had stored on Charlie Radcliffe and he wondered, as he had so many times over the past few days, just what Moira had done that had led to her death and if, as he suspected, it really had been because of what he'd told her about Radcliffe's business.

There was nothing to connect directly.

Moira had been found in a little alleyway at the back of a local supermarket. She'd been left only ten or fifteen feet from what, in daytime, was a busy road, and which was, even at night, well lit and pulsing with regular traffic of both the pedestrian and vehicular kind. A single blow had killed her, smashing the side of her skull; it looked as though she had been turning to face her attacker when the blow had been struck. Her bag was lying beside her, but her wallet and mobile phone were gone. Had she not been a policewoman it was likely that the incident would have been logged as a mugging that went pear shaped. A tragic but common-place crime.

After leaving Colin, she had gone home. They knew that because a neighbour had seen her and she had made two phone calls during the day, one to her mother about nothing in particular – Colin recalled that she spoke to her parents nearly every day. The other to work, calling in sick at three fifteen.

John Moore had tried to call her back an hour hater, but there had been no reply.

Colin dumped the empty crate on the counter and picked up another full of bottled water. As he turned back towards the door, he noted that Charlie Radcliffe still stood there, alone now, apart from his personal security. They scanned the crowd from the

35

raised vantage point of the metal stairs that led down from the entrance into the pit below, but Radcliffe was watching Colin. Colin met his gaze, held it for just a moment, then looked away. He noted in passing that Radcliffe smiled. Suddenly, Colin's days of wondering coalesced in that one moment, his thoughts confirmed by Radcliffe's smile. He'd had Moira killed. His hands tightened on the sharp plastic of the crate rim. The hardness of it bit deep and felt good. He looked back, the anger surging through him so great that he longed to shout a challenge at this man, get up there and rip the smile from that smug, satisfied face, but as Colin looked up towards the entrance landing, he realized that Charlie Radcliffe had gone. He had seen Colin, assessed him and, Colin felt, somehow found him wanting. A nothing man, prepared to know what he, Radcliffe, had done and just to let it go.

'Got a minute, Col?'

'Sure,' Colin stripped off the red shirt and threw it into the laundry. It stank of sweat and other people's beer. Micky Pryce was grinning at him.

'You see the big man was in tonight?'

'Charlie Radcliffe? Yeah I saw him.' Colin shrugged into a fresh shirt and shut his locker door with a clang. 'What about him?'

'Well, more to the point, he saw *you*,'

Mickey Pryce was still smiling, but Colin's stomach knotted itself so tightly he felt sick.

'Oh yeah?' his voice trembled only slightly. Mickey Pryce didn't seem to notice.

'Well, I told him about you a while back. How you were so good with the punters and suchlike. Subtle, I said. You were subtle.'

Colin nodded, not sure where this was leading. He was surprised Mickey knew the word subtle.

'Seems he was impressed. You handle yourself well, we all know that and Mark reckons you can smell trouble long before the rest of them get a whiff of it.'

'I try to do my job,' Colin hedged. He was smelling trouble now, but didn't think it was the time to say so.

'Anyway, Charlie, well he's looking to expand his other business. You know the casino he operates over on the Strand? Looking for security staff, he is and they have to be, well ... subtle. Different class of people you get over there.'

He sounded vaguely jealous, Colin realized suddenly. And concluded just as suddenly that he was supposed to be feeling flattered by this information. Excited, even.

'Erm, I'm quite happy here, you know. I've no plans...'

'And we're happy with you,' Pryce assured him. 'But when the boss wants someone,' he shook his head as though failing to comprehend how Colin could be so slow about this. 'When the boss hand picks someone, that someone ought to jump at the chance, if you see what I mean?'

Colin sighed and nodded. 'Sorry,' he apologised, deciding it was easier to go along with the game. 'What with Moira and that, I've had a lot on my mind, you know.'

Pryce nodded with what was meant to be understanding, his features creased in what Colin supposed was an expression of sympathy. 'That's what I told him, Col. See, we've talked about you before and he was interested then but when I happened to be over at his place a few days ago and the papers were full of your ex. Moira, I mean,' he amended, as though Colin might need clarification. 'And I said to him how broken up you must be, seeing as how you still got on so well. You know, we both agreed, we admired that. You being able to move on with no acrimony, like. And we got talking about how you could do with cheering up and Charlie, seeing as how he was coming down tonight, he said he'd take another look at you. And, so, there you are, don't you see. Landed a good job. Promotion, you might say.'

He paused and gazed expectantly at Colin, who struggled to respond in a way that Mickey Pryce would see as appropriate. 'Thanks,' he managed at last. 'I'm grateful. It sounds like a good move, you know, time

I got into something a bit more stable and that...' He trailed off, hoping that was enough.

Mickey looked fairly satisfied at any rate. He thumped Colin painfully on the upper arm and nodded enthusiastically. 'He'll be expecting you Wednesday next,' he told Colin. 'He said to tell you he'd be in touch before then. Well before.' He smiled again and then strode away, happy that his news had at last been received with almost the expected reverence. Colin slumped down onto the bench and hugged himself as though trying to keep warm. He was shaking as though he had a high fever and his body ached about as much. 'Oh my God,' he whispered. 'Oh my God. He knows it was me that told her. He bloody knows.'

He'll be in touch, Mickey had said and Colin was under no illusions as to what that might mean.

5

Both the police and Charlie Radcliffe had pictures of Moira's funeral and even of one another recording the event.

Colin featured heavily in both sets.

Radcliffe had studied his at great length.

He had also acquired a copied set of those snapped by the police photographer. They made an interesting comparison, but added little to his knowledge or to his impression of what had gone on. It amused him that several of the frames his own agent had taken had no parallel in the police selection; they featured Colin and John Moore brawling in the mud like a couple of badly behaved school kids. Charlie thought about posting copies on the internet, maybe even emailing a couple to the chief constable or the local papers, but he decided to forego the pleasure, for now at any rate.

'You think he knows anything?' Brian Henshaw was Radcliffe's most trusted associate, both in the running of the casino and in other, more private business. Charlie, seated at his antique desk, glanced up at him. Brian was still, Charlie Radcliffe mused, a good looking man, with his almost Mediterranean looks and a body that was fit and honed without being over muscular. Henshaw made a good frontman, not least for those attributes.

'No,' Charlie told him. 'I think he might suspect she came here, but I don't think he's taken it no further than that.'

'Even so...'

'Which is why I'm bringing him into the fold,' Radcliffe told him. 'From what I've seen of him and what Mickey said, the bloke's a bit of a loser. Twenty nine and doesn't even have a proper job, still lives in some crummy little bedsit.' He tapped the image of Moira's coffin being lowered into the grave. 'Little wonder she divorced him. Rumours are she was bailing him out money wise left, right and centre. No, he's a worm, is my opinion. I'm just taking steps to make sure the worm doesn't turn and to get rid now would be to draw too much attention. Two bodies in a small place like this is a bit much, I'd as soon not add a third.'

Brian Henshaw nodded. 'We could have disposed of the other woman elsewhere,' he said.

Radcliffe shook his head. 'No. I want her found, she's the one link we've got to what that policewoman might have come here for.' He tapped a forefinger on the little black disk that had been sitting on his desk since the night of Moira's death. 'Someone's going to react when they find the other body. I want to know when they do.'

'She didn't tell us anything,' Brian observed. 'And there's nothing to connect her to either the policewoman or, her ex, this Colin bloke.' He frowned. 'Pryce reckons he's into computers big-time,' he added.

'I take your point,' Charlie Radcliffe nodded. 'Way it looks to me is that Colin Grainger gave this disk to his ex wife. *Why*, I haven't figured out yet. Something on it struck a chord, she started nosing around here.' He picked it up and stared at the square of black plastic. 'What I don't get is what. It's just semi nude shots of this Alice woman.'

'Why don't we ask him direct?' Brian wanted to know.

'Oh, we will,' Radcliffe assured him. 'But I want him good and scared first and Alice here, I think she might just help us to do that. Meantime, we've got a business to run.' He glanced meaningfully at the large wall clock that ticked solemnly opposite. The casino was due to open in less than an hour. Brian Henshaw took the hint and left.

6

There were aspects of Moira's death that Colin did not know about. It had been released that Moira had been killed by a single blow to the head and as far as it went that was true. But John had seen the pictures from the post mortem examination and he knew about the bruises. Finger marks dug so deep into her arm they could almost have left fingerprints, and the broken ribs and internal bleeding that told him she had been kicked and punched viciously in the hours prior to death.

The images filled his dreams when he tried to sleep. He'd seen murder victims before, of course, but never someone he had been so close to. At the time her body had been found, no one knew about his relationship with her. He'd been forced to confess to it, declare his particular interest, but not before he'd seen too much, been involved too much for the scars not to have been fashioned.

Colin must be feeling the same way. In his more generous moments, John Moore was forced to acknowledge that, but for all his embryonic sympathy, Moore still reckoned Colin Grainger to be a waste of space and definitely never good enough for a woman like Moira. And besides – and, if you were competing in the tournament of grief such *besides* were important – Colin had not seen those pictures, the ones that gave an insight into the last hours and minutes of Moira's life.

There were times when John would cheerfully have lost that particular contest.

The young woman lying at the edge of the school playing field reminded him so forcibly of this that he damn near disgraced himself by vomiting in the long grass. He'd not been sick at a crime scene since his days as a probationer and it was sheer pride that helped him to hold it together now.

She lay face down, her body half on, half

43

off the verge that separated the football pitch from the area of long grass and scrubby trees now designated as a nature garden.

She was partly clothed, her skirt rucked up beneath her hips and her upper body covered only by a red lace bra. The rest of her clothes had been bundled roughly together and thrown down a few feet from her body.

She had fair hair, like Moira. Was slightly built, like Moira, and she wore red polish on her nails the exact shade, he reckoned, that Moira wore on her days off. And she'd been kicked and beaten, the imprint of a hard-soled shoe clear on her naked back, then finished with a blow to the head ... just like Moira.

He watched from the path laid out by the first officer on scene, while the SOCO, a young girl who looked as though she should be still in school, carefully bagged her hands, preserving possible evidence within clear plastic bags. She wore no tights and her feet were bare. The girl bagged those too and John wondered for a moment, if, like Moira, this young woman painted her toenails.

He felt he had to watch, as though in watching this woman he was somehow watching Moira's body being carefully prepared ready to be taken away, but he turned away gratefully as Morantz appeared at his shoulder and told him they thought they'd found her purse. In his mind's eye though, he could see what would happen next. The SOCO easing clear plastic over the woman's head and sealing it carefully about her neck. She'd be careful with her, gentle – he'd seen this girl work before – making sure to tuck in the odd strands of hair before closing the opening with tape, as though she was worried the hair might be caught, might pull and hurt... Angrily, he shook himself and tried to get a grip.

'Over there in the bushes,' Morantz was saying.

'So, what, fifty feet from the body?' Moore had still not fully entered the metric age.

'About that, yeah.'

'Why dump the purse over there and leave the clothes close by the body? You sure it's hers?'

Morantz nodded. 'Driving licence,' he said. 'With a photo. It's her. Name's Alice Sanders. Rigby Street. No bag, just her purse, no bank cards, no cash.'

'So you think robbery? A mugging?' John demanded.

Morantz looked sideways at him. 'No, I don't,' he said in an undertone. 'SOCO reckoned she'd been dumped here. I figure same as you do, they want it to look like a robbery on the face of it, but they want us to know who she is and took steps to make sure we had no doubt. Take a look.'

The crime scene photographer had already taken shots in context and was hanging around to see if they wanted anything more. Morantz crouched down a few feet from the blue leather purse and John dropped down beside him. The purse was a billfold type. One compartment for notes and cards and a zipped section for cash. It lay open, the note section flat against the floor, weighted down by a small stone. The driving licence placed carefully on top, similarly weighted. The surface of both was wet.

'Grass is trampled slightly over there,' the photographer pointed. 'I've taken positioning shots and close ups. Anything else?'

Moore shook his head. 'They're getting ready to move the body,' he said. 'Get over there and take me some more contextual shots once she's moved will you. Then come back here and do the same once it's been bagged and tagged.'

The photographer nodded and retreated the way they had all come, careful to keep to the marked path.

'When did it rain?' John wanted to know.

'Didn't start 'til after midnight, so we might be able to pin our time quite closely. Can't have been before ten thirty, anyway.'

'Oh?'

'Yeah, dog walker who reported the body, he was here at around half ten last night, reckons he'd have seen her.'

'It was cloudy last night and there's no lighting here. He might have missed her in the dark.'

Morantz smiled grimly. 'Reckons he always carries a torch,' he said. 'Walks his dog along the back of the field here, then through the nature reserve and back onto the York Road. He lives just off there.' He dug in his pocket for his notebook. 'Mr Albert Finch, Albermarle Road. Had a mobile phone with him this morning and the sense to stand still until someone got to him, thank Christ. I had Morrison mark the path along the line Finch reckons he walked.'

Moore nodded and got wearily to his feet, glancing back to where the body was now being lifted carefully onto a gurney ready to be wheeled away. The photographer was taking the last of his pictures with PC Morrison much in evidence making sure that they moved the body out along his sacred path. Morrison was just out of his probation, Moore recalled. 'How's he handling it?' he asked the older officer.

Morantz laughed. 'By the book,' he said. 'He's holding himself together alright, though my bet is he'll go home to Mama and cry into his dinner.'

John grunted an acknowledgement. Privately, he thought that Morrison was perfectly within his rights to do just that.

'Mr Finch? Detective Inspector Moore. I wonder if you could spare me a few minutes.'

'Oh, of course. It's about that poor girl, isn't it? They said someone would call round.'

'Who is it?' A reedy, anxious voice called from the back of the house.

'It's all right, Millie. It's the police. You know, about that girl.'

'Oh...' The door at the end of the hall opened and a pale, grey haired woman in a light blue sweater and dark blue skirt came out into the hall. Her hand strayed nervously to the blue beads she wore at her throat and she stared at John as though he were some strange species of creature she had never before encountered. It was probably close to the truth, John Moore guessed. Albermarle Road was the height of respectability. Quiet, well tended and almost exclusively occupied by the affluent retired, a band that in John Moore's experience were rapidly dying out.

'Please, come in,' Mr Finch stood back from the door. A small dog came rushing through from the kitchen and began to sniff at his shoes. It was some kind of Jack Russell cross, John guessed, mainly white, but with odd ears, one black and one brown.

'Oh, leave off, Charlie,' Mr Finch ordered. 'Millie, shut him in the kitchen, there's a dear. And make some tea, would you. I'm sure you'd like a cup, wouldn't you, Inspector?'

John agreed that he would and watched, gently amused, as the couple ushered the dog back into the kitchen and Mr Finch closed the door rapidly, shutting both dog and wife inside. 'He's a lovely little chap,' Finch assured John, 'but so lively. Walks the legs off me, he does. We told them at the rescue centre we wanted a small dog and I have to admit they did warn us how much energy he'd have, even though he's only tiny. I'm afraid I didn't believe them. Go on through. Go on through.'

Moore found himself in the front room of a standard nineteen thirties bay fronted house. 'You must have found all this very upsetting,' he said.

Albert Finch paused and then sat down signing for John to do the same. They occupied two dark red fireside chairs, in a style contemporary with the house, though the upholstery, John thought, looked new. New and not really in keeping.

'I couldn't quite believe it, you see?' Albert Finch was saying. 'There she was, lying in the open. Not hidden in any way. At first, I thought, there'd been an accident, then as I got closer... Well, it was obvious she was dead, so I called the police. Your people I mean. You know, I've hardly ever used the thing before, the mobile. Our son bought us

49

one each, made us promise we'd carry them just in case and I must admit, once or twice they've been very useful. I don't suppose he had anything like this in mind though.'

'No,' John agreed. 'I don't suppose he did.' He nodded towards a couple of framed photographs that decorated the mantelpiece. The Finches still had an open fire, he noted. It glowed warmly, crackling peaceably in the grate.

'Yes, that's Martin, and his wife and the grandchildren. They'll be coming over next week, staying for a few days. The children have a teacher training day or some such at school, so it's a long weekend. I had hoped the weather would be better for them, but they don't seem to mind. We all go out anyway. You can't let the weather stop you. And then we'll be there at Christmas.' He smiled, pride showing in his faded blue eyes.

Millie chose that moment to arrive with the tea tray. Charlie followed her, but seemed content to sit beside the fire and observe. 'My officer, PC Morrison, he says I should commend you. You remembered exactly where you'd been walking and didn't disturb anything.'

'Oh, well,' Albert Finch looked pleased. 'We watch the television you see, probably more than we should, but when the nights draw in, we're not so keen on going out. Other than to walk the dog,' he glanced at his wife for confirmation and Millie nodded, then bent her head over tea tray and cups.

'I really don't like him walking out at that time of night,' she commented. 'But usually he walks with Bill from down the road, so I suppose it's not so bad.' She looked up and shuddered extravagantly. 'I've told him,' she said. 'I want him to keep to the roads from now on. At night at least.'

John Moore nodded thoughtfully and, he hoped, sympathetically. 'This other man. Bill, did you say? He wasn't with you last night?'

'Not for the past few nights,' Millie put in quickly. 'He fell off the step ladder and broke his leg. That was what? Wednesday, wasn't it?'

'No, no, dear. He didn't break it,' Albert reminded her. He sighed, and glanced over at John as though to ask indulgence. 'He *sprained* his ankle, that's all.'

'Well, he had to have an X ray,' Millie insisted.

'And the X-ray showed it wasn't broken. Anyway,' he went on, 'Bill wasn't with me. But, as I was saying, we watch all these things on television and they say you shouldn't move anything. You know, not at a Crime Scene.'

John could hear the capital letters as the man spoke the words. 'Quite.' he said. 'You did the right thing, Mr Finch. Did you see anyone, either last night or this morning? Anyone or anything unusual.'

Albert Finch shook his head. 'I've been asking myself that,' he said. 'And there's nothing I can tell you. I spoke to a few people, just to say "good morning". I bought the morning paper as I always do. Nothing more.'

'Did you let Charlie off the lead?'

'No. He's a good dog, but he likes to wander and I'm not up to chasing him. When Bill's with me, we let both the dogs go, once we reach the field, but on my own, I just daren't do it. We've got one of those retractable leads,' he explained, 'so he can run and sniff and do all the things he likes to do, but I can still keep a hold. I'm glad I did this morning,' he added. 'The thought that he might have run up to that poor young woman, started sniffing around and interfering in the Crime Scene, well. I wouldn't have been happy at all about that. Not at all.'

Again that capitalisation. John smiled. 'Maybe you could give me a list of the people you talked to,' he suggested. 'It might be that they saw something,' but even as he said it and the Finches exchanged an eager look before Millie got up to find a pad and pen, John knew that it would mean nothing. Whoever left the body would have made sure not to be seen. They had left a message, though, he thought, remembering the driving licence, weighed down by the smooth brown stone.

7

Colin heard about Alice's death when he got to work that night. Mark was waiting for him at the locker room door, the evening paper in his hand.

'Look, mate. It's her.'

'What's who?' Colin didn't click at once. Then he took a second look at the picture emblazoned on the front page. It was a different Alice from the pretty young woman who'd posed for the glamour shots. It looked like a picture taken for a passport in one of the automatic photo booths ... but it was unmistakably the same woman.

'Christ!'

'Keep your voice down, man. Jesus, Colin, what's going on here? You think the guy who took those pictures went too far? Or what?'

Colin shook his head. 'No,' he said. 'No, I don't think it's that.'

'Well, what then?'

'I don't know. How the hell should I know?'

He was getting loud again and heads

53

turned to look their way. The rest of the team, changing into uniform and wondering if Colin, old Mr Reliable, was about to throw a wobbly. Last thing they needed on a Saturday night.

Mark took his arm and gave him a not too gentle shake. 'Get a grip, Col,' he hissed. He seemed about to say more but Mickey Pryce banged on the door, stuck his head around to tell everyone that it was five minutes to show time. Colin moved away, out of Mickey's line of sight, Mark following him. He shoved the offending newspaper into the locker and pulled out the clean red shirt that lay inside.

'You OK?' Mark asked him in an undertone. 'God almighty, was I shocked when I saw her. I've got her frigging pictures on my PC.'

'Then get rid,' Colin told him 'Delete them from your hard drive and chuck the floppy disk I gave you away.'

'Yeah, but I mean, will that be enough? You told me, man, even if I reformat the hard drive, stuff's still there.'

Colin sighed, tried his best to sound calm and reasonable for Mark's sake. 'There's nothing to connect you to Alice,' he said quietly. 'No one else knows I gave you those pictures, do they?'

Mark hesitated just a fraction too long.

'Do they?'

'I sent a copy to my brother,' Mark admitted at last. 'Told him ... look, I've not had a girlfriend in months, Col. He was winding me up like every time I talked to him on the phone. So, I kind of told him...'

'You told him Alice was your girl,' Colin said flatly. 'Oh, nice one, Mark. And what happens if your brother sees the paper? Or the news on TV? You think this will stay local? "Attractive Young Model Found Beaten to Death in City Park." It'll be everywhere by tomorrow morning and he's bound to recognise her.'

'You think?' Mark ran his hand across his face as though to clear the thoughts away. 'You're right, I know it. God, I never should have told him nothing.'

'Well, you'd better *untell* him and do it tonight. And you'd better make sure he doesn't mention it to anyone else.'

Mark leaned against the lockers, they rocked back and hit the wall. 'I was only a kid when I got that assault charge, Col, but what if they find out, what if someone finds those pictures and they think...'

Colin reached out and put both hands on Mark's shoulders. He barely reached the other man's chest and had to look up to meet his eyes. 'Look, mate,' he said. 'Go and call him now. I'll cover for you. Tell him to get rid of the pictures and make sure he didn't show them to anyone else.'

'What if he already has?'

'She looked a lot different in those other photos. Chances are, no one who'd just had a quick shuftie would make the connection.' He let Mark go and jerked his head towards the door. 'Call him now, before the crush starts. You'll have no chance later on.'

Mark sighed heavily, then nodded. 'Yeah, you're right,' he said. 'Guess I got myself in a right old panic. I'll be back in five.'

Colin watched him go, then slammed the locker door and fell back heavily against it. It didn't move for him the way it had for Mark. He wasn't quite sure what to think, but one thing was for certain, Alice's death was no coincidence and it deepened his conviction that Radcliffe had had Moira killed. Moira was, most likely, still carrying the disk with Alice's pictures on so Radcliffe had found her, murdered her too.

The locker room door swung open again and a blast of music followed Mark back inside. He came over to where Colin sat, obviously still tense and anxious, he nevertheless looked slightly more relieved.

'I got through to my brother,' Mark told Colin. 'Just as well I did, he'd copied her pictures, planned on showing them about when he went to the pub tonight.'

'How much did you tell him?' Colin wanted to know.

'Much as I could standing back there in

56

the corridor. I'd a nipped outside, but Mickey was on the prowl and would have asked questions.' He got up and dragged Colin to his feet. 'Come on, Col, we've got work to do.'

But, suddenly, Colin could not bear the thought of it. Of going out there into the hot and noisy club, spending the night surrounded by the life sweat of young bodies, so alive and heedless when two women whose lives he'd also touched had wound up dead. It sickened him. He could feel the anger mixed with nausea churning in his stomach, rising into his throat and he knew he had to get out of there.

'Col?' Mark was staring at him. 'You all right?'

'No, no, I'm not all right, I gotta go, Mark. Sorry, but I've just got to go.'

He pulled the locker door and fished his jacket from the depths, dragging it on over the bright red shirt. 'I can't do this, Mark. I'm sorry, there's something that needs ... something I have to do and I have to do it now.' He shrugged off Mark's constraining hand, and headed for the door, almost knocking Mickey Pryce off his feet in his rush to be gone.

8

Had Colin stopped to think at that moment, life might have turned out very differently for him. But, as Moira had often observed, it was Colin's abiding principle that he should act first and consider the consequences later – if he bothered to consider them at all.

Blind to those who tried to stop him and deaf to Mickey's shouts of 'What's going on, Col?' he had left the club and dived into the dirty little alley that ran alongside. From there he had climbed the wall into the yard of the adjoining pub and made his way home the fastest way he knew. Once in his flat he had paced impatiently, still in the thick fleece jacket, while the computer fired up and he established his internet connection. Minutes later he had entered Radcliffe's IP address into the programme and forced his way through the inadequate firewall and onto his machine. The message he left was unambiguous and unequivocal.

'Bastard,' it read. 'I know you murdered them and I'll make sure you bloody pay.'

Then he retreated and shut down his computer, pulling the plug in his impatience to be gone, as though suddenly afraid that Radcliffe might track him back.

It was only then, sitting in his shabby little room, his dark blue fleece pulled tightly and protectively across his chest, held closed by hands that shook and turned white at the fingertips so hard did he clasp the fabric, that Colin realised just what he had done. He might as well have *signed* his accusation. Invited Radcliffe round, said, here I am, come and beat the living daylights out of me – or worse – and the action he had taken, which he had supposed in some idiotic way might be cathartic, had been nothing of the sort. The sheer stupidity of his actions caught him breathless, like a fist in the gut, and Colin slumped forward over the keyboard and began to weep, weak, choking sobs, for himself, for Moira, for Alice, the woman he had never known, for all the ripples of pain that would travel outwards from this spot on the world that was Colin Grainger and the mess he had made of it all.

Maybe it wasn't too late to undo?

The thought crept almost unbidden into that part of his consciousness still attempting to think clearly. He could go back in, remove the message and no one would be the wiser.

With fingers that felt twice their normal size, Colin groped for the connector, plugging it back into the tower and rebooting.

The blue screen that warned him of an improper shutdown and the computer's intention to check for errors mocked his impatience and took, it seemed to Colin, an age to finish its examination and return access. He logged back on, only to be thrown off again almost at once. Cursing the dial-up connection, Colin tried again, this time it worked. He called up his program and ran Radcliffe's IP, contacting the remote machine for the second time inside a half hour. Such was his state of nerves that he found himself glancing over his shoulder, fearful of some physical presence in the room as he, ghostlike, snuck into Radcliffe's domain and removed the evidence of his incursion. Again, he logged off fast, then slumped back in his chair, relief flooding through his limbs until they felt weak with the force of it.

Had he been in time? Surely he must have been. He glanced at the faulty alarm clock, then at the numbers on the corner of his screen. Ten fifteen. For once, both clocks agreed. Surely there would be no one in Radcliffe's office at this time of night? But the fact remained that he had gained access to Radcliffe's office computer and that meant the machine must have been on. Fired up, logged on ... many people did leave their computers on twenty-four seven and, for it to be so easy to access, Radcliffe must have a broadband connection of some sort, but was that the only explanation?

Colin racked his brains, trying to remember if ever there had been a time when he'd been unable to log on to the other man's machine, searching for evidence that someone might have been there to have seen his message. He couldn't remember, not for sure.

Despairing, he reminded himself that this particular computer was most likely in the office in the casino and that casinos, by their very nature, tended to be open at night and that people working in them might well be using the computer at a quarter after ten.

His relief, short-lived and drenching, was replaced by an equally incapacitating dose of fear. For a moment he sat, head in hands, wondering what the hell to do next. Reluctantly, he accepted the fact that, now Moira was gone, there was only one person left who could advise him. Before he could change his mind, he plugged in the phone and dialled John Moore's number.

'I've done something really stupid,' Colin said.

9

After waiting at the airport for much of the afternoon, James Sanders and his wife, Mel, had finally collected his mother from the airport at seven fifteen, her flight having been delayed. The trip home had been taken up with stories of Cousin Ellie's wedding to a Greek she'd met on holiday the year before.

'Oh, it was beautiful,' Annie Sanders said for the umpteenth time, clearly taken by the Orthodox ceremony, so different from her own little registry office affair and her son's marriage to Mel in the tiny non-conformist chapel up the road from where they lived.

'All the incense and the candles and the family dancing and she looked so ... like an angel, she was. I wish you could all have come. I can't wait till our Alice decides to take the plunge.'

'She's got any sense, she'll elope,' James teased.

'Wouldn't bloody dare!' his mother told him. 'She's marching up that aisle in all the froth and fancy I can lay my hands on.'

Mel laughed. 'Well,' she said. 'If she can hang on a bit longer, there might just be a little flower girl...'

'Or a page boy,' James interjected, then, 'do they have page boys any more?'

'Flower girl? Page...? Oh, you don't mean?' She reached over the front seat, constrained by her seat belt, to hug Mel. 'You're expecting? Oh love, when?'

Mel returned the hug as best she could with the seat back in the way. 'I'm only a couple of months gone,' she said. 'We wanted you to know first, I only found out this morning.'

'Oh, love. I wish your mam could have been here to see it, she'd have been that proud. Oh look at me, crying like a burst pipe. You got any tissues, darling?'

But the crying had changed to another sort from the moment they'd pulled up outside her door. Neighbours had been looking out for them and, seeing the tears, they thought she must already know.

'The police have been trying to reach you. They left a number for you to call, we told them James had gone to pick you up.'

'Police?' James stared at the woman. 'What do the police want with Mum? What's going on?'

The neighbour, realising her mistake, blanched and fell silent. She gripped her fists and carried them to her mouth as though to force the words back in. 'It's Alice,' she whispered. 'Alice. They found her this morning.'

John Moore had walked into the aftermath and was still trying to calm things down.

'We had no way of reaching you,' he said again. 'We had the address of Alice's flat and the girl she shared with was out at work. Neighbours told us where they thought she worked, but ... she got it wrong and we had no idea who Alice's next of kin might be.'

'Couldn't you have got it from her flat?' James demanded. 'Broken in or something? She was dead, for god's sake.'

John didn't bother to reply to that. They had eventually forced entry to the little flat that Alice shared with an old school friend only to find that they hadn't been the first to examine the place. Whoever had killed Alice had taken her keys, waited until her flatmate left for work and then let themselves in – which meant, he thought absently, that they'd been pretty sure of not being disturbed. It crossed his mind that Mr Finch's discovery of the body and the subsequent arrival of the police might well have been observed. Carlie, Alice's flatmate, had left for work before seven anyway and Alice had not been discovered until eight. It had been well after nine before they had an identification. More than enough time for the untidy but thorough search that had taken place.

What, he asked himself, had they been looking for?

'By the time we knew where to find you,' he continued softly, 'neighbours told us that you were away. No one seemed sure what time you'd be back...' He hesitated. 'Or if you'd be aware of what had happened before we reached you. We tried to make contact at the airport...' he tailed off again. That had been an almighty cock-up too. The officers had been sent to the wrong terminal, the delayed flight coming in to a different gate. He sighed. 'I can't tell you how sorry we are. If you feel you have a complaint, I'd be happy to...'

'Complaint!' James had roused himself again. 'My complaint is that there are perverts on the streets who prey on kids like Alice. That's my bloody complaint. That and you seem to be doing sweet F.A. about the bastards when you do catch them. Sorry Mam,' he added in a small, despairing voice. He gathered her to him again and held her, both weeping while John Moore looked on.

The opening of the living room door broke the tension. Mel Sanders came in with a tray of cups, followed closely behind by a female officer carrying milk and tea. They set the trays down on the low table in front of the sofa. John caught DC Morgan's eye.

'Anything?' he asked silently. She pursed her lips and shrugged leaving him none the wiser. Mel began to pour the tea, hands

65

shaking. Her eyes were red from crying, John noted and she was trying hard now to keep her tears in check.

He sighed. He needed to know so much and yet, he knew from experience that this would not be the time for answers. Tonight was the time to ask the questions, to sow the seeds that might lead, if he was very lucky, to a flowering of information when the bereaved relatives had time and space to talk amongst themselves. Time and space to allow themselves to think anything but good of their precious dead. That, John knew, could take an age of time. And he would be coming back to them with further questions, further intrusions and, this he also knew from bitter experience, further evidence that they did not know their dead one as well or as completely as they might once have believed.

It would be a painful journey.

Just like the one he had embarked upon in respect of Moira.

It was PC Morgan who broached the next requirement.

'We'll need someone to make a formal identification,' she said softly. 'I've already...'

Annie Sanders raised her head. 'Formal...?' she said. She pulled away from James and looked at them with sudden hope. 'You mean you can't be sure. You mean...?'

'No, Mrs Sanders,' John told her. 'Your

daughter's driving licence was found at the scene, it had her photo on it. There's no doubt, but we still have to have someone ... someone close to verify it.'

'I've already said I'd do it,' Mel told them. 'Mam, I couldn't bear for you to have to go through that.' She turned towards John. 'I'm a nurse, you see,' she explained shakily. 'I've seen dead bodies. I know what to expect.'

'Dead bodies,' Annie Sanders said. She stared at her daughter-in-law as though she couldn't quite believe she'd spoken about her Alice in that way.

'What I don't get,' James's voice was harsh, 'is, if you didn't even have any of us to talk to, how you could have told the bloody press about it all. Neighbours said it was all in the papers. On the bloody telly! How come? When you hadn't even told her next of kin?'

It was a good question, John thought, and one he didn't have the answer to. 'It shouldn't have happened,' he told them, allowing a touch of anger to creep into his reply. 'We're not yet sure how the press got hold of the picture,' he admitted. 'The editor of the *Hillford Guardian* believed – had every reason to believe – this was in the public domain. That you already knew about Alice.'

'In the public domain,' James echoed. Stony-faced, he glared at John Moore. 'That what this is, then? Our Alice, public property now? Whose decision was that? I suppose we should be grateful we don't have bloody journalists camped on the doorstep.'

John grimaced and exchanged a swift glance with PC Morgan. 'Is there somewhere you could all stay for the next few days?' he asked softly. 'It might be for the best.'

James stared at him a moment longer. 'Jesus wept!' he exploded finally. 'What a bloody mess.'

John Moore felt that he could do nothing but agree with him.

At that moment, his mobile phone rang. It had been set to divert calls from his home and from his desk. John didn't recognise the number, but he answered anyway. It was Colin Grainger.

'I've done something really stupid,' Colin said.

For several seconds, John Moore said nothing. What the hell was Colin Grainger doing calling him and why should he be interested in the latest act of stupidity the man had committed? He felt a surge of anger, felt the blood from it rushing to his face and was aware that not only was Colin repeating his name over and over like some trained parrot but that the others in the room were staring at him.

'You OK, guv?' PC Morgan's face showed her concern.

'Excuse me for a moment,' John Moore apologised. He went out into the hall and gently closed the door.

'What the hell do you want?'

On the other end of the phone he could hear Colin hesitate.

'Your help,' he said finally. 'As a policeman, you understand. Not as a friend or anything. I know you don't think...'

'You want a policeman, phone the station.'

'I don't want just anyone. I want you.'

'Colin, are you drunk, or what?'

'What,' Colin confirmed. 'Definitely what. Look, I know, given the choice, you'd forget I'd ever been born and you'd certainly forget I was ever married to Moira. And I mean, I can respect all of that, but this is *because* of Moira, you see. The stupid thing I've done. I did it because of her, but... Oh God, I'm not making much sense, am I?'

That, John Moore thought heavily, was the only comprehensible thing he'd said so far. 'Colin, I'm in the middle of an interview. I've got enough on my plate without your problems. You have something useful to say, then say it. If not, get off the bloody phone.'

'I know who killed Moira and I think I know why.'

The words came out in a rush of breath and stopped John dead in his tracks for all of a half minute. Then he remembered it was Colin who had said them and he

69

sighed, leaned back against the plum striped wall.

'Go on,' he said wearily. 'You've got two minutes, Colin, I've got more important...'

'More important than who killed Moira? I don't think so. And he did the other one too, that girl, Alice. They're all linked up, you see. I gave Moira... OK, OK, let me get this straight.'

John could almost hear him collect his thoughts. He was about to end the conversation, switch off his mobile and leave Colin to stew when the other man began to speak again. John listened, at first with disbelief then with growing anger and finally with real concern. 'You did what!' he demanded finally as Colin told him of his abortive act of vengeance. 'I always knew you were a bloody fool, but that about tops the lot.'

He broke off, thinking quickly, trying to plot the best course of action. Radcliffe was a dangerous man and John had no illusions about what he would do to Colin Grainger should he realise who had left him that little message. And, John figured, it wouldn't take him that long to work it out.

'Colin, pack a bag and get out of there. Do it now.' He glanced at his watch. There was an all night café up on the main road a couple of miles out of town. 'Meet me at the Road House, you know it? On the Ashford Road.'

'Yes, I know it but...'

'Just get there. I'll be with you soon as I can.'

The living room door opened as he rang off. PC Morgan, eyes inquiring, stood in the doorway, silhouetted against the too bright light.

'Everything all right?' she murmured as he stepped back inside. John nodded, took a deep breath and sat down again in the easy chair, sliding back into the role he had left only minutes before but, it felt, like a lifetime of complications ago.

'There are some things I need to ask,' he said quietly, wondering how he could phrase his question in the light of what Colin had just told him. He tried to equate the woman he had seen lying dead and battered on the playing field with the description Colin had given of the photographs. Tried and failed, nevertheless, he had to know.

'Did you know Alice had an interest in modelling?' he said carefully. 'Did you meet the photographers she posed for, see her portfolio, perhaps?' The query, gently put, nevertheless evoked a strong response. PC Morgan stared at him as though he had gone mad and the shock on the mother's face made him feel suddenly dirty and ashamed.

'Modelling!' James's face told him the answer to that one. 'What the hell are you trying to say?'

'We've reason to believe,' John told them, the sudden anxiety that Colin might have got it wrong again nagging at his mind. 'Information we've received,' he tried again, 'suggests that Alice might have posed for...' What could he call them? From Colin's description, she wasn't nude, well not quite anyway.

'Glamour shots,' PC Morgan caught on fast and John blessed her for it. 'You might have met the photographers, perhaps. Or Alice might have shown you her portfolio.'

John looked gratefully in the young woman's direction. Her face was a picture of innocent curiosity, as though it were normal for you to ask a dead girl's family if they knew she posed undressed and had her pictures strewn across the internet.

'You're telling us,' James returned, his voice tense and harsh. 'You're telling us that some bloody pervert maybe got her drunk and took mucky pictures of our Alice? 'Cause I'm telling you that's the only way they'd get pictures like that.'

He stood up and opened the living room door. 'And I think we've answered enough of your filthy questions for one night. You'd best get out, now, while we can still be civil.'

John and Morgan rose to leave. He could have insisted on remaining, but John didn't see the point. He made a mental note to talk to Mel when she came to identify the body.

Maybe one young woman would take another into her confidence.

'Thank you for your time,' he said. 'We'll see ourselves out. And, Mr Sanders, we are deeply sorry.'

James said nothing, standing with clenched fists beside the door. Behind him, his mother had begun to weep again.

10

'Thanks for that,' John said as they got into his car. 'I admit, I wasn't sure how I should phrase it.'

'Not like you to be lost for words.' She paused, studied him with interest. 'You going to tell me, then?'

'Tell you what?'

'Aw, come on! Tell me how come we're suddenly asking the bereaved family about mucky pictures?'

'I didn't say they were mucky pictures.'

'Whatever. It was that phone call, wasn't it? You came back into the room looking like you'd seen a ghost and wanted to throttle it.'

John smiled at the analogy. 'Not far off the mark,' he admitted. 'And yes,' he added, starting the car engine, 'it was the phone call. An informant suggested she might be

73

involved in ... well, in glamour modelling, as you put it.'

'Oh?' She was staring at him, eager to know more. John pulled out, switching his windscreen wipers onto intermittent. Rain was falling again. Half hearted rain, drizzling from ragged clouds.

'An informant,' he said. 'I can't tell you more than that 'til I've checked it out.'

Her eyes widened. 'So you decide to throw that particular sordid little ball into the court, and you're not even sure of your facts yet. Nice one, guv.' Her tone somewhere between admiration and contempt. An interesting balance, John thought.

'I wanted to ... give them something to consider, I suppose.'

'I'd have said they had enough to think about already.'

'Oh, I agree. But this way, they've got tonight to talk about it. To talk among themselves, see if, maybe, Alice was behaving strangely. If she had boyfriends she didn't bring home ... and I get the impression that would have been unusual.' He glanced in Morgan's direction. She nodded briefly in reply. 'You get anything useful from Mel?' he asked. 'While the two of you were making tea.'

She shook her head. 'Nothing concrete, but she's got something on her mind. Something niggling.'

'Oh? Any notion as to what?'

'No, not really. I don't think Mel can put her finger on it yet, but it's there. You know, she found out this morning she was pregnant...' She trailed off.

John winced. 'You think she's up to making the I.D?'

'Yeah, I think so. She strikes me as tough and she's got a protective streak a mile wide when it comes to Annie. Seems Mel's mum died of cancer a couple of years back and Annie's been good to her.' She fell silent for a moment and then asked tentatively, 'are you all right, guv. I mean ... we didn't know about you and Moira ... DS Barker, at the time, but now we do, we're all really sorry. Maybe Weaver was right and you should have taken leave.'

'Leave would have given me more time to brood,' he told her. 'I can't be doing with that. I'm better working.'

'But a murder like this. I saw both of them, sir...'

'And you noticed similarities?'

'Well, yes and I just thought, you know.'

'I'm coping,' John told her. 'So you can pass that on to anyone who asks.' He smiled, softening words that had been spoken far more angrily than he had intended. 'I know everyone's been talking,' he told her. 'And if it gets so I'm not doing my job, I expect you to tell me.'

She laughed at that. 'Oh, right,' she said. 'I'm really going to tell a senior officer, Look guv, I think you're messed up and should go home before you screw the case for us.'

'Well, no,' he admitted. 'I expect you to put it in a report, on the official form and in triplicate and allow me time to consider all points before taking action.'

She laughed again. 'I'll just bet there *is* an official form,' she said, then she sobered and he felt her change of mood. 'You reckon they're linked, don't you? DS Barker and this Alice.'

'Is that what you think I think, or what *you've* decided?'

'Bit of both, really. The similarities are striking, for one thing. Both women suffered pre mortem beatings and both were killed by a single blow to the head.' He felt her glance across at him, assessing how well he was dealing with her bluntness. John's stomach churned, but he managed to keep his expression blank. This was Moira she was talking about. Moira.

'For another thing,' she went on, 'two murders in the space of a week in a little place like Hillford is a bit of a coincidence.'

'They've been known to happen.'

'Yeah, but...'

'I hear you're taking the Sergeant's exam.'

She shrugged. 'Yes. I thought it was about

76

time I gave it a shot.'

'Oh, I agree and a case like this, even if it gets handed over to the regional crime squad, there's plenty of opportunity to prove yourself.'

'I wasn't thinking that.'

John smiled. 'Of course you were. At your age and in your position I'd have thought it too. But watch yourself, Morgan, don't put yourself out on a limb. Yes, for what it's worth, I think these two deaths are linked. Closely linked. And I also have reason to believe that Moira got herself killed because she was trying to prove herself. She felt badly after that cock up with the information on the so-called drug delivery. I think she wanted to prove a point and, if my informant is correct, she was acting on information received the night she died.'

She stared at him. 'Information about what?'

John shook his head. 'I can't tell you that yet,' he said. 'Once I have more confirmation, I'll make my report. Meantime, we focus on the job in hand and in your case that's being there when Mel Sanders comes to identify the body tomorrow. And I want you to organise the family liaison officer. Not tonight, first thing will do. I think they've had enough of us for one night, but tomorrow they're going to want someone or something on which to vent their emotions.'

He pulled up in front of Morgan's house. 'Get in early, write your report and get ... Andrews, I think, to act as liaison. See who she recommends as second. You have a time for seeing Mel?'

'I'm meeting her at St Gerard's Hospital, eleven o'clock.'

'Good. So you should have time between the morning briefing and your meeting to discuss things with the liaison.'

'Yes, sir.' She put her hand on the door handle but made no move to get out.

'Something on your mind?'

She nodded. 'If Alice's murder does prove to be linked to the murder of DS Barker...'

'Then I'll step down like a good boy and twiddle my thumbs elsewhere for the duration,' he told her.

'That won't be easy though, will it?'

'No, it won't,' John admitted, 'but if these two deaths are linked ... I'll be too involved.'

She nodded and then got out of the car. 'Night guv,' she said and bolted through the damp haze to her front door.

John watched her inside, then drove away deep in thought. The rain was heavier now and he increased the speed of the wipers, half listening to the *sheesh thump* as they passed across the glass.

He glanced at the clock on the dashboard, surprised that only an hour had passed since Colin had phoned. Would that have given him time to get to the Road House? John had given little thought to how Colin might get there. Did buses go out that way at this time of night? Would he have got a taxi? Walked even?

John sighed deeply, misery settling in on him again now the business of the evening had passed. He was OK, well, sort of OK, when he kept busy, but the times when he was left alone, off duty or waiting around at home – and, this past few days, any time not spent at work had been spent just waiting around ready to go – had been the worst of times. Depression was settling over his mind like a thick black cloak that stifled his thoughts and made the simplest of tasks seem complicated, and he knew what they were saying at the office. Questioning whether or not he was up to the job at the moment, wondering who should suggest he take compassionate leave.

Right now, John told himself, compassion was the last thing he had wanted. Too much of that and he'd break down completely.

He found himself, much against his will, wondering if Colin felt the same.

Phil Jones and Rose Morgan had been seeing each other for close on a year and, though he hadn't officially moved in, he spent a good deal of his time with her and stayed over maybe three nights a week. Rose wasn't yet ready to completely take the plunge. This was her first home of her own and the little house – one bedroomed, mid town house, tiny garden – was *her* space. She wasn't yet sure about either sharing it or moving to something that wasn't completely hers, especially as she knew Phil had previous debt problems. Growing up with a father who could never get his financial act together and watching her mother struggle with the consequences had left her suspicious of such incapacity.

Phil had a key and, as he often got in from work well before she did, he often cooked for them both. The scent of food greeted her as she opened the front door.

'Hello,' he said. 'I'd about given up on you. Hope you don't mind but I was starving. I've had mine.'

She shook her head. 'One of those nights,' she said.

'I thought you might be late when I saw the papers.'

She nodded, unutterably weary now. 'Shouldn't have been in the bloody papers,' she exploded angrily. 'Next of kin hadn't even been informed!'

'What?'

'Too right, what. They've got any sense they'll make a formal complaint. Thankfully, they hadn't actually seen the report. I mean, can you imagine that? Seeing your daughter's picture on the front page and finding out that way some bastard's beaten her to death.'

'Is that how she died? The report just said a blow to the head.'

Rose shrugged. 'Same thing,' she muttered, knowing she shouldn't have given vent to her feelings that way. 'I hope whatever you cooked is microwaveable, I'm starving.'

He smiled at her and wrapped both arms round her, drawing her into the kind of warm and total embrace she had come to like so much.

'You sit down, I'll bring food, maybe open a bottle of wine and you can moan about a policeman's lot.'

She laughed. 'Yeah, maybe.' It was the last thing she wanted to talk about just now. She shed her coat while he went back through to the kitchen and she wandered into the living-come-dining room that finished off the plan of downstairs. It was nice, she thought to have someone to come home to and despite his past problems, Phil was good company. The sort of man she could think of settling down with.

She sat down on the sofa and curled her feet beneath her, allowing the warmth of the house and the quiet sounds of preparation coming from the kitchen to soothe her nerves.

She was asleep when Phil came through with a tray and set it on the table. He studied

81

her for several minutes, then, certain she would not wake, went back into the hall where she'd shed her coat and dumped her bag. Glancing back over his shoulder, listening close to be sure she'd not stirred, he took her notebook from her bag and read the entries for the day.

11

At first Charlie Radcliffe had been puzzled by what the woman was saying, but Sandra wasn't someone who made things up and she swore the message had been there.

Brian Henshaw looked as confused as Radcliffe felt. 'You said it just appeared?' he asked again.

'I told you,' Sandra insisted. 'One minute it was there, the next it was gone. Well...' She hesitated. 'I came through into the other office to shout for someone and when you came back in with me it was gone.'

'So, how long would that have been?' Charlie wanted to know.

Henshaw shrugged. 'I had to come up from the floor,' he said. 'I was over by the Blackjack table when Security said Sandra wanted me. Five minutes, maybe a bit more.' He glanced at his assistant for confirmation.

She nodded.

'Something like that.'

'So,' Charlie went on. 'In the space of say, five, ten minutes, a message accusing me of murder pops up on the screen then takes itself off again.'

'It happened, Charlie,' Sandra sounded offended.

'I'm not doubting you,' he told her. Sandra had been his PA for too long for him to do that. Pushed, he'd have ranked her above Henshaw in terms of reliability. 'Just trying to figure out how and who.' He frowned. 'Brian, give Mickey a ring at the club, find out if our friend Colin Grainger turned up for work tonight.'

With a nod, Henshaw left the room.

Radcliffe stared at the offending machine. 'We got anyone on the staff that might know how it was done?' he asked Sandra. She knew his staff better than anyone, including himself, making it her business to be interested in their personal lives, remembering birthdays, that sort of thing. It made her popular and didn't do Charlie any harm at all in terms of the information that flowed back through Sandra.

'There's young Sam Warner. Trainee Croupier,' she told him. She crossed to the bank of screens that filled one wall and switched cameras to show the Roulette wheel.

Radcliffe watched him. 'Reliable?'

Sandra laughed. 'He's a student,' she said. 'Works for us three nights a week. Honest to the core, living off student loans and what he earns here. He's a nice boy, helped me out a time or two.'

'Discreet?'

'Frankly, he's not interested enough to be anything else. He's here to earn a few bob, rest of the time he's studying to be a geologist or something, seeing his girlfriend, being young.'

'Feeling your age, Sandra?'

'Only when I look in the mirror.'

Radcliffe laughed. 'Well, get him up here. Julie can relieve him, she's in tonight.' He saw Sandra frown. 'Something still bothering you about that girl?'

'Something, yes. I wouldn't like to say what, but she's been jumpy this past week, ten days. And Brian's still not sure she didn't see him with that Moira.'

'Always did strike me as the nervous type,' Radcliffe commented. He made a mental note to check it out. Sandra was rarely wrong about these things and if she was worried, then he should be too.

He went through to the outer office and called down to the floor, arranging for the changeover on the table. Henshaw came back in as he was finishing his call.

'Grainger turned up for work,' he said.

'Seemed upset about something and cleared off. Mickey's having a word with his mate, Mark Harris. That's the black guy, works the door.'

'I know the one,' Radcliffe frowned. 'So it could have been him,' he mused. There came a knock at the door and Sam Warner, looking a little apprehensive, came inside.

'Ah, Sam,' Radcliffe smiled his most expansive smile. 'Sandra tells me you know a bit about computers. Someone's been playing silly buggers with that thing in there,' he pointed through the open door at the offending terminal. 'I was hoping you might be able to tell us how.'

Colin had arrived before him. John saw him through the Road House window, sitting at the back of the restaurant, beside the kitchen doors and the rear exit. He had a white coffee cup on the table in front of him and a teaspoon in his hand which he twizzled back and forth between his fingers, all the time gazing warily at the door. His relief was palpable as he saw John arrive.

John went to the service area and ordered a pot of tea, then carried his tray over to Colin's table. He said nothing as he busied himself with pouring milk into his cup and stirring the tea in the pot to speed its infusion.

'Have you been here long?' he asked, his

voice neutral.

'About a half hour. I had to walk.'

John eyed the soaked jacket hanging on an adjacent chair. 'So I see,' he said. Colin's hair had flopped wetly over his forehead. It dripped into his now empty cup.

'I left, like you told me to. I didn't have time to pack much.' He kicked at the holdall lying on the floor beside his chair, 'but I made you a copy of what I gave to Moira.' He dived into his pocket and produced a floppy disk. It had, John noticed, been re-labelled several times, the previous contents crossed out in bright green marker pen.

Somewhat reluctantly, as though in taking it he crossed a bridge into Colin's world, John took the disk from him and looked at it briefly before tucking it into the inside pocket of his jacket.

'You'd better start at the beginning,' he said.

'The beginning.' Colin laughed nervously. 'I'm not sure I know where that is any more. I mean...'

'Colin.' John held up both hands as though in self defence. 'Start with how you got this information. With what you told Moira and how this ties into Alice Sanders.'

He'd given him too many options, John realised. He realised too, that Colin was shaking with more than the damp and cold. The man was scared. Scared and looking to

John for a lead.

He tried again. 'Tell me about the night Moira came to see you and I'll ask questions as we go along. That help you?'

Colin nodded. Went to lift his empty cup, then replaced it with a sharp little crack against the saucer.

'Here,' John poured half the tea into the empty vessel. It mixed unpalatably with the coffee dregs, but Colin, adding milk and then heaped spoons of sugar, didn't seem to notice.

'It was the night when it all went wrong with that tip off I'd given her,' he began. He lifted his gaze as though pleading with John not to judge him for that. 'She came over. She was mad as hell, said she'd never listen to me again and I mean, who could have blamed her.' He trailed off and blinked rapidly as though trying hard not to cry. 'I wish she'd kept to that,' he said, this time meeting John's gaze full on and holding it. 'I wish she'd had the bloody sense just to walk away. Tell me to go to hell and go off home. But me, well, I wanted to show off. I'd got this feeling, you see, that this time I'd really found something. Something maybe she could use. Something she could take seriously.'

'You still wanted her back, didn't you?' John asked softly.

Colin's laugh was loud and manic enough

to turn heads. 'What do you think? Best thing, maybe the only good thing ever happened to me and what do I do? I chuck it away by being ... pathetic. And then, she asks for a divorce and, you know, it didn't even occur to me to fight it. To fight for her. I knew she deserved better, I knew...'

'Colin, spare me the self pity. I've had a long day and I've better things to do than hear you rant about what might have been. For what it's worth, Moira never stopped caring about you. She thought ... thought you were a nice bloke, someone worth ... well, worth... Look, she went out on a limb for you often enough.' John paused, sighed, regretting his having to be here, wanting his bed and a few hours precious sleep before he started over again. 'You gave her some info that night, Colin. What was it? You said you put it on a disk with pictures of Alice Sanders.'

'Yeah, yes I did. That's right, I did.' Colin took a deep breath and took hold of himself. 'I told her I'd found something about Charlie Radcliffe. I down-loaded what I had and I hid it in the boot sector of a disk with Alice's photos on.' He shrugged, embarrassed. 'I'd got the pictures for a friend from this guy, like I told you on the phone. This photographer, does some glamour shots and his computer, he leaves it wide open, anyone could walk in.'

John bit back the challenge about it being not everyone that would want to and denied himself the tirade on the criminality of hacking. 'So, what?' he said. 'What you're telling me is that anyone looking casually at this disk, all they'd get is nude pictures?'

'Semi nude,' Colin corrected him. 'She never went more than topless, at least, not for Mr Tyler.'

'Mr Tyler?'

'Don Tyler. He's the photographer.' He took a quick drink of his tea and then mumbled, 'I had a good look through his files while I was there.'

'Christ, Colin!' John leant back in his chair and closed his eyes. None of this was admissible of course. It was illegally gained and laid Colin open to prosecution. John wasn't totally sure how he would be able to use it. But it was potentially a lead and they were thin enough on the ground. 'OK,' he said slowly. In for a penny. 'You wouldn't have an address for this Don Tyler?'

Colin shook his head. 'No, but I know what photo club he belonged to. Bishopswood, across town. They meet at Westwood College and use the darkroom facilities there. The Alice pictures and the others like it, I think he must take those at home though. There's the same background stuff in most of them. I think they're slides. He could process colour slides at home – Moira

89

and I used to do it...' He trailed off, colour reaching his cheeks.

John opened his mouth and closed it again, the flush on Colin's cheeks telling him what kind of slides they might be.

'Um, you can put slides onto a computer?' he asked. 'I thought they had to be digital images if you wanted to save them to PC.'

'No. You can buy a scanner specially for negatives and slides. Expensive, if you want a good one, but I guess it would be worth it for someone like Don Tyler. He, er, he has quite a collection.'

John fell silent, considering. 'These payments you found. On Radcliffe's computer. What made Moira think they might be dodgy?'

Colin shrugged. 'Don't know for sure. You see, there were two sets of figures. One looked legit – orders for spirits, catering costs, all the normal stuff, but the prices,' he paused and whistled, 'high or what? I got to thinking, I wouldn't want his liquor bill. Then I thought, well, you hear about bottles of vintage stuff that sells for a fortune and I looked some of the names up on the internet. You know what some bottles of vintage wine sell for? And the mark up ... you know a typical restaurant mark up is about 68%? But anyway, it still didn't seem quite right. I mean, this is Hillford, for Christ's sake, not Kensington, so I looked a bit further.' He glanced nervously at John. 'I wasn't going to do anything with it, you know. What I found out. I was just being nosy. Then I found the other set of accounts. It was in a file marked AOB, you know, like Any Other Business? In the other set of accounts the figures were the same, but the payouts didn't go to caterers. The same names came up over and over again. And when I showed them to Moira, she seemed to know some of them. She got excited, said I should give her a copy, then delete the information and forget all about it.'

'But you didn't,' John tapped his pocket.

'I didn't get round to it. Then there was ... Moira died and I didn't know what to do.'

'Is this the only copy?'

Colin shook his head. He dug into a pocket once more and brought out a bunch of keys. On the ring was what looked like a blue enamel keyfob. Colin's name had been crudely painted across its surface in silver paint. As John watched, Colin pulled on one end of the 'fob'. It came away, leaving the short end attached to the ring and revealed a silver connector of some sort. John vaguely knew he'd seen something like it before.

'A hard drive,' he said. 'Stick drive, or whatever it's called.'

Colin nodded. 'I figured, one copy could be lost, corrupted. It's never safe to just have a single copy. You should always back up your data, you know.'

John thought that in this instance probably the less copies there were the better.

A thought seemed to strike Colin. 'You have *got* a computer, haven't you?'

'I've got a laptop,' John told him. 'Anything I need to know about the disk?'

'No,' Colin told him. 'Like I said, I put the data in the boot sector for Moira. She could access it via her old DOS machine, but then, Moira knew what she was doing. I've left it in the clear for you, so...'

'I'll be careful,' John assured him, not sure whether or not to be insulted at the inference that he was ignorant as regards things technical. He decided to let it pass. It was, after all, pretty close to the truth. Most of the time, his laptop sat, unused, in the corner of his bedroom. He remembered to charge it occasionally, but that was often the only exercise it got. He made use of the technology at work, acknowledged its usefulness, but had no wish to play with it in his spare time the way many of his colleagues did. He'd far rather go for a long walk or lose a round of golf.

'Have you got anywhere to go?' he asked.

'Not really thought about it.' Colin shook his head. 'Where do you think I should go?' He looked hopefully at John.

John Moore thought about it. There were safe houses, used to house witnesses, but that couldn't easily be organised tonight and he wasn't certain that Colin would qualify. Certainly not until John had checked out the evidence. The Road House had rooms. Its usual clientele being long distance drivers and the odd motorist who found he couldn't make it home. They were used to folk checking in at all hours. It was one of the few places John could think of where that wouldn't raise comment.

'Stay here at the motel,' he told Colin. 'Do you have money?'

'Some.'

John took out his wallet and found two twenties. 'Look,' he said, 'pay cash in advance, tell them you don't want to be disturbed. I'll call you tomorrow and we'll sort out something better.'

'When will you call?'

'I'm not sure yet. You just hold on here. Register under another name.' He thought for a moment, trying to think of the last time he'd used anywhere like the Road House and if they were likely to check ID. He decided it was unlikely but they might want a car registration. It was usual to ask in the hotels attached to service station cafes. If the number wasn't recorded, the guest would be charged for overnight parking and, as no one usually *walked* to a place like the Road House, not having a vehicle *would* be likely to make someone sit up and take notice.

He said as much to Colin and then scribbled his own car registration on a scrap of paper.

He got to his feet, scraping the chair back from the table.

'You're going?'

'I need to get some sleep. It's been a long day.'

'Oh. I suppose it has, yes. When will you call me?'

'I told you, I'm not sure. I've got some things to do first and other things to check out. Just stay put. If you need to, book another night. Do you have enough money?'

'Yeah, I think so. I've got my credit card and my bank card. There's an ATM here so I can draw cash,' he reassured John. 'I'm not quite daft enough to sign in under one name and use a credit card with another.'

John smiled wanly. 'Right,' he said. 'Just keep your head down and I'll get back to you as soon as I can.'

He left then, going back through the glass doors and out into the pouring rain. As he glanced back, he could see Colin still seated at the table, staring down into the depths of the empty cup.

Charlie Radcliffe stared at the young man. 'So, basically, what you're telling me is that as long as I'm connected to the internet, other buggers can waltz right in and fuck around with what's on my machine?'

'Well, yes,' Sam shrugged. 'You can stop them, Mr Radcliffe, but I think whoever was leaving obscene messages in your files must have been using a port scanner of some kind. You see, every computer has its own unique number, like a name and address that just relate to it. So, if someone with a port scanner has that unique number, the IP address, they can, well they can dial straight into your computer.'

Radcliffe stared at him. 'Why did no one tell me about this when they installed the damn thing. Or when they came and connected me up to bloody broadband?' He sat down, suddenly annoyed with more than Colin. 'Does this happen a lot?'

'I believe so, but no one wants to admit it. Service providers like to stress the idea of privacy and security and they sell their systems on things like parental control and net nannies.' He paused. 'I ... what I mean is, when people buy a computer and connect it to the internet, they're usually more concerned with stopping their kids accessing sites from the computer – you know, things getting out, so to speak, that they don't think about other people getting in.'

'But you can do something about it? I thought they'd installed a firewall or somesuch.'

'They did. Well, someone did, but it's not

95

the best you could get and it doesn't look as if it's been updated since it was installed. There are ways round a lot of them and it's … it's kind of a challenge to some people to find the holes. Dealing with security is like dealing with viruses, you need to keep on top of things, do regular updates.'

Radcliffe looked at Sandra. 'And do we?'

She nodded. 'That's one of the things Sam helped me with before.'

'Well thank fuck for something. This other problem, you know how to fix that?'

Sam nodded. 'I can install a bit of software that'll stop the scans,' he said 'and set up an alarm so you can tell every time anyone tries. You'd be surprised how often it happens.'

Henshaw had been listening. 'How do they get this unique number? What are we saying here, we've got business rivals who…'

Sam was shaking his head. 'Probably nothing as organised as that,' he said. 'It's usually well, kind of cold calling. You know how some people muck around with mobile phones, dialling random numbers, just to see if they get a hit?'

Radcliffe shook his head. 'Can't say that I do, but go on.'

'Well, people with scanners just put in random addresses, see what they come up with. I'd guess you were just unlucky, Mr Radcliffe.'

'Do you have this software we need?'

'No, but I can get it for you.'

'Do that. Sandra, give this young man some money out of petty cash. Sam, I'd appreciate it done as soon as. You'll be paid, of course, double time if you can make it tomorrow.' He paused and then went on, 'I'm running a business here, Sam and I'm sure you can appreciate some of my files are confidential.'

Sam looked surprised. 'Oh, yeah, of course. I don't need to look at anything anyway. You just install the barrier and alarm and it runs in the background. You'll not even notice it.'

'Good enough.' Radcliffe extended a large, square hand and shook Sam's. 'You'd best get back to the game,' he said. 'Sandra says you're doing well for us.'

Sam smiled at the woman and she smiled back warmly. 'Oh,' she said as though as an afterthought. 'Sam, when you get down there, check that Julie's feeling all right? I noticed she was looking a bit peaky earlier on.'

'OK, will do. I think she's been a bit upset, that's all.'

'Upset?' Sandra's voice filled with concern. 'Is Ian not well? She should have said something.'

'I don't think it's her little boy,' Sam told her. He shrugged. 'Sorry, I don't know her that well, I just got the impression there'd

97

been a death in the family or something. She mentioned going to a funeral. Sometime last week, I think.'

'OK, love, I'll have a word later,' Sandra told him. She waited until he'd gone then looked across at Radcliffe.

'A funeral?' Henshaw said. He reached into the desk drawer and pulled the photographs of Moira's funeral out onto the desk. It took them fifteen minutes of searching, she'd kept away from the main party, but there, close to the church wall, was a small figure dressed in a dark blue coat. She wore a scarf tied over her hair and had her face turned partly from the camera but Sandra was in no doubt.

'Julie,' she said. 'Now what the hell was she doing there?'

12

Morning briefing and John was almost late, arriving at eight fifteen and slipping into the back of the room. DS Morantz noticed and nodded in his direction.

DCI Weaver stood at the front of the room, listening as the duty officer delivered a resume of the case so far. It didn't amount to much. Body of a young woman, twenty-five years old, name of Alice Sanders. Found on recreation ground at eight forty five yesterday morning. He pointed out the crime scene photos arranged artfully on a group of pin boards and made special note of the way her wallet had been laid out with the drivers license on top and finished by saying that Inspector Moore had spoken with the family the night before. Across the room, facing these photographs, John could see a similar board. He looked away quickly, focus back on the duty officer. Seeing Moira, displayed in this way, bruised and battered and very dead was so much harder than looking at this other woman. Someone whose death was now in his hands but whose life he had not known.

The duty officer peered around the room, not having noted John Moore's entrance, his gaze finally alighting on the Inspector as John stepped from behind the filing cabinet he had been leaning upon. Weaver had been looking for him too.

'Get anything useful from the family?' Weaver was straight to the point.

'Nothing helpful. DC Morgan,' John nodded in the young officer's direction, 'is due to meet the sister in law at eleven so she can make the formal identification. The family was too shocked by the news to tell us much last night, but I gave them something to think about and I'm hoping it will bear fruit.'

'Oh?' Weaver looked sceptical, but then Weaver always looked sceptical.

'An informant tells me that Alice Sanders used to pose for one of the local photo clubs. Maybe more than one. Glamour shots, I believe is the official terminology,' he paused for the burst of raucous laughter issuing from the back of the room to subside. Weaver turned his head and glowered at the offenders.

'Glamour shots?'

'Bikini, fancy underwear, that sort of thing.' He hesitated. He'd been up all night wondering how much to tell, but now he decided. He pulled an A5 envelope from his raincoat pocket and extracted two of the images he had printed out. Colin had been kind enough to leave these two on the disk. The quality wasn't brilliant. The images had been compressed, zipped up and it'd taken John an hour to figure out how to unpack them. His printer wasn't that good either, but even so, they were undoubtedly of Alice Sanders.

John pinned them to the board, aware that every eye in the room was looking at him expectantly, including Weaver's.

'And you got these, where?' Weaver bent close to the board, frowning. He glanced back over his shoulder. 'Can we get these cleaned up a bit?'

100

'Should be able to. Do you have the original source, sir?' This last addressed to John.

He looked to see who was speaking, recognised Morrison, the probationer from the day before. He looked keen, almost too eager.

'I'll talk to you after,' John told him. He'd no intention of surrendering the disk. Yet. Didn't feel safe even admitting its existence. Yet. He'd looked at the figures in the accounts Colin had downloaded and understood, now, why Moira had been so excited. John had recognised three names. Two were local dignitaries and one, Billy James, was a real blast from the past for John. *If* it happened to be the same man and instinct told John that it would be.

Alone, it was not admissible as evidence. Alone, it was less than nothing.

'Your ... informant,' Weaver was asking him. 'How did he get these pictures? Is he a happy snapper?'

A second ripple of laughter trickled across the room.

'I don't believe so, no. But he knows who took these. A man called Don Tyler, member of the Bishopswood photographic club. They meet at a local college on a Wednesday night.'

'And your informant? He fancies this Tyler for it?'

John shrugged non-commitally. 'I don't

101

think so,' he admitted, 'but Alice's family claim they knew nothing about it. If she kept her ... modelling assignments a secret, there may have been other things.'

Weaver fixed him with a cold stare. 'There's always other things,' Weaver said.

John found it suddenly hard to meet his gaze.

Brady Timms had been editor of the local paper for as long as John could remember and had been balding for almost all that time. John figured that the process must have started when Brady was still a young man, then at some self appointed moment, come to a complete halt. Brady's bald patch had been in roughly the same tonsorial state for the past ten years, the only difference now being that it was edged by a fringe of greying hair rather than the chestnut brown the man had previously owned.

Brady, unlike some journalists John had dealings with, was a likeable man. He was honest and open and still bore that unmistakable mark of the idealist. The badge was so clearly born he might as well have had it tattooed across his hairless scalp.

He greeted John warmly and offered him a seat. Shouted through to the boy in the outer office to fetch some coffee. Brady seemed to employ an endless procession of school leavers in that outer office. They generally lasted six months or so before departing for pastures new; though the odd one had stayed. Brady's staff boasted three or four reporters that John could name, whose humble beginnings had been in making coffee and filing according to Brady's incomprehensible system. Brady Timms was of the old school. You started at the bottom and you worked your way up, learning your trade as you went. He had no truck with the new-fangled notion of university for journalists. Brady's crew started where it mattered, making coffee for the boss, until he was sure they'd absorbed enough of his worldly wisdom to be allowed to try something new.

But even the likes of Brady Timms could get it wrong, and John knew from the instant he sat down that this had rankled.

'I don't need to ask what you're here for,' Brady said. 'Bloody mess or what?'

'It is that,' John admitted. Publishing a deceased's name and picture in the local paper before her family had been informed was something beyond a social *faux pas*. 'What happened?'

Brady shrugged. 'We got wind of the story first thing, got onto your press office. I was a bit surprised when Chrissie said there was an officer here to see me about the murder. Normally your little girl in the press office would give me a call, but, it'd happened before, you'd sent someone round when you wanted my help, so...'

Little girl in the press office. John laughed inwardly.

Linda was at least thirty-five and mother of three.

'And his ID checked out?'

Brady nodded. 'Plausible all round,' he said. 'He introduced himself as DC Sandford, had the right papers, said you wanted to strike while the iron was hot, as it were.'

'He used that phrase?'

'Well, no.' Brady frowned. 'He said something like, you wanted to get a jump on the bastard. He seemed pretty steamed up, but then, second murder in Hillford ... enough to get anyone steamed up. Not the sort of thing that happens here,' he paused, looked at John. 'I heard... you and DS Barker were an item. I'm sorry, John, deeply sorry.'

John Moore nodded briefly. 'And he asked you specifically to print the photo.'

'He had the photo and details of the finding and some other images, looked like crime scene shots. I mean I couldn't print those and I told him so, but it seemed he wanted me to see anyway.' Brady paused again. 'Like I said, he was pretty steamed up.'

John nodded slowly. 'And it all looked legitimate.'

Brady opened his desk drawer and reached inside. He withdrew several plastic wallets and laid them on the desk for John's inspection. 'They'll be covered in prints,' he said apologetically. 'God knows how many of our lot handled them while they were in the office. Soon as I got word last night I rounded everything up and put it in my drawer.' He shrugged. 'Not going to be of much help, is it?'

'I don't know,' John told him. 'We're going to need...'

'Prints for elimination. Yes, I've already primed my lot.' He fished in his drawer again. 'Descriptions of the man from anyone who had anything to do with him. They're fairly consistent. We take this personally, John. It makes us look unprofesional and aside from any considerations sympathy wise, that's bad for the circulation.'

John wondered briefly if Brady meant his own or the newspaper's. 'Headed notepaper,' he commented. 'Whoever put this together had access to the press office.'

Brady nodded. 'I thought that too,' he said. 'At first. But think about it. How many places do the normal press releases go to? I've a filing cabinet full, then copies will go out to social services, mayor's office, I don't know, a dozen places on a regular basis. All anyone has to do these days is blank off the copy and scan the heading into a computer. Dead easy. One thing's for sure though, whoever it was knew what they were doing and went to a lot of trouble to make sure we printed those pictures and ran the article. They wanted the world to know that little Alice Sanders was dead.'

He looked pointedly at John, unasked questions hanging in the air between them. John nodded. He got to his feet and reached across the desk to shake hands with Brady Timms. 'You come up with the reason why before I do, Brady, be sure and let me know.'

Colin wasn't good at waiting around. His life may not have amounted to much in a material sense, but he had always kept busy.

Now, he just had too much time to think and, of course, he thought of Moira.

Separated they might have been, but they had remained close. They had spent last Christmas together. Or a part of it at least. She'd played the dutiful daughter and had lunch with her folks, then come over to his flat and the two of them had spent the evening with mutual friends they'd managed to hang onto from their university days.

For a brief few hours Colin had forgotten – almost – that they were no longer a couple. He had been able to pretend to himself and, almost to the others, that everything was as it had once been. Before Moira grew up and Colin didn't.

It wasn't that Colin lacked inner resources or the ability to keep himself amused; just that he had so little with which to do it.

Almost all of his possessions had been left behind in the flat.

He had tried watching television, but the daytime diet of cookery advice and house makeovers failed to excite. Colin owned a television, but rarely watched it. It lived in a cupboard and he dragged it out only when there was something absolutely specific that he wanted to see.

He thought, briefly, of going home. The intense fear of the previous night had worn thin through over-use and Colin now settled into a state of restless anticipation.

He sat, staring at the television and willing the phone to ring.

It occurred to him that John Moore might not contact him. Might just leave him in the lurch. Or worse, somehow betray his whereabouts to Radcliffe. Only the fact that Moira had trusted the man sustained Colin enough to do the same, though the thought nagged at the fringes of his consciousness that she had not trusted John enough to go to him that night with the information Colin had given to her.

That Moira might simply have been acting like an idiot or that she might have been trying to prove herself to her colleagues, or some combination of those things, they fought with the logic of her telling John. So far, Colin's mental argument was pretty finely balanced, but as ten thirty came and

John Moore still had not been in touch, Colin felt himself losing the battle against the irrational.

He sneaked another look at the telephone and at his mobile, plugged in and charging beside it, as though they might have rung and he somehow not have noticed. He even checked for missed calls and text messages, took his mobile with him to the bathroom and left the door open so that he could still hear – and watch – the phone. But John Moore still did not ring and Colin could feel his hold on sanity ebbing away under the pressure of alternating fear and pure boredom.

Finally, he could stand it no longer. Figuring that John could still contact him by mobile should he finally decide to do so, Colin left the hotel and, without any clear idea of where he might be going, began the wet and dreary walk back towards the town.

With Colin safe at the hotel, John had decided to take the chance to look around his flat in his absence. At that moment he was parked outside the building, reading through the descriptions that Brady Timms had given him.

Brady was right, all three witnesses – Brady himself, Chrissie, his long standing, long suffering PA, and the latest office boy had seen a sandy-haired man of about five feet eight to ten in height. Brady estimated his age at early thirties and, knowing Brady's habit of down grading everyone in terms of physical maturity, John was inclined to add a decade. The office boy – whose name turned out to be Tom Clarke – was only eighteen and therefore assumed that everyone over twenty-five was ancient. He guessed the man's age at forty plus, describing him as middle aged or oldish, but, more usefully perhaps, noted that he had a small scar on his left cheek and that he wore a fancy and very expensive looking watch. He didn't actually label it a Rolex, but John could guess he had wanted to. He modified the young man's description, taking an average age of around forty and guessed that maybe the watch was analogue rather than digital and that the boy wouldn't know a Rolex from a Pentax.

He was more inclined to give credit to Chrissie's notes. Chrissie was a shrewd woman, observant and smart and if she stated that the man was probably in his late thirties and that there was grey in amongst the sandy-blond of his hair, John would accept her word. She mentioned the scar – small, she said, more like a pock mark than a wound – and the watch also. Expensive, she noted, classy, but not overly flashy. She thought it might have been a chronometer, showing several dials. She noted that because, she said, she could never quite see the point. Not unless you were the type always to be jetting off to a different time zone, from which observation, John implied that this man definitely was not that type. He made a mental note to talk to Chrissie about that, then tucked the statements back inside his raincoat and got out of his car.

The steady November rain had soaked his hair and the jacket beneath his open coat even before he reached the door. He rang the bells in sequence until, on the third try, he found someone home.

'Here to see Colin Grainger,' he said, speaking into the grill, but the owner of flat three had buzzed him inside even before he had finished Colin's name. Colin's flat was on the second floor of the converted house. There were two bedsits on the ground floor and another two on the first.

Colin's flat was on the floor above and a Miss Bryce apparently occupied the attic rooms. She had been the one to let John in and he wondered if she'd be worth talking to.

Colin's door was closed, but the lock was old and John remembered Moira telling him that a good thump would often as not bump the sneck out of the hatch. Colin, apparently, was always forgetting his keys.

Glancing around and feeling a little guilty, John tried her method and found, somewhat to his surprise, that as the door jerked back, it did indeed spring open.

'So much for security.' Though he supposed that Colin felt safer, knowing that anyone wanting to come into the building would have to get a resident to buzz them inside. Not, as John had just found, that this would prove much of an obstacle.

He pushed the door and frowned as it seemed to snag on something, refusing to open fully. With difficulty, he squeezed inside. He wasn't the first to have been there. The tiny flat had been well and truly turned over and whoever had done it didn't care a fig for discretion.

John pushed the door closed behind him and stood on the threshold looking around. One space for living and bed, with a tiny bathroom and kitchen leading off it – factors that turned it, in rental terms, from bedsit to studio flat. He could see these other rooms through the open doors. The contents of Colin's cupboards had been strewn across the floor.

Bed stripped, mattress slashed, television lying on its imploded screen beside the desk. The computer monitor had been left in place and the keyboard and mouse simply slung onto the floor. John could glimpse them beneath the tangle of bedcovers. But the computer itself had gone, dangling cables beneath the desk illustrating, along with a line of fluff, where it had once been.

Careful not to disturb anything, John took a further step into the room. No floppy disks, no CDs, nothing that indicated data storage. It looked as though the only information Colin had left was on the disk he had given John and the little keyfob thing he carried with him. He smiled, at a half memory of Moira's exasperation with her ex. He'd bought the stick memory, she said, carried it everywhere with him, but still forgot his keys. It was Moira who suggested he attach it to the ring.

John's hand moved to extract his mobile from his deep raincoat pocket. Then he hesitated. He ought to report this; but not yet. It would involve too many explanations right now and he still wasn't ready. He was now convinced that Moira's death and Alice's murder were closely linked and he'd have to talk to Weaver about that ... soon. He needed to think, first, put it all together in his own mind so he could advance the case without having to contend with Weaver's scepticism when he learned that John's informant was none other than the infamous Colin Grainger. And, sooner or later, he would have to tell him. If only to bring Colin under Weaver's protection. John was not looking forward to that moment.

John frowned. He had no liking for DCI Weaver and yet it was ... nothing he could put his finger on. There were rumours, but then, it was hard to rise so high and fast as Weaver had and there not be rumours. Shrugging, he put his worries to one side for the moment. He could hear the resident of the flat above moving about, her feet sounding where she walked on bare floor-boards, silenced again when she presumably stepped back onto carpet.

He doubted whoever had broken in here had been quiet enough for her not to have heard something.

Closing the door carefully behind him, John took himself upstairs to interview Miss Bryce.

Mel Sanders looked pale but was admirably in control, Rose Morgan thought as she watched her crossing the car park towards the main Hospital doors. Only when she got close could Rose see the dark shadows beneath her eyes and the redness of a night of tears.

'Are you all right?' Rose asked her. 'I mean, are you ready for this?'

Mel shrugged. 'As I'll ever be,' she said. 'Look, I don't mean to be rude, but I've had all night to think about this and I'd rather get it over now.'

DS Morgan nodded. 'They're waiting for us,' she confirmed. Then added, as though it might help, 'It won't take long.'

Immediately, she regretted the crassness

of the remark, but Mel just smiled wanly. 'I know,' she said. 'It's afterwards that takes the time.'

Alice had been removed from the mortuary and laid tenderly in the chapel of rest. The post-mortem had been done and the body washed, then a plain white sheet arranged so that it covered all but her face. Someone had taken the trouble to comb out her hair.

Relatives had two choices at St Gerard's. It was possible to view the body through a little window or to go inside. Rose, whose experience of these things, she had calculated, now ran to an even dozen times, had found the split to be equal. Some relatives needed to be at one remove, as though the pane of glass and sheet of white linen somehow made it ... if not less real, then at least more manageable.

Others needed to touch. To see close up that this was really their loved one. That only touching the face, stroking the hair, could convince them that this was it. An ending.

Mel had no hesitation, she opened the door without Rose asking and she went inside.

'Has the Post been done?' she asked.

Rose nodded.

'When can we have the funeral?'

'I'm sorry, I don't know.'

Mel nodded and then crossed the few feet of space between the door and the gurney on which her dead sister in law lay.

'Poor little bugger,' she whispered softly. 'Oh, Alice, what the hell did you do to deserve this?' She shook her head.

'No one deserves that,' Rose said, surprised at how harsh her voice sounded. Mel looked at her in some surprise. 'This really gets to you, doesn't it?'

'Every time.'

'And you're right, no one deserved this.' She paused and then reached an unsteady hand to caress Alice's hair. Her fingers paused over the bruises on the dead girl's face. And then, she gently turned the head until she could see the wound that had killed her. Rose instinctively moved to stop her, then let her hand fall back to her side.

'What did they do to her first?' Mel's voice was harsh.

'Mel. I don't think...'

Slowly, Mel pulled back the linen sheet and looked long and hard at the mass of bruises covering Alice's pallid skin.

'God,' she said. Then turned away, one hand covering her mouth as though to stop herself from being sick.

'Mel,' Rose took her arm and led her away and out of the room. 'Come on,' she said. 'I'll see about a cup of tea.'

It was some time before Mel said anything. She accepted the tea and loaded it with sugar, then stared down at her cup. 'Don't know why I did that,' she said. 'I gave up drinking sweet tea over a year ago.'

'Are you all right now?'

'Yeah,' she managed a wry, bleak smile. 'I didn't expect ... I mean I thought I'd cope. I just needed to know ... Mam and James, they needed to know. They *said,* they needed to know.' She shook her head.

'And what will you tell them?'

'Not that.' Mel's gaze seemed to search every inch of Rose's face as though looking for something. 'It's enough for one of us to know the bastards beat her black and blue before they killed her. A beating like that, it doesn't happen in minutes.' She paused again and poked at her tea with a spoon as though checking the sugar had dissolved. 'I ... did some voluntary work in a crisis centre,' she explained. 'Women who'd finally got the guts to walk out. We documented their injuries for if they got it together enough to press charges. Half the time they just went straight back, but... Some of them looked like that. Like Alice. There was one woman, said her husband had taken three solid hours over that final beating. She'd been barely able to walk after, but he'd been ... kind of systematic, eking it out so it could go on longer without her passing out. You know?'

Rose nodded. She'd seen it all. 'Mel, would you say Alice's is a close family?'

Mel exhibited some surprise at the question, but then she nodded. 'The dad left when Alice was about five. Not been in touch since, so it was Annie and the kids from then on. Truthfully, I don't think they even missed him, not after the first shock and he's certainly never mentioned. Alice was always a pretty girl. Lots of friends and boyfriends, but nothing serious.' She hesitated again. 'Look, I had Mam and James make a list last night. It gave us something to do, I suppose.'

'A list? Of friends?'

'Yeah. From school and after. I don't have all their addresses and so on, but they all more or less knew one another, so it shouldn't be difficult.' She raked in her bag and handed Rose three sheets of lined paper.

Rose glanced at the list and thanked her. 'Did you know about her modelling?'

Mel glanced down at the table, then she sighed. 'Not exactly,' she said. 'I knew Mam would be upset and Alice seemed OK about it all, so I didn't mention it. She told me this man had asked her to pose for him. Made a joke of it and when I acted kind of shocked, I suppose, she laughed it off and assured me she'd told him where to go.'

'And you believed her?'

'Yeah, yeah I did. Like I said, Alice was pretty. Men, and women for that matter, they looked at her. But she wasn't vain or anything, she was just ... just Alice. And

117

when she said that, about this man, it was in the middle of a conversation one night about, well, I don't know, girl stuff.' She smiled. 'We'd have at least one night out a month. See a film or go for a meal, then spend an hour chatting somewhere. It was said in passing and I didn't take the bait.'

'Bait?'

'I thought about it a lot last night. I think she thought she'd try saying it to me first, see what reaction she got and if I was OK, then she might get around to mentioning it to Mam. Obviously, I didn't give her what she wanted. I don't remember sounding very shocked, but I can't have sounded too happy about it either.' She stared down once more into the cooling tea. 'If I'd acted differently. If she'd been able to tell me...' She looked back at Rose and DS Morgan wondered if she'd ever seen such despair in anyone's eyes. 'If we'd known about it, she might not be dead.'

13

John had returned to headquarters to find Don Tyler had been brought in and was waiting for interview.

He was a small man. Tired looking and with an unmistakable air of anxiety that seemed more second nature than merely due to the circumstances.

John sat down at the table opposite and DS Morantz stood slightly back from them both, a clip-board in his hands to which was affixed the photographs John had printed. Strictly speaking, they could not be used in a court of law but as equally strictly speaking, John did not know exactly how they had been obtained and was inclined to ignore what he did know. He was quite prepared to bring them in here, see what happened when Don Tyler was confronted.

Morantz also had crime scene pictures. Images of Alice. After. But John wanted those kept in reserve. If Tyler had nothing to tell, John felt he would soon know.

'Mr Tyler?' John allowed a question to creep into his tone.

'Er, yes. That's me?' The man sounded uncertain, returning the questioning tone.

'Thank you for coming in.' He reached over and set the tape player, announcing his presence and that of Morantz along with Tyler in the interview room. 'The time is twelve forty on November seventeenth.' He glanced across at Tyler as though for confirmation and was not surprised when it came.

'Oh yes,' glancing at his watch. A Chronometer, John noted. 'Yes, it's the seventeenth and I make it twelve forty-two if that's any help.'

Out of the corner of his eye, John could see Morantz stifling a smile.

'I understand you're a photographer, Mr Tyler.'

'Yes, man and boy. It's a nice hobby.'

'Do you have a speciality, Mr Tyler?'

'Landscape,' he said without missing a beat. 'I enjoy landscape. And industrial archaeology. We went up to see the remains of the Alum works a month or so ago. You wouldn't know it, but there was once a thriving industry on the coast down from Whitby, ships used to come right up onto the beach. They cut deep trenches in the shale...'

'I'm sure that's fascinating, Mr Tyler, but a history lesson isn't what we're here for. You know a young woman by the name of Alice Sanders.'

Tyler thought about it. 'No, I don't believe so. No.'

'Oh,' John said. 'Then I'm to assume you photograph your models without asking their names, Mr Tyler?'

'Models? We use models down at the photography club sometimes. Figure work, you know.'

'Figure work.' John let the silence sit. Tyler had paled visibly and John knew he would keep up the pretence only for so long. He gestured for Morantz to lay the pictures flat upon the table. 'The quality isn't good, I'm afraid, Mr Tyler. In fact it does neither Alice nor your skills any favours, but I believe you took these pictures.'

'Where...?' Tyler looked at him slack jawed.

'Information received, Mr Tyler.'

'I want my lawyer.'

'Do you have a lawyer?'

Tyler gaped at him then blinked rapidly, totally flummoxed.

'Why would I have a lawyer?' he said at last. 'I've never been in trouble. I've got a wife and family. I...'

'We'll be happy to provide you with a lawyer, Mr Tyler. I just enquired in case you had a preference.'

'I... I...' Tyler stared at him. 'What's this all about, Inspector?'

'Do you read the papers, Mr Tyler? While I agree that the picture that appeared in the *Hillford Times* may not have been as flattering as your pictures, I'm sure if you saw it you'd have recognised the young woman. The young, dead, woman.'

Tyler was stunned 'You can't be serious,' he whispered. 'I had nothing to do with that. I just took her picture, I didn't kill...' He lifted both hands and rubbed his face so viciously that it left pink marks behind. Bright spots of colour where the blood had been dragged to the surface of his otherwise pale and pasty skin.

'So, you knew Alice Sanders?'

'I knew her, yes. She did a life class for us at the college. It was this combined thing with one of the art groups. Their regular model didn't want to be photographed.' He barked what must have been a laugh, but it was hard to tell. 'It was alright, apparently, to be painted in the altogether, but you take a photograph and suddenly, it's one step from pornography!'

'And you came to a private arrangement with Miss Sanders?'

Tyler nodded. 'I never did anything but take pictures. I'm not like that and, anyway, I have a wife. I never...' he broke off. 'My God, what's she going to say?'

'She doesn't know about Alice?'

Tyler shook his head. 'No, I chose nights when I knew she'd be out and Alice came in through the back way. I knew my wife wouldn't understand. She didn't understand about any of it anyway.'

'About any of it?'

'Photography. To Sharon, photos are what you take on holiday with an instant camera. Not ... not the sort of thing I was doing. Anyway, I had my nights at the camera club and she ... she went out to Bingo.'

'And the nights she was out, you indulged your hobby at home?'

Tyler gave him a look that told John that his sarcasm had found its mark. 'When did you last see Alice, Mr Tyler?'

'November the sixth. She came over on November sixth. Sharon was out at a bonfire party with her sister and her sister's kids. They'd put it off until the Saturday so no one had to get up the following morning. I knew she'd be home late, so I arranged for Alice to come round.'

'Weren't you expected to go along?'

Tyler shrugged. 'I don't get on with her sister,' he said.

'And did you pay Alice?'

Tyler nodded. 'Twenty quid an hour. Usually it didn't take much more than an hour. Sharon spends more than that on Bingo.'

'You processed your own pictures?'

Tyler nodded. 'The other stuff I did at the club. We used the college darkroom. The pictures of Alice...'

'Alice and the other girls.'

Tyler jumped as though he'd been stung.

'I'm assuming those pictures, you did as slides? I'm told you can scan slides directly into your PC.'

Tyler nodded.

Morantz, John noted, looked impressed. John Moore's lack of technical know-how was somewhat legendary in the department.

'Did Alice meet the other girls?'

Tyler shook his head, violently. 'Never. Never,' he asserted angrily. 'I just took her picture. Oh my God.' Again, he buried his face in his hands and rubbed hard. John fought the impulse to reach out and pull the hands away.

'Mr Tyler.' It was Morantz this time. 'Did Alice pose for anyone else?'

'I wouldn't know.' The voice muffled behind the palms. 'We never talked about it.'

'What did you talk about?'

'Nothing. Really nothing. She'd tell me about her family. Little things, like how she'd had a night out with her sister. Might have been sister in law, I don't recall. What film they'd been to see, that sort of nonsense. Nothing important.'

'And did she ever seem frightened? Anxious about anything.'

Again that laugh. The harsh, humourless bark. 'Alice? Scared? Alice ... Alice didn't have enough of a brain to be scared or enough imagination to be anxious. She had the easy life, did Alice. Oh, I know, wrong to speak ill of the dead and all that, but it's the truth Inspector.' He let his hands fall back onto the table. 'She was like Sharon that way. Like my wife, Sharon.'

John let the pause following sit for so long that Morantz shifted restlessly as though worried that the tape recorded nothing but their breathing.

Eventually, it was John that broke the silence and his voice was hoarse with an emotion he scarcely recognised. He was

124

uncertain, too, whether he spoke of Alice or Moira, both so closely linked in his consciousness. 'She was scared in the end,' he said heavily. 'She might have had an easy life, Mr Tyler, but, let me assure you, her death was anything but.' Whether it was mischief born of a sudden dislike for this man, or an unreasoning anger that there should be anyone left in the world that didn't witness such ugliness, John reached over and took the crime scene photos from Morantz.

'Guv.' Morantz was puzzled. Disturbed. He cleared his throat. 'Um, Inspector Moore is showing Mr Tyler some pictures of Alice Sanders,' he said. Then fell into a troubled silence as John laid the new photographs down on the wooden table.

For a moment Don Tyler stared, transfixed by the images. Transfixed for so long that John almost wondered if he were examining them with a critic's eye, judging the work of a fellow professional. Then he broke down, sobs rising to his throat so violently that he was soon gasping for air. 'Oh, God,' Tyler wailed. 'Oh my dear God.'

Morantz could take no more. He stood up, reached over and stopped the tape, then almost forcibly dragged John to his feet and out of the door, shouting to the young P.C who stood outside to get back in.

He pushed his boss back against the wall and moved in close, standing toe to toe, hands clenched as if about to strike out.

'What the hell did you think? With respect, sir, what sort of game are you playing?'

John blinked at him as though waking and finding himself lost. He stared hard at Morantz trying to fathom what the man was saying and then looked back at the slightly open door. Inside the room Don Tyler wept, howling with shock and pain as though Alice's wounds had somehow become his own.

Weaver pointed John into a seat on the opposite side of the desk. There was only the one extra chair and Morantz perched on the low cupboard across the room. John still felt shaky. He had brushed Morantz's anger and concern aside, but he knew in his heart of hearts it had been justified. He had been out of line.

'Well?' Weaver questioned.

Well what? John thought. Then, collecting himself, 'I don't think he knows more than he's told us. He took pictures, of Alice, of others. We could seize his computer.'

'He's probably wiped the hard drive.' Morantz commented. 'Guilty conscience.'

'Even if he has, the data can probably be recovered,' Weaver noted.

Morantz shrugged. 'I'll get a warrant,' he said. 'But I agree with Inspector Moore. He's pathetic, but I doubt he's a murderer.'

'Anything from DC Morgan,' John asked.

He'd suddenly remembered she had been due to meet Mel Sanders.

Weaver nodded. 'The sister-in-law recalls Alice mentioning a man who wanted to take her photo, but she didn't say any more. Morgan reckons Alice was scared her family might disapprove. The sister-in-law's now on a guilt trip. Reckons she should have taken more notice.'

John nodded.

'What do we do with Tyler?' Morantz asked.

'Cut him loose, for now. Get a warrant and we'll see if there's anything incriminating on his computer. Apart from that...'

Weaver looked at John, his eyes hard and probing. 'Your informant tell you anything else?'

'Not yet, no.'

'Is he likely to?'

John shrugged. 'To be truthful, sir, I don't know. He came by this information by accident, then when he saw Alice's picture in the local paper, he realised it might be significant.' He could feel the stoniness of Weaver's gaze upon him. Suddenly, he felt very tired. That incident just now with Tyler, well, John knew he'd stepped beyond the bounds. He fully expected Morantz to tell his boss about it. He'd do the same had their roles been reversed. John Moore's losing it, that's what they'd say. Understandable, for sure, they'd add, and he knew what they'd be thinking. He should take some time out. Give himself a chance to grieve. See the counsellor. Get signed off on the sick for a week or a month or however long it took. The thought of being away, of being cut off and stranded, unable either to influence events or be a part of them was more than his brain could cope with. He'd be all right, just needed to get some sleep. He made a promise to himself that he'd not be late home.

'Anything new?' he found himself asking. He didn't need to elaborate.

'I'm sorry, John. No.' Weaver made an effort to sound conciliatory. 'We're still trying to piece together where she went after the neighbour saw her at five o'clock.'

Radcliffe, John wanted to say. She went after Radcliffe. He nodded at Weaver, acknowledgement and brief thanks, he supposed, wondering what was stopping him from telling Weaver about the disk. About Radcliffe. About the things that Colin had given Moira on the day before she died. He had thought, or had been telling himself, that it was fear of ridicule that kept him silent. That he needed more proof before he went public with Colin's evidence. But, he realised with a sudden unpleasant flash of insight, it was more than that. It was purely and simply a need to sort this out himself. If Radcliffe was responsible for Moira's death, then John wanted to be the one who exacted vengeance and he wasn't sure he cared if it were within or outside of the law.

Impatiently, he shook the thought away and was about to make his excuses and leave when his mobile rang. It was Colin.

'You need to take that?' Weaver enquired as John hesitated.

'I ... Yes, I suppose I do.' He got up. Moving across the room as he flipped open the phone. 'Yes.'

'It's me.'

'I know.'

'You said you'd phone. I waited for you.'

'I've been tied up. I'm sorry.'

John was aware of Weaver's eyes upon him. Morantz was staring at the cracks in the ceiling. John turned his back on both of them, wishing he could leave the room but knowing it would attract even more comment should he try. He wondered why Colin was using his mobile when there would have been a landline in the hotel room. 'Where are you?' He asked.

'Out. Just out. I walked. Look, you said you'd help me. I want to go home but...'

'No, you mustn't do that,' John said quickly.

'Why? They've been there, haven't they?'

Colin's voice had risen and John wished fervently the audio on the phone was less clear. He glanced back at Weaver whose gaze had narrowed. 'Look, I'll meet you.'

'When.'

'I don't know. Later.'

'Later!' Colin's voice rose again. 'And in the meantime, what am I supposed to do?'

'Stay calm,' John told him. He wanted to add, stay off the streets, but Colin had hung up on him. He closed the phone and slid it back into his pocket.

'Problem?' Weaver demanded. 'Your informant, was it?'

John shook his head.

Weaver continued to look at him, waiting for a proper response. When none was forthcoming, he sighed. 'John, we all know what you've been going through, but frankly, I'm concerned. Your man gives you anything more, however vague or small, I want to know about it. You've always been a team player, something about you I've always known could be relied upon. Don't mess up now.'

He dismissed them shortly afterwards and John left the office. Morantz, as John knew he would, hung back and he was aware of both men staring after him, their expressions speaking of both suspicion and concern.

John walked away, not sure even in his own mind if he was just being careful or paranoid. Or if they were right, those voices that said he was losing it and he really should be taking their advice to just walk away.

Meanwhile, across town, Colin was busy conclusion jumping. Moira had always reckoned that, had it been an Olympic sport, Colin would be a world class star.

Was it just bad timing? Had John been where someone might overhear? Or was it something more?

Radcliffe's men had been to his flat. Invaded his space. Colin groaned. He'd half expected that, but still, it was a blow and not just that, it brought home to him like a fist in the gut just how much trouble he was in.

He tried John's phone again only to find it engaged and, somehow, that just added to his feelings of despair. Surely, the man would ring him back. Any minute now, tell him it was all OK and arrange somewhere they could meet that was warm and dry. He thought about returning to the hotel, but the thought of the long walk back and all that open space along the main road ... well, he quailed at the thought of it.

So, just where should he go? He had no car, little money and no clear plan and, as though to insult him even beyond all that, it had once again begun to rain.

14

Julie was scared. Julie had been scared for days but last night, after Sandra and then Charlie Radcliffe had approached her with their questions and concerns, the fear had tipped over into pure terror and the feeling had not left her.

Truthfully, Julie could not recall the last time she had been free of fear or at least unease, but from the evening she had seen Moira Barker with Brian Henshaw in Radcliffe's Casino, what had once been a manageable baggage of insecurity and anxiety had become a bundle heavy enough to have frozen her leadenly in her tracks and was now threatening to drag her all the way down.

She had tried John Moore's number three times so far, but each time someone else had replied, told her that he was unavailable and offered to take a message. Julie couldn't trust anyone else. She was barely able to trust DI Moore and was willing to talk to him only on the basis that Moira had been his girlfriend and had mentioned him in passing a time or two. Julie, therefore, had a name and, also via Moira, a reputation. That she was prepared to risk everything trying to contact someone she knew only by these flimsy devices was a measure of her desperation. The fourth time Julie called, promising herself that this would be the last, she was in luck. John had set his phone to divert and calls from his office desk were routed directly to him.

'Moore,' he said.

'Oh, thank God. Look, you don't know me, but I knew Moira. DS Barker, I mean.'

She paused suddenly at a loss now she had him on the line. John's reply was cautious and non-committal. 'How did you know her? May I know who I'm talking to?'

'My name's Julie,' she said. 'And I knew her ... I knew her because I talked to her sometimes. You know, passing stuff on.'

'What sort of stuff?' John asked her.

'Oh God, do I have to spell it out? I work for Radcliffe, in the casino. God, I thought I'd die that night she came in. And then she was dead and I've been so bloody scared since I've not known what to think and then...'

'Hold on,' John demanded. 'She came to the casino?'

'Yes, she came. Next day she was dead. I don't want to end up the same way. Look, I need to talk to someone and yours is the only name I've got. Moira – mind you, look what trusting her did for me, she said you were OK I need help and I need it now. I've got no one else and I've got a little boy.

133

Anything happened to him and I'd...' She broke off, choking on the words.

'Meet me,' John told her. 'Fifteen minutes. You name the place.'

He felt her hesitate, knew she was in two minds whether to cut him off or to agree.

'Please,' he said. 'Meet me. I can't help you unless you do.'

'All right,' she said. She named a place on the other side of town and John knew he'd have to shift to make it in the time. He thought about calling Colin, but he had just reached his car and, looking at his watch, decided Colin could wait. If her timing was to be believed, this woman claimed to have seen Moira far later than anyone else on the night she'd died.

He climbed into his car and started the engine, forcing himself to be calm as he backed out of the awkward space he'd parked in – the end of the row, nearest the wall. Always certain to be empty.

Moira had hinted once that she had someone inside Radcliffe's, but she'd refused to tell him more and John had not pushed. He remembered what it had been like for him as a newly appointed Sergeant and slowly building up your own network. Some of them, narks you'd cultivated in the early days in uniform; others came into the picture now, knowing they could approach a little more discreetly now you were in effective civvies;

still others who would deal with nothing less than CID. Even informants and grasses had their hierarchy. Back then, John would as soon cut off his little finger as give away his sources and he knew that Moira felt the same. Even so, even if this Julie was inside Radcliffe's organisation, even if she was feeding Moira odds and sods of information, it still begged the question. What the hell was Moira doing in the casino on the night she died? Why go there alone, when she knew Radcliffe was dangerous? And, if he were honest, most painful of all, why hadn't she come to John and told him what she knew?

The meeting place Julie had chosen was in the middle of a park. The pavilion, once a small concert hall, now a cafe, was Victorian and ornate. It seemed to John that its architect had been unable to decide if he were emulating a Kew Garden's glasshouse or a classical Georgian house. It fell short of both. Ten years or so ago, someone had decided to paint the brickwork white and the ironwork deep bottle. John remembered reading that this was an authentic Victorian shade known as Invisible Green. He couldn't for the life of him think why. The green had chipped and showed bubbles of rust. The rust had bled out onto the now off white surface of the walls. The whole was stained and unhappy, paint peeling in the habitual winter rain and washing down to lie like dirty snow.

Surrounding the pavilion, the remains of a formal garden, forlorn in its state of winter abandonment. In summer, laid out with vibrant bedding, it was cheerful, if a little garish. In November, stripped bare, it took on the appearance of a formalised mud bath. Two flights of stone steps led from the narrow path and in through french doors. These had once run the length of the wall and, in summer, could have been opened wide to allow the scent from the roses to waft inside. The roses. John remembered them from childhood, remembered his mother's sadness when at last they had been grubbed out. All but one door had now been sealed shut and tables filled the spaces, wall to wall. John wondered in passing what fire regulations they might be breaking. During the summer, the tables would be packed with parents and their children, sticky with ice cream. In winter, the cafe was as forlorn and abandoned as the gardens beyond.

Only two tables were in use today. At one, a man and woman sat. They seemed to be mid argument, their posture stiff and awkward, both seated on one side of the table, but with a distance of miles between. They spoke in tense, tightly articulated whispers, their eyes shifting, seeking distraction, looking anywhere except the other's face.

A woman sat alone at the table furthest

from them. Back to the wall, facing the door. In her obvious isolation she reminded him for one guilty moment of Colin.

'Julie?'

'Yeah. Look, you'd better get something.' She jerked her head towards the counter. 'She gets real snotty if you sit in here without buying.'

'You want anything?'

'Thanks, I'll have another tea.'

Obediently, John crossed to the counter, trying to keep Julie in his field of vision. He had a feeling she was still not sure whether or not to bolt now, or to stay and talk. He decided the by play about the tea was to give her time to figure it out.

To his relief, she seemed to have decided in his favour. The thought of chasing this slim, nervous looking woman out through the pavilion and across the mud of the unmade beds was not one he had relished.

'Do you have another name?' he asked her as he sat down.

'Julie will do,' she said. Then sighed. 'Wise,' she said. 'Julie Wise.' She picked up one of the sugar packs he had dropped onto the table and tugged at it. It split in half and she swore irritably as most of it missed her tea. John pushed another towards her and she picked it up, then held it, poised as though his contact had somehow contaminated the contents.

'You saw Moira the night she died,' John prompted her.

'Yeah, I did. Look, I've got a little boy. His dad's long gone and I don't have much to do with my family. They didn't approve, not of me and his dad and then when he ran off ... well nothing much changed. We manage on our own, but I'm all he's got and I want protection.'

'What makes you think you need it?'

'You stupid or something? I told Moira things and then she shows up that night, ends up dead, and Radcliffe and that woman that works for him, his secretary or whatever she calls herself, they've started sniffing round, asking questions about me. A week ago, Charlie Radcliffe didn't even notice I existed, suddenly he's all over me. Saying stuff.'

'What kind of stuff?'

'Oh, you know, like he's noticed I haven't been myself lately and have I got something on my mind? I let slip ... I let slip I was going to a funeral and someone must have mentioned it and all of a sudden he's asking if I've had a death in the family and how tragic it would be if anything more happened to upset my little boy.' Her lips trembled and she twisted the sugar pack between her fingers before dropping it unopened on the table. John had the feeling she'd like a cigarette. He wondered if she smoked or if she'd recently given up. If so, the sugar pack

138

would be a poor substitute. It had been three years since he gave up, but there were still times ... now for instance.

'Funeral?' he asked. 'You went to Moira's funeral?'

She nodded. 'Stupid or what? I don't know why I did it. It's just that, well, she was decent to me. Gave me money for the stuff I told her, even though we both knew it was nothing. She knew I was managing on my own.'

John nodded. That would have been like Moira. 'I didn't see you there?' He would have remembered her. Strikingly pretty. A melange of white and Afro Caribbean he guessed, her hair, falling to her shoulders, was light in colour and twisted into tight ringlets and her skin was what his mother used to call, one of coffee two of cream in a way that was purely descriptive, but, he guessed, would have not been considered PC. Her eyes were hazel, flecked with green and the curve of her lips was full and dark. She wore little makeup and, though she was a tad too thin for his taste, he could see that many men would find her attractive and that Radcliffe would notice her, whether he'd given sign of it or not. Dressed in the casino's uniform – a neat, black shift dress smartly fitted, with a white linen collar – she would be hard for any man not to notice. He knew that Charlie chose his girls as much for their looks as any brains they might possess.

'You say he's paid you no attention before?'

'Oh, he was polite enough, but it's all strictly business in the Casino. He doesn't even like employees to date each other. Says it's distracting. And he'd know if we did,' she added. 'Sandra would make sure of that.'

John had heard this before. It made him even more curious as to how and why Julie had become involved with Moira. He asked her next.

She shrugged. 'Stupid, I guess. Look. I earn pretty good money now. I've taken every training course they've offered me and being a croupier pays better than you might think. But when I first started, I was behind the bar. I had to work two jobs to try and make ends meet plus the bit of top up I got from the social. You any idea how much it costs to look after a kid?'

John shook his head.

'No. Well. I didn't have a lot growing up, and I wanted it to be different with Ian. He didn't ask to be born and he's a good kid. I want the best for him.'

'Who looks after him while you work?'

'I don't leave him on his own, if that's what you mean.'

'I didn't mean that.'

'My next door neighbour. Her daughter sometimes sits, or she does. I pay her for it. Ian goes to sleep in his own bed and she keeps the baby monitor. Look,' she added, suddenly defensive. 'I know it's not right, maybe, but what else am I supposed to do? He's ten and very grown up for his age.'

'I'm not judging you.' John told her. 'Look, you were telling me how you and Moira met.'

She sighed. 'I was working this other job. Cleaning. The health centre at Bishopswood. You know it?'

John nodded. Bishopswood again. Don Tyler's photography club was based in Bishopswood.

'She'd call in ... this was when she was still in uniform. The health centre became one of those twenty-four hour things ... a walk in clinic. Sometimes we'd get drunks and the centre manager, he encouraged whichever copper was on duty to call in, have a cuppa, scare the trouble-makers off.'

Again John nodded, calculating. 'So you must have known her for, what, five years?'

'Yeah, before Ian's dad took off.' Her hand swooped suddenly to the table and she had the sugar pack again, twisting it between her fingers. 'He was a bastard,' she said. 'Violent. One night, Moira came in and I'd ... he'd been hitting me. This time, he'd been careless, given me a black eye. I'd had enough. You know,' she lifted her gaze and fixed John with it. 'She was so nice. Just so kind. Two days later, he was gone. She said there were

141

ways of pressing charges even if I didn't feel able to. She got the clinic manager to look at me and took pictures and ... and she went to talk to Tony. I don't know what she said, but then, he was gone. He's not been back since. I felt I owed her and when I started at Radcliffe's, I passed on bits of gossip. Stuff I'd overheard. You know.'

John nodded. Thinking back, he was pretty sure why Tony had been so fast to disappear. More often than not, Moira would have been double crewed with Phil Marksman. Phil had since left the force and gone off to work security somewhere, but he was a bruiser of man. Actually very slow to anger, but once you had him well wound, you'd best stand back. He didn't differentiate much between friend and foe once he'd passed a certain point. Phil and Moira in combination would have been enough to put the fear of God into anyone.

'Did she ask you about anything specific?'

Julie hesitated and then nodded. 'Yeah,' she said. 'Stuff like, who bought heavy. Who won on the high stakes games? If they took their winnings in cash or banker's drafts, that sort of thing.' She shrugged. 'A lot of the time, I didn't know. I mean, if they played my tables, then I'd have an idea, but I told her what I could and of course, someone got a big win, it would be all over the club.'

John nodded. He could see where Moira

had been going with this. Casinos were good places to lose dodgy money and win it back clean and they'd suspected for some time that Radcliffe was a big player in this particular game – locally, at least. UK casinos were still not subject to the money laundering regulations that had been implemented since '93. They still weren't required to identify their clients or keep the kind of records other businesses were forced to keep for anti money laundering purposes. 'Mr Smith' could turn up and, provided he had the funds, register as a member and no one was required to check him out or keep a record of what stakes he played. He could come in, buy his chips in cash and take his winnings away as a nice new banker's draft. Clean and squeaky and, even in a relatively small business like Radcliffe's, often for a pretty sizeable amount.

A small commission would be charged, of course – the punter had to lose from time to time, just to keep things looking straight – and everyone went home satisfied. It was all about to change. New European regulations meant that soon all transactions over the equivalent of 1000 Euros would have to be registered and identification shown when the chips were bought. But even after this becomes law, there will be nothing to stop Mr Smith bringing a couple of non gambling friends along as guests, who could each buy just below their limit of chips for Mr Smith to play with, or for Mr Smith himself to buy in several different transactions, as his luck and funds allowed. John doubted the new regulations would upset the likes of Charlie Radcliffe one little bit. He thought back to the rows of figures and transactions in the so-called accounts Colin had downloaded. John didn't have the skills it would take to pick them over and make the necessary links. For that, he'd have to co-opt someone both skilled with IT and in the complexities of fraud. But he had recognised those names mentioned in the second set of accounts and their 'bar bill' ran into the tens of thousands. Then that particular name. John could not but hope that this was mere coincidence. He had no wish to become involved with the owner of that third name. Not unless he had to.

He wondered if Charlie's clients would be happy, knowing that he kept his own, unofficial records of their currency exchange. He wondered too, why Charlie Radcliffe would keep such lists. What pressure could he bring to bear?

Two of the names John had recognised were local businessmen. One, in fact, was also a magistrate.

Blackmail?

John had been silent for so long that Julie was becoming restless. He felt her shift across

144

the table, crossing her legs and leaning back in her chair. Then shuffling forward again.

'So,' she said finally. 'You going to help me or what? I need to get out of here. I don't want to end up like Moira.'

John frowned, thinking. He agreed that she couldn't stay. Knew she was right; Charlie Radcliffe was getting too interested. But he wasn't certain he had enough to persuade Weaver that she should be moved to a safe house. He could go over Weaver's head. Superintendent Caldwell was an old ally, but Caldwell was away and John wasn't certain when he was due back. It would all take far too long.

'You know what Moira reckoned?' Julie leaned towards him, then glanced around as though to make certain no one could hear. The couple at the far end of the café were still there. Lapsed now into stony silence, the man reading through the paper, the woman glaring out at the heavy rain as though willing it to stop so they could leave.

'No,' John said. 'Tell me.'

'She reckoned Charlie has someone. One of your lot. Someone high up.'

John frowned. The idea that Radcliffe had someone on the take was not a new one. It was an accusation that came up, almost inevitably, from time to time, but two internal inquiries had failed to find any evidence of it.

'She ever mention any names?'

Julie shook her head. 'I don't think she knew,' she admitted. 'It was just something she let slip one day. But what if she's right? What if...?'

'It's OK.' John raised a placating hand. He had made his decision. 'Look, you seem to trust me, I've got a place you can stay that has nothing to do with the police. No one will know about it until you want them to.'

'Oh, where?'

'It's a B&B. It's more or less closed this time of year, but I know the owners and they'll take you and ... Ian?'

She nodded.

'If I ask them to.'

Julie started to protest. 'I can't afford a...'

'I'll take care of it.' He smiled in what he hoped was a reassuring way. 'They owe me one,' he said. 'You'll like them.'

She argued a little longer, but finally agreed. John got the impression that this had caught her somewhat by surprise. That she'd been hoping – irrationally, perhaps – that he'd dismiss her fears. Tell her that everything was all right and it was just her imagination. Not that she would have believed that, John guessed. Julie was too bright to believe that. But she must have wanted it to be true. She'd been holding back the worst of her anxiety, keeping it in check on the off chance that she was wrong and everything in Charlie Radcliffe's garden was green and good after all. By believing her, John had torn down her last defences.

'Now,' he said. 'Tell me, where was Moira when you saw her? Was she with anyone? Did Radcliffe know she was there?'

She nodded, miserably. 'He must have done. I get a break around midnight. Only long enough to grab a coffee and use the ladies. They were on the stairs up by the offices. I was so shocked when I saw her that I dodged back into the toilets and I only came out when I was sure they'd gone.'

'They?'

'Moira and Brian Henshaw. He's Radcliffe's right hand man. They were arguing, I could see that and he had hold of her arm.'

'How was she dressed? Do you remember that?'

Julie frowned, then nodded. 'Black jeans and a plum-coloured sweater, I think. It might have been a fleece jacket or something. I can't be sure.'

John nodded. When Moira was found, she'd been dressed like that, her jeans bloody and the fleece top she'd had on over a long sleeved t-shirt had had the zipper broken, as though someone had grabbed hold and pulled hard while she'd struggled to get free. The description of the clothing and the implication that she had been killed shortly after Julie had seen her wasn't proof. It was all circumstantial. It did, however,

147

make Julie's testimony even more pertinent.

He took a deep breath, blocking from his mind all of the possible images this conjured. 'How fast can you get away? Today?'

She had a car, she told John, would meet her son from school and go straight away. She listened while he called his friends, the Matthews and arranged for her to stay. She spoke briefly to Jan and seemed cheered by the older woman's manner, even smiling when she said goodbye.

'Call me soon as you're there,' John told her. He made sure she had his mobile number and that of his home phone. Glancing at her watch, she told him she had just over an hour before collecting her son from school. Enough time to pack.

'Just one more thing,' John said. He found a piece of paper in his pocket and wrote three names. 'Do you know any of these men?'

Julie read them and nodded. 'These two are local. In about once a week. They use the restaurant for business lunches too, so Sandra says and sometimes bring their guests to dinner then the casino.' She glanced up. 'There are a lot like that, use the place like a social club. Always in and out.' A wry smile. 'A few even bring their wives.'

John laughed. Lance Spencer, the property developer and Chris Vincent, the magistrate. John vaguely recalled that he was something to do with building too. 'And the third name?' he asked.

She shook her head. 'Mr James? He prefers roulette to blackjack,' she said. 'So I don't often have him on my table. He's not from Hillford and only comes in once a month or so, but the nights he does, he plays like he's making up for lost time.'

'Win often?'

'Got a good average, as I remember. Not as lucky as some, but I think he usually comes out on top.' She paused and tapped the name again. 'He tips well,' she recalled. 'One night, I was just going on my break and as I went past him he asked if I'd mind getting him a drink. I got it for him and he gave me a tenner, just for getting his drink.' She smiled again. 'He was on a winning streak, mind, so I suppose he was celebrating.'

'Are you allowed to accept tips?' John asked. He'd always understood that wasn't permitted.

She nodded. 'We don't have pockets in our uniforms, but if anyone offers us a tip, we show it to the camera and there's a spare ashtray on every table. We put the money under that, end of the day, after the count, someone checks what we've got and we get to keep it. Tips can double your wages sometimes. I know a lot of casinos don't allow it, but, like Sandra told Mr Radcliffe, the place is so full of cameras, we may as well make use of them for our benefit too.' She paused, her face pained, caught up in some divided loyalty. 'She was good like that. It was a good job.' She sounded suddenly angry as though it was all so unfair, this disruption of a life it had taken her so long and so much hard work to build.

'I don't know what I'm going to do now,' she said softly. 'I really don't know.'

The rain had eased and the argumentative couple left. John walked with Julie to the door and then watched as she ran through the puddles towards the north gate, impatient now that the decision had been made. Impatient and fearful.

John sighed. The feeling that this was rapidly getting beyond his control and that he should ask for help, come clean about the whole damned business, weighed upon his mind, worrying it like an ill behaved dog. And the introduction of Bill James into the equation was not one he welcomed.

It was, he noted, checking his watch against the pavilion clock, one forty-five. Still a full half day to go, though it felt as though he'd been awake forever. And the next question, he thought as he delved in his pocket for his mobile phone, was where the hell was Colin?

15

Julie had more brains and basic street smarts than many had given her credit for. She'd learnt from her own mistakes and also taken note of those other people had committed. Result was, there were very few people Julie really trusted and even those she was inclined to believe – like Moira and John Moore – still carried, in Julie's eyes the risks of stupidity, carelessness or sheer ill luck. Julie didn't like to take chances and the best way, she figured, of not taking chances, was to rely on herself.

She went home and packed a few things into a spare backpack that belonged to Ian. He didn't have much with him at school today, just his reading book and his PE kit, and they could be left in the car. Ian might take a bit of persuading to carry the bag but a kid – or even his mum – carrying a Taz backpack wouldn't draw attention in the way a suitcase or a holdall would. Anything else, Julie figured, they'd have to buy as they needed. She made sure Ian's Game Boy was tucked inside the front pocket, together with what games she could find and his favourite jeans and hooded sweatshirts. Then she changed her small shoulder bag for a leather shopper, tucking her own essentials inside in a plastic carrier bag.

Ian was ready at the gates when she got there.

'Can Tom come round?'

'Not tonight, love. Sorry. I've got to go to work early and we've shopping to do first.'

Ian groaned. 'Tomorrow then?'

'Yeah, I should think so.' She smiled at Tom, who grinned back.

'I've got a new game for my PS2,' he told her. 'Ian wanted to have a play.'

'Sounds good,' Julie told him. 'I think your mum's waiting, love. Catch you later.'

She waved to Tom's mother, just arriving, late as always and with the younger two in tow, then ushered Ian into the car.

'I'm sorry, love,' she told him as they pulled away.

'That's OK. It'll do tomorrow.'

'No, I'm sorry, but I had to tell Tom and you a lie.'

He stared at her. 'A lie? What about?'

'You can't play tomorrow either.'

'But...'

'Ian, I need you to be really sensible here and not make a fuss. Something's come up and we've got to go away for a few days.'

Ian stared harder. 'What?' he demanded. Then. 'Has dad come back?' He sounded scared. He only just remembered his father,

152

but the memories still woke him from his sleep at night sometimes.

'No,' she said quickly. 'It's nothing to do with him.' She took a deep breath and wondered how to explain.

'Someone I know got killed,' she said. 'Her name was Moira. You met her once?' She glanced sideways at him, and he nodded at her.

'The policewoman,' he said. 'I saw it on the news. You went to the funeral and came back crying.'

'How did you...?' She glanced at him again.

'I'm not stupid, Mum. I do notice things,' he told her pompously. Then, 'What's that got to do with us though?'

Julie sighed. 'I'm hoping, nothing,' she told him. 'But the people who are trying to find out who killed Moira, they think we should go away for a few days.' She forced a smile. 'It'll be fun,' she said. 'A seaside holiday in term time.'

Unconvinced, Ian regarded her with too wise eyes.

At the supermarket she got them both out of the car, dumped the PE kit and book bag in the boot and took his backpack out. 'I've put some things in there,' she told him. 'Can you carry it for a bit?'

He shrugged into the straps. 'You bring

153

my Game Boy?'

'Sure.'

'OK. What games did you pack?'

She tried to remember and was relieved to find she'd not done so badly in the packing department. Ten-year-old boys, she knew, had their own set of priorities.

'What are we shopping for?'

'A few spare clothes, some snack food for the journey.'

'Better get bread and milk and stuff,' he said. 'You always buy those and if they're watching, that'll make it look normal.'

'If who's watching?' she tried, and failed, to sound casual.

'Oh, Mum. Get real. The bad guys we're running away from.'

Julie stared at him and forced herself not to look around, seeking those invisible watchers her son just assumed might be there. He was almost enjoying this, she realised. Had adapted to it the same way he slipped into the world of his computer games. The thought rose sharply to her lips that this wasn't play, it wasn't just a game. She'd seen two men following her earlier. She bit it back. Why scare him, why make it harder than it was?

Then he took her hand, just for a moment. It was something he'd not done in months. Not since some kid in the playground had shouted abuse at Ian when he'd kissed his mum goodbye one day. That touch told her that she'd read him wrong. This wasn't fantasy. He knew that it was real, but he was doing his best to protect her feelings as she was his.

'It'll be OK, Mum,' he told her quietly. 'Don't you worry. It'll all be OK.'

For the next half hour they shopped. Trying to be as casual and as normal as they could be. Bought milk and bread and doughnuts and the chocolate bars she usually got for his packed lunch. Bought extra socks and under-wear and a t-shirt Ian took a fancy to, just because. And when they'd finished with their shopping, they went to the café and ordered tea and Coke and the sort of sticky cake Ian always wanted but could never finish. Ian carried the tray while Julie struggled with the bags. He carried it carefully, without spilling a thing, to the table for two at the rear of the café, screened by the pot plants and close to the fire door where they always sat when they came here. In summer, the door was left open and the scent of flowers from the giant tubs that stood outside drifted into the always too hot café. This time of year the door was closed, but it opened easily enough and outside all was dark and still, the narrow path leading in one direction back to the car park and in the other out of the shopping centre and back towards town. On the other side of the path, flower beds had been planted with robust evergreens. Beyond that was the waste ground that had once been allotments and was now awaiting the developers trenches. Julie knew that there were little pathways tracked by kids taking short cuts from the shops back to the estate beyond the waste ground. In the light shed from the cafe windows, she was pretty sure she could find the way through. Even more convinced that Ian would be able to.

For a little while they sat and chatted and shared the cake. Julie drank her tea and glanced around in that disinterested fashion parents do when waiting for their kids to finish up. Then she gathered their bags together, handing the back pack to her son and arranging everything else into the smallest space she could.

'You ready?'

'Yeah.'

'Then let's go.'

They were out through the fire door in an instant, pushing it to behind them and then hurrying away into the dark, leaving the path and pushing their way through the shrubbery beyond, taking the short-cut kids had made and slipping away into the bushes.

'What about the car?' Ian wanted to know. 'You think they'll be watching it?'

'I think they might.'

His pale face told her that the reality of

their situation was really hitting home.

'What do we do?'

Julie took a deep breath. There were a few items of knowledge learned from her ex that she'd never figured on needing ... until now. 'Then we get ourselves another one,' she said.

Ian's eyes widened. 'Cool,' he said.

16

'You've lost her.' Radcliffe's voice was flat and cold.

'She gave us the slip. We think she left her car in the car park and went out through the fire door in the café.'

'We think,' Radcliffe echoed. 'You mean you know sweet F.A.'

The two men shuffled uncomfortably.

'We'll find her,' Crowther said, running weary fingers through his sandy hair. 'Look, she's on foot and got the boy with her. She can't have gone far.'

'You've no way of knowing that. You don't know if our DI Moore hadn't arranged a pick up for her? You don't know that she's not on her way to a safe house by now. You wouldn't know how to tie your frigging shoe-laces without an instruction book.'

He gestured heavenward as though seeking divine inspiration. 'And I suppose it's too much to hope there's any word on Grainger?'

Crowther and Jones exchanged glances. 'Nothing yet,' Crowther said. 'But we've got a watch on Inspector Moore. Colin Grainger's bound to make contact sooner or later.'

'I hope whoever's watching Moore's got more about them than you two,' Radcliffe told them. 'Get the fuck out. Now.'

Sandra poured him a drink and set it on the desk in front of him. 'Like they said,' she agreed, 'Colin Grainger's bound to contact Moore eventually.'

'Eventually,' Radcliffe echoed. He sighed. 'I know you're right, San, but ... simple job, that was meant to be. Watch one woman and a boy for a couple of hours ... and what frigging happens? I mean, San, how do you manage to screw that one up?'

'Cleverer than she looks, our Julie,' Sandra commented. She sounded oddly satisfied, Radcliffe thought.

'So,' she went on, 'we wait it out.'

'I suppose we do,' Radcliffe agreed. But he was rattled. Rattled and irritated in just about equal measure. Charlie Radcliffe had got used to having things his own way and just lately they'd been anything but. It was a state of affairs he didn't intend getting used to.

17

John Moore arrived home at seven fifteen after what had been a frustrating day. He hoped Julie and her son had removed themselves to the safety of the Matthews's guesthouse, but he would have to wait until either Julie or the Matthews' contacted him to tell him they'd arrived safely. And, he reminded himself, it was quite a drive.

He worried at the Julie problem. What to do, who to tell. Should he go to Weaver and come clean about everything? But what if Julie was right and Radcliffe did have someone in the department on his payroll?

Weaver? John didn't see it. Not really. Weaver was known to be an awkward cuss on occasions – a reputation John shared, for that matter – but no one had ever suggested he was anything less than straight.

Sitting in his car, outside of his house, John made a decision. He'd wait until he knew that Julie and her son were safely with the Matthews and then he'd go to Weaver and tell him all he knew, take the flak that would bring.

He thought of Moira and how it still made no sense to him. Why the hell go to confront

Radcliffe on his home turf? Going to the Casino in those circumstances classed as an act of madness.

But, having seen the list of names and the money the figures must represent, John was beginning to guess just why she had taken such a risk. Begun to think that, in some perverse, Moira-thinking way, it was because of him and what he'd told her about Billy James.

He shrugged impatiently, telling himself that Moira had always been her own person. That she was over eighteen, an adult well able to make her own mistakes without it having anything to do with him. Moira had only herself to blame.

But that wasn't true, no matter how much easier it would make it for John. Problem was, John had seen that name on the list. He knew she would have recognised it, knew she would have understood.

And that brought it back to him again. To John. To things John had been doing his damnedest to forget these past however-many years.

John had only stepped over the threshold, but he felt it. He knew the way his house should feel and this wasn't it. Someone had been here ... or was still here.

Aware that any intruder would already have heard the key in the lock, he kicked the

160

door closed behind him and then listened to the ensuing silence.

'All right, come on out. I know you're there.'

'That's right, tell the whole street, why don't you?' Colin's voice, sullen and annoyed came from the living room. A moment later and Colin himself appeared in the doorway.

'What the hell are you doing here?'

'Waiting for you, what do you think?'

'Anyone see you come here?'

'I don't think so. I arrived about a half hour ago. Came in through the back. You really should get that window fixed.'

'What window?'

'The small one in the kitchen. Climb on the ledge and reach through, you can unfasten the main transom. My mum's used to be the same and she was always leaving it open. Ventilation, she said...' Colin trailed off, eyeing John nervously.

'I lock my windows,' John told him.

Colin followed him through to the kitchen and they inspected the lock. The small transom had been forced and the larger window opened from that access point.

'You might lock them,' Colin pointed out, 'but there's not a lot of point if you're going to leave the key hanging on the handle, is there?'

John felt he had to concede the point. 'So,' he said. 'Who was here before you and how long ago?'

'You still got the disk?'

John patted his pocket.

'Right,' Colin glanced around the room as though expecting Radcliffe or one of his henchmen to be hiding in a cupboard. 'You think Radcliffe's been here?'

'Not in person. No.'

Colin followed as John inspected his domain. The search had been careful, skilful, but he knew it had taken place. Things were slightly out of place. And anyway, there was that feeling. The way his house shouldn't feel.

'You think he found anything?'

'There's nothing to find.'

'Oh. Then what was he looking for?'

'How the hell should I know? The disk, probably. If he knows it exists.'

'Why should he know?'

John shrugged. 'Why did you leave the hotel?'

'Why didn't you call me? I didn't know what the hell was happening.'

'You were safer there.'

'I was bored,' Colin admitted. 'Anyway, where have you been all day? Why couldn't you talk to me when I called? What's going on, John? I've a right to know. I need to know.'

John nodded. He had to concede that much. 'The name Julie Wise mean anything to you?'

162

Colin squinted, thinking. 'Works at the casino,' he said. 'Moira had a soft spot for her. Had a son, I think.'

That was more than John had known a few hours ago. 'Right,' he said, trying not to feel hurt ... irritated cheated ... or whatever it was it made him feel that Moira had told her ex husband more than she had told him.

'Any chance of a cuppa?' Colin eyed the kettle.

'Sure,' John sighed. 'Sit down, I'll get us both something to eat.'

'Great,' Colin approved. 'Now what's this about Julie Wise?'

For the next half hour, John filled Colin in regarding the information Julie had given him.

'You need to get out too,' John told him.

'Where would I go?'

'Where Julie is. North, to my friends the Matthews' B&B at Staithes.'

'Where the hell is that anyway?'

'It's about ... what was that?'

Colin shrugged. 'I didn't hear anything.'

'Something outside.'

John got to his feet and moved towards the door but that was as far as he got. The back door burst inward, almost knocked off its hinges and John was hurled to the floor as the first man thrust his way inside.

John hit the deck hard. He heard Colin shout. Painfully, he twisted round, trying to

163

see what was happening. There were three armed men invading his kitchen and one of them had hold of Colin.

Had John thought about it, he would have stayed down, let them go and then raised the alarm. But John wasn't thinking. His house had been invaded and on top of everything else, it was more than he could take.

He was on his feet and making a grab for the nearest man.

Afterwards, he was never sure if he had heard Colin shout a warning or if he had imagined it, but the shot and then the pain in his right shoulder was searingly real.

John lay on the kitchen floor, hearing the scuffle of feet and Colin's shouts as he was dragged away. He had a vague hope that the neighbours might hear, or see. Might call the police. But the thought faded as soon as it formed. No one saw or heard anything in this quiet street. The inhabitants retreated behind their high hedges and net curtained bays and, should the rudeness of the outside world threaten to intrude they simply increased the volume of their television sets and clucked their disapproving tongues.

Truth was, it was this level of anonymity and insular behaviour that had induced John to move here. No one knew or cared who he was or what he did and his usual level of contact with his neighbours was little more than a polite good morning.

No. No help from that front.

He was sick with the pain radiating from his shoulder and now spreading across his chest. For an irrational moment, he wondered if he might be having a heart attack. His breathing was painful and his ribs felt constricted and over tight. His face felt sticky against the laminated floor and for another irrational moment, he found himself asking when it had last been mopped and what he'd spilt there that should feel so wet and warm against his cheek. Then it registered that what he was feeling was blood. His own, spreading outward from the gaping hole in his back.

And it hurt. It bloody hurt.

He had to move.

Awkwardly, John eased himself onto his uninjured side and then pushed up so that he sat with his legs straight out in front of him. The effort caused another wave of pain.

He looked down at his blood soaked shirt and then at the kitchen floor, Christ! Where was it all coming from? How much had he lost?

Enough to make his head spin and his stomach heave with nausea as he struggled to his feet. That was how much.

There was a phone on the kitchen table. A cordless that should have been mounted on the wall, had John ever found the time. He was grateful now for his own inefficiency.

The table was closer, easier to reach than the wall would have been. The phone ... please let it be charged ... felt cool and reassuring in his hand. He sat down heavily on the kitchen floor. He dialled, asked for police and then, on second thoughts, an ambulance. 'I've been shot,' he told the controller. 'I've lost a lot of blood.'

He managed to tell her his address and then fell back against the cabinet, the phone still in his hand.

18

Colin didn't know if John was dead or alive. They'd bound his wrists with a plastic tie that cut into the flesh when he struggled and then bundled him into the back of a large grey car. Colin wasn't good on cars, but he thought it might be a BMW of some description. The windows were tinted and, with one man seated either side of him, Colin had little room to even struggle, never mind a chance to escape. Then, about ten minutes on, the car had stopped. Colin recognised the street behind Radcliffe's casino, which put paid to any doubts he might have had concerning the identity of his abductors. They hustled him out of the car and up the fire escape. Moments later, he was seated in Radcliffe's office and his pockets were turned out and their contents dumped on the table. Colin eyed his keys, nervously, wondering if anyone would recognise the stick drive for what it was, but the men who searched him had maintained their silence all the way here and they passed no comment now.

The fact that they made no attempt to hide either their identities or his location worried him. It wasn't, Colin decided, a propitious sign as regards his own survival. Neither was the fact that they'd been prepared to shoot a police officer to get him. It spoke either of carelessness, determination or sheer bravado and whatever way you looked at it, any combination of those motives was likely to be bad.

The men left. One stood just outside of the half open door. Colin could just see the grey of his suit. But the others were hidden from view. An outer door opened and then closed. Then nothing.

Colin looked around. He'd been brought through an outer office into what was clearly Radcliffe's inner sanctum. In front of him stood a large, old-fashioned desk. Colin guessed it was a genuine antique. The swivel chair, decked out in bright blue leather, looked out of place behind it.

On the desk was a rolodex-type address

book, a blotter with Colin's worldly goods strewn across its surface, a couple of pens – one, a deep blue and expensive looking fountain pen – and an ivory paper knife. Otherwise it was empty; not even a telephone, though Colin had noted two on the desk in the other room and wondered if either was an outside line and if he'd have any chance of reaching them. He thought of all the action films he'd seen. Man trapped in building filled with hoodlums, stabs three with paper knife clenched between his teeth then dials for help with the end of his nose. He tried to picture himself in such a heroic role, and failed.

A filing cabinet stood in the left corner, near to the door and to Colin's right as he sat in the big leather chair – one of two, facing the desk – was a bank of monitors. Three were switched on, the rest blank. The active screens showed the front doors of the casino and a staff area with a half dozen cleaners gathering their equipment together and replacing it in cupboards. Colin tried to guess what time it was and figured it must be somewhere close to nine.

So. What now?

Colin took a deep breath and tugged at the plastic binding his wrists. His efforts did nothing, only served to make it more painful. He thought about the way they had brought him in, through the fire escape and across a narrow corridor, into the outer office and then here. None of the doors had been locked and none, judging by the fact that one man had been left to watch the door, were locked now. Could he make a run for it? Had his hands been free, Colin would have tried. Physically, he was neither the bravest nor best co-ordinated of individuals and, even had he had both hands to use against this one man; one bigger, stronger, both-hands-free-to-pull-a-gun-or-throw-a-punch type man, he didn't reckon he had a snowball's chance. But it would have been preferable to try than to sit and wait for whatever Radcliffe had in store.

Colin sighed and laid his head back against the chair, feeling suddenly drained of energy. How had Moira felt, he wondered. She must have been in this same position. Knowing she'd got herself in too far and there was no clear way out.

Colin was pretty convinced that, barring a miracle, he was going to die.

His reverie was interrupted by the opening of the door as two men entered. One, Colin recognised as being the short, thick-set thug that had shot John Moore. The other was Charlie Radcliffe.

Radcliffe did not look happy. He seated himself behind the desk while the short man cut Colin's bonds with a penknife.

'Mr Grainger,' Radcliffe said. 'We've been

looking for you. You're not an easy man to keep up with.'

He paused, surveying the scatter of possessions on the desk, prodding at them with the end of the blue pen.

Colin eyed him anxiously but tried to keep his expression bland and unconcerned. It wasn't easy. The blood was returning to his hands and bringing with it excruciating pain. He tried to rub his hands together, speed the process, but that just made things worse and in the end he sat, writhing inwardly, with his dead hands in his lap, waiting for the circulation to return to normal, and all the while watching Radcliffe poking his things around as though they were too contaminated to touch.

Radcliffe stared hard at Colin and then glanced sideways at the other man.

'Out,' he said.

'Boss?'

'Mr Grainger and I have to talk. I'd like you to go.'

His tone told Colin that Radcliffe was not best pleased about something. 'You know he shot DI Moore?'

Radcliffe eyed him suspiciously. Hungrily, Colin thought. Like Colin was prey.

'I'm aware of that,' Radcliffe growled.

'It was totally unnecessary, you know. There were three of them and only two of us and if you take usefulness into account,

170

John was pretty much on his own.'

Radcliffe said nothing. The short gunman hovered uncertainly.

'He could be dead, for all you know. All I know, for that matter,' Colin pressed on. He knew this was probably a bad move, but he was getting to Radcliffe. He could see that in the man's eyes and right now, that felt pretty good.

'Not a sensible thing to do, I wouldn't have thought. Killing a police officer. But oh, I was forgetting. You've had it done before, haven't you, so I suppose ... you know ... may as well be stuffed for a sheep as a lamb, or whatever the saying is.'

Radcliffe pointed at the exit and this time the other man took the hint and left. Colin heard him close the outer door and, as far as he could see through the opening into the other office, that room too was now empty. Colin was alone with Charlie Radcliffe.

'What I don't get though,' he continued, 'is what she did to deserve what your lot did to her. Moira, I mean...'

'I know who you mean.'

'Moira didn't deserve to die. She didn't deserve any of it.'

'Why did she come here?'

'Why? Oh, I don't know. Moira always did her own thing. Maybe she thought she could talk you into becoming a model citizen.' Colin paused and closed his eyes.

'But she didn't do anything to deserve you killing her and neither did that kid, Alice, neither did John Moore.'

'And you?' Radcliffe asked. 'You deserve to die, Colin?'

Colin shook his head. 'Who knows,' he said. 'Maybe I do.'

Radcliffe made no comment. He opened the top drawer of the desk and removed a floppy disk with a blue edged label. Colin recognised it as the one he'd given Moira. His handwritten scrawl across the label was clearly visible even from where he sat. It said simply 'photo', written in bright red ink.

Colin stared at it, drawn as though the thing were magnetic. That disk. That little square of black plastic was what had got Moira killed. How the hell could death look so damned innocent?

'I put this into my computer,' Radcliffe said 'and all I found was pictures of some little tart. Her name was Alice – but you know that already, don't you, seeing as you mentioned her.'

Colin didn't reply His hands were almost back to normal now and his brain, no longer distracted by the pain, was working overtime.

'So, what was your ex doing with mucky pictures?' Radcliffe demanded. 'Funny that way, was she? That why it didn't work out between the two of you? But no, I was forgetting, she'd taken up with that policeman, hadn't she? Or maybe she was 'that way' and it was a case of a real man showing her what she was missing? Are you a real man, Colin?'

Colin refused to be riled. Radcliffe, he figured, couldn't even imagine the kind of insults that would reach Colin's psyche. 'Depends who's asking, I suppose. Look, I don't know what Moira was doing with that disk. She must have taken it off my desk. She asked me if I'd got a spare and I told her to help herself.'

'Really?' Radcliffe looked unimpressed. 'And I suppose you know nothing about the accusations that popped up on my computer the other night.'

'Accusations?'

'Don't play games with me.'

'Never was one for games,' Colin said. He took a deep breath and stared back at Radcliffe, hoping he looked less terrified than he felt. If Radcliffe looked closely, he'd see the sheen of sweat Colin could feel breaking out across his forehead and the fact that he was, quite literally shaking in his shoes. He was amazed and somewhat gratified that his voice was as steady as it was, but the only thing really keeping him together was the thought of Moira. She'd have been solid to the last, he told himself. Faced Radcliffe down, come back with that smart mouth of hers every chance she got.

Colin, even now Moira was gone, wanted her to be proud. He might not have made that happen in life, but he was sure as hell going to give it his best shot now that she was dead and Colin himself not likely to be far behind.

It was as though Radcliffe sensed his thoughts.

'She squealed like a stuck pig,' he said. 'Begged me to let her go. Practically wet herself. She might have come on all tough to start with, Colin, but in the end she was just like everyone else. Crying for her mamma.'

Briefly, the image of Moira as Radcliffe was painting her infiltrated Colin's thoughts and threatened to undermine him, but even as he allowed them entry, he knew he had to slam the door and force them away. The thought of Moira, weak, frightened, in pain.., he couldn't handle that. Not now, not yet. Moira was his hero and, if he was to get through this, her pedestal was where she had to stay.

'Moira... Moira wouldn't beg,' he said quietly. 'She never begged for anything in her entire life. She wouldn't have given you the satisfaction.'

'No? You don't think so? Well let me tell you this. It took a long time to do what my people did to your Moira and at the end, she didn't know or care what she was saying.

174

But... well... why am I bothering to tell you when I can show?' He picked up the disk again and turned it between his fingers. 'You put something on this disk and you hid it then gave it to her. She thought she'd get one over. Maybe she was eager for promotion. Maybe she wanted to impress her new lover. Whatever it was, she *knew* something or thought she did and I want to know what that something was.' He dropped the disk onto the table and stood up. One of the phones in the outer office began to ring.

Radcliffe cast an irritated glance in its direction. Looked as though he'd like to ignore it, but the ringing, persistent and shrill in the otherwise silent room, continued and Radcliffe, not troubling to hide his annoyance went out to answer it.

'What?' Colin heard him say. 'Can't you buggers sort any bloody thing out for your-selves? OK, I've done here. Send Brian up.'

It was now or never, Colin thought. The fact that Radcliffe had finished meant he was ready to hand the job of interrogation over to whoever had killed Moira and Alice, and Colin was under no illusions that even if he told them everything, up to and including his life story so far, he'd still be dead at the end of it. He had, he felt, one thing in his favour. Charlie Radcliffe saw him as no kind of threat. The fact that he'd chosen to speak to Colin alone meant two

175

things; the gunmen he'd sent to John Moore's house probably had no idea why Colin was wanted – and Radcliffe wanted it keeping that way – and it also meant that Radcliffe had him down for a nothing man who couldn't defend himself.

Was he right? Colin shook his head. Not now. Not while there was a chance he might get out of this alive.

He heard Radcliffe replace the receiver and closed his eyes, then drew in several deep, sharp breaths as though preparing for a deep dive into freezing water. It took less than a second for Colin to be out of his chair and across to the desk, grabbing his keys and wallet from its surface before dropping his head and charging an astonished Charlie Radcliffe as he came back through the office door.

Radcliffe let out a yelp of surprise, and made a grab for Colin's arms, but Colin had seized the one weapon available to him. The nib of Charlie Radcliffe's very expensive pen drove upward into his jaw, hitting bone and then deflecting into the softer part of his neck.

Radcliffe yelled in pain, hands flailing momentarily as the shock of Colin's attack hit home. Colin knew he wouldn't be off balance for long, but he was on a roll now. He stabbed again with the nib of the pen, this time aiming for Radcliffe's face. He

176

missed the right eye by a fraction, but with his other hand he'd grabbed at Radcliffe's thick and beautifully groomed grey hair. Acting through instinct and desperation born of pure unadulterated fear, Colin yanked Charlie Radcliffe's head right down even as he brought his left knee up. The impact of Radcliffe's chin in the top of his knee sent a crushing pain through Colin's leg, but he was too mad to really notice. He stabbed again with Radcliffe's pen and this time it found its mark. Charlie Radcliffe howled as the iridium nib pierced his eye. One last kick and Colin ran, praying that the doors would open – they did. Praying he could reach the fire escape before whoever this Brian was came up the stairs.

Behind him, Radcliffe was still screeching in pain, clutching at his bloody face and ruined eye. Colin barely heard. He had before his own eyes an image of Moira. She was smiling at him, urging him on.

'I did good,' he told her as he thrust through the fire door and pounded down the metal stairs. 'I did OK, love, I got him. Got him for the both of us.'

19

John Moore was having trouble keeping focus on what was being said to him. He had vague memories of the paramedics questioning him at the scene, asking his name and if he could hear and understand. John had given them some answer, but it wasn't the one they wanted. For a brief time, they'd been convinced his name was Colin, so, John figured dimly, he must have been repeating Colin's name.

He knew he must have lost a lot of blood, knew the shot at such close range would have done a lot of damage and he lifted his left hand to his shoulder, trying to feel for the wound. The paramedic gently but firmly moved his hand aside.

'Lie still.'

'Collar bone?'

'I'm sorry. I can't tell.'

'Exit wound? How big is the exit wound?' She looked away, glancing at her companion, then looked back at John. 'I don't know,' she admitted. 'It's a bit bloody. So it's hard to see what's going on.' She patted his hand. 'You'll be all right,' she told him. 'Try to lie still.'

John lay still. The siren, muted inside the ambulance, drifted in and out of his consciousness, now louder, now more muffled as though he heard it from under water and the voices of the paramedics sounded now clear, then muffled as though his ears were filled with wadding.

'Colin,' he said. Where was Colin? 'They took him.' Where was Colin?

Next thing he was aware of was the crash of opening doors and the metallic rattle of the gurney as they lifted him from the ambulance, wheeled him into a place where more doors crashed and the walls moved past at nauseating speed. Then a familiar face as DCI Weaver swam into view, mouthing his name.

'Colin,' John said. 'Radcliffe's people, they took Colin.'

'Colin,' Weaver's face was the picture of confusion. 'Who the hell's Colin?'

'Grainger. Moira's ex. Radcliffe's men came for him. Shot me. Took him away.'

It was taking such an effort to say this. John closed his eyes. Dimly, he could hear Weaver's voice asking him something and another voice arguing, saying it would have to wait.

'John, what the hell would they want with that loser? Is he hallucinating or what?'

'I don't know, sir. I don't think so,' the paramedic answered. 'He was asking about

179

someone called Colin when we got there.'

'John. Talk to me. What the hell's going on?'

John dragged his thoughts into as clear, sense making lines as he could manage. 'Moira,' he said. 'Colin gave some information to Moira. She, stupid bugger, she went and faced Radcliffe with it. He had her killed. They found out it was Colin.'

Weaver was almost purple with disgust and disbelief. 'And she believed him? Colin Grainger's a bloody waster. John, you're...'

'No.' John reached out and grabbed Weaver by the lapel. 'Not this time. She found something about Billy James. She went to Radcliffe. My fault. I shouldn't have said anything.'

'John. You're not making sense.'

'That's enough now, sir. Please...'

The gurney was moving again, the walls chugging by at a sickening pace, the crash of doors, that unfamiliar yet familiar smell of disinfectants and blood and men's toilets that John associated with hospitals and, briefly, the stomach turning scent of food.

He moved his head, nauseous. 'Going to be sick!' he warned.

Too late.

The man pushing the trolley swore under his breath. Another door crashed open. Bright lights shining in his eyes. Hands moved beneath him, lifted him and the pain hit with a renewed force, striking deep into his shoulder, back and side, surging through him until it even pulsed, viciously, behind his eyes. John gave in and allowed himself to slide into the dark.

Colin couldn't stop shaking. He had run through the empty streets, putting as much distance between himself and the Casino as possible, instinctively heading towards the centre of town, where there would be people and lights and places to hide.

Eventually, cold air scalding his lungs and legs threatening to give way beneath him, he slowed to a walk, then came to a full stop on the bridge crossing the canal. He was horrified by what he had done, even though, he kept telling himself, there had been no choice. He felt tainted. Shocked, he realized that he still held the pen in his right hand, the fingers in spasm, so tightly had he gripped the smooth barrel. He dropped it over the parapet of the bridge, peered down into the black waters as it fell, then looked at his hand. It was bloody. Radcliffe's blood.

He began to examine himself closely under the yellow street light, trying to see just how much blood there was, but his fleece jacket was dark and damp from the light rain and he couldn't tell.

What now?

John. He still didn't know about John. Was

181

he still at the house?

Colin dare not go back there, but he had to raise the alarm. He found a phone box and dialled emergency services, asking for an ambulance and giving the address. 'He's been shot,' he told the controller. 'No, I don't know how badly. Look. I've got to go. Just get someone there.'

Feeling slightly relieved, he turned his mind to what he should be doing next.

There was a small train station in Hillford, but the platform would be near empty at this time of night and, as far as Colin could recall, it was unmanned. If Radcliffe had his people out looking, they'd be sure to go there. The bus station was close by and that was busy right up until the last service around midnight. He stood more chance there.

Colin set off at a quick walk. Once there, he went straight to the men's toilets and washed his hands, checked for bloodstains on his clothes. To his relief, he'd got off lightly. He washed his face, dragged damp hands through his tangled hair and went back outside.

There was a coach in the bay close to the washroom. Its engine running, the driver just about to leave. The destination, propped in the front window, said Leeds. It was, Colin figured as good a place as any and at least it was heading North. The boarding house was North. That would do.

'Can I pay you?' he asked the driver. 'The ticket office is closed.'

'If you pay cash.'

Colin fiddled with his wallet. He had just enough. Gratefully, he handed it over and found a seat. Only then, positioned beneath the warm air vent above the seat, did Colin realize how cold he felt. He was shaking like a man with high fever.

He started to put his wallet away and then frowned. His bank card wasn't there. His credit card, hardly ever used, was still in the zip pocket, but the ATM card... He thought back to the last time he'd used it, how he'd just slipped it inside the billfold and not put it away properly. It was in all likelihood still there in Charlie Radcliffe's office.

He sighed, tried to remember how much he still had on his Visa. In cash, now he'd paid for his ticket, he had two pounds and twenty pence, which wasn't going to get him very far.

Comforting himself with the thought that there was bugger all in his account anyway, Colin tucked the wallet into the pocket of his fleece and closed his eyes. The bus was moving now, picking up speed as it passed through town towards the motorway and Colin didn't think that even Charlie Radcliffe had the power to search all coaches heading North. With luck, Radcliffe would, in any case, have other, more painful and pressing concerns.

Flexing his fingers, fancying that he could still feel the smooth casing of the pen against his palm, Colin drifted into an exhausted sleep.

Weaver had been undecided. John Moore had seemed so insistent but none of it made much sense.

However, the fact remained that someone had shot Detective Inspector Moore. The fact also remained that Moore had been playing things pretty close to his chest since Moira's death and both Morantz and Rose Morgan had been certain that he'd been hiding something or other.

Weaver made up his mind. He called his boss and told him what he knew.

Superintendent Caldwell was not best pleased to be disturbed at home. He had guests. He had a disapproving wife. But he listened as Weaver told him he might have a head on the death of Moira Barker and that John Moore had been shot.

'Get a warrant,' Caldwell authorised. 'Home and office.'

Weaver wasted no more time.

An hour hater, he was leaving the home of Christopher Vincent, a local magistrate, warrant in hand. His officers were already in position. Less than two hours after Colin Grainger had been taken from John Moore's home, both the Casino and Radcliffe's own house were raided.

Charlie Radcliffe, however, was not around to enjoy the fun.

20

John Moore woke with what felt like the mother of all hangovers and a mouth like glass-paper. He'd been roused by the sound of an electric floor polisher. Looking through the glass panel in the door, he could see the cleaner slinging the offending machine enthusiastically from side to side. He could also see the ward clock. It told him it was half past six.

John groaned.

'How are you feeling?' Weaver sounded cheerful. Cheerful and loud.

'How do I look?'

'Ah. That bad. You want some water? The nurse said you'd be thirsty when you woke up, said I was to call her.'

'Can't you get it for me?'

'No. I don't think so.' Weaver shook his head. 'She said you were likely to throw up, first drink you had.'

John smiled. It was hard work. 'Would I do that to you?' He sounded like glass-paper too.

The nurse arrived and bustled efficiently, checking the drip, easing his position against the pillows and, finally, offering iced water. John had never realized that water could taste so good. He waited for the nausea to hit. Was relieved when it didn't, though the pounding in his head worsened second by second. Why, he wondered did his head hurt so damned much, when he'd been shot in the shoulder?

'You been here all night?' he asked Weaver when the nurse had gone.

Weaver shook his head. 'Got here about a half hour ago.' He jerked his head in the direction of the door and the offending polisher. 'I arrived with your morning alarm call.'

'Did you find Colin?' John closed his eyes against the pain. The beating inside his skull had taken on the rhythm of the polisher, whining in his brain and thumping against the walls each time she reached the edge of the floor and bashed against the skirting.

'No, but he'd been there. I got a warrant and we searched the place, Radcliffe's home too. Colin had been in Radcliffe's office, though of course, they're all denying it. His ATM card was under Radcliffe's desk.'

'Not good,' John said.

'Maybe not so bad. You'll never guess who was admitted here last night. Not long after you, as it happens.'

186

John opened his eyes again and stared, mystified. 'Who?'

'Our friend Charlie Radcliffe.' Weaver was grinning as though about to share a massive joke.

His smile was not pleasant, John thought. Probably lack of practice. Weaver looked like the last sight Red Riding Hood's grandmother had ever seen.

'Reckons he was mugged,' his boss went on. 'Shallow stab wounds to his face and eye socket and a section of his scalp looks like someone had serious hair envy.' He grimaced. 'I'd say whoever went for him was aiming for the eye. Didn't blind him, unfortunately, but he looks like he's just gone ten rounds with Ali, when Ali was on form.'

John's smile spread slowly, but the final grin matched Weaver's. 'Colin,' he said. 'It had to be Colin.'

'Wouldn't have thought he had it in him,' Weaver commented. 'I thought you considered him a waste of space anyway.'

John nodded, then wished he hadn't. 'Part of me still does,' he admitted. 'But I feel I owe Moira. She never stopped caring about him. Anyway, whatever I feel about Colin Grainger personally, he's still the key to all of this and Radcliffe knows it.' He grimaced. His shoulder was starting to hurt, joining his head in a cacophony of pain. 'Think you can find that nurse?' he asked.

'Surely, but while I've got you so obviously at a disadvantage, I'd like a few answers. It seems to me you've been playing silly buggers. So. What the hell's been going on and who's this woman, Julie, that keeps leaving messages on your answerphone?'

'Julie. Oh God.' John was shamed to find he'd almost forgotten about her. 'Painkillers first,' he pleaded. 'Then I'll tell you anything you want.'

'Truth would be a good start,' Weaver told him. He reached over and pressed the buzzer that had been left close to John's hand. John had been unaware of it until that moment. He cursed Weaver under his breath, but his boss ignored it. 'Your trouble is you don't know who your friends are,' he told him.

'Yeah. Right.'

The nurse came in, listened to John's complaints and went off to fetch him some pills. 'Five minutes,' she told Weaver when she returned. 'He needs to get some rest.' And went again.

'Better make it quick then,' Weaver told him. He sat down beside the bed and rested his hands on his knees. Weaver, John thought, always looked slightly lost without a desk in front of him.

'It began,' he said. 'On the night before Moira died. You remember, Colin gave her that info about the Chinese takeaway.'

'Don't frigging remind me.'

'Well, it seems like he was trying to make up for things. Moira was reluctant to listen at first. I wish,' he said fervently, 'she'd trusted her instinct and just told him to shove it, but she listened and she saw the information he had on his computer and, far as we can figure it, she went to Radcliffe to confront him with it or maybe just to snoop around. Whatever, she was caught. Julie saw her with Brian Henshaw and next we know, she's in a back alley.'

Weaver listened as John summarised what he knew. Twice, the nurse came back. Twice, Weaver glared at her and she went away. The third time, she'd brought reinforcements in the shape of a very weary looking Houseman. 'Go,' she said. 'Doctor wants to examine his patient.'

'My things,' John asked her. 'In my jacket pocket, there was a floppy disk.'

She frowned, opened the locker drawer. 'If you had it, someone would have ... Ah, this what you're looking for?'

'I want a copy of it,' John told Weaver.

His boss shook his head. Mock despair or just plain irritation, John couldn't tell. 'OK, OK. I'll see to it. I'll even give you a frigging receipt. Now, rest. Do as you're told. It'll be a first.'

John was glad to see Weaver go. He felt like he wasn't sure what it was, but it was awful all the same. Worst of all, he felt like he wanted to cry. Howl like a baby and he wasn't entirely certain why.

For Moira? For himself? Relief for the fact that he was still alive, guilt that she wasn't? He couldn't have told anyone had they asked. He realised, belatedly, that the doctor was talking to him, describing what had been done the night before.

'You're lucky. I'm told the bullet was a .22 and had it been a 9mm, you'd have felt like half your back was missing.' He looked pleased with that bit of knowledge. John would have liked to contradict his assumption that half his back missing wasn't how it was feeling at that moment.

'The bullet entered your shoulder here.' He indicated the top of his shoulder. 'Behind the clavicle and passed down at a bit of an angle to the outside of the shoulder blade. Then it exited here, lower back, just below the rib cage. You'll feel like you've been run over by a train,' he added cheerily. 'And the ribs will be bruised and sore, so don't be alarmed if you find it hard to breathe. Rest and try not to worry about anything.'

He smiled and took a last look at John's chart. 'I'll be in later,' he said and departed before John could ask him anything, like when could I go home.

He closed his eyes. The painkillers must be having an effect, he thought. The agonised thumping in his head was easing to a fainter but still insistent drum beat, the only thing cheering him up, the thought of Charlie Radcliffe nearly losing an eye.

By lunchtime, Charlie Radcliffe was home, accompanied by Brian Henshaw, arriving just as the last of Weaver's officers had departed. Radcliffe lived alone, his wife having gone some years past, her sights set on a respectability she felt Charlie couldn't offer. She was married to a doctor now, so he figured she had her respectability. He wondered if it rankled that Charlie was making more money.

He looked at himself in the hall mirror, removing the pad and plaster dressing the hospital had applied. His left eye was bloodied and the lids almost closed by bruising. They'd told him there'd be no long term damage. Colin, Radcliffe thought wryly, hadn't even managed that properly, the pen nib penetrating the socket but only grazing his eyeball.

It was bad enough though, he thought. It looked bad. Both ways. He'd misjudged the situation and that was something Charlie Radcliffe was not known for doing. He was angry with himself as much as Colin Grainger. Felt he had been humiliated and that, far more than any physical damage, was something Colin would have to pay for.

'Want a drink, boss?' Henshaw asked.

'Yeah. Better make it coffee though. The Doc said no alcohol with the painkillers.'

Henshaw nodded and disappeared into the kitchen.

Charlie Radcliffe stared into the mirror, turning his head better to examine the damage and to build his rage. This was no longer just about the information Colin may or may not have had; this was now personal. Charlie had a reputation to maintain and he wasn't going to let some little bastard like Colin Grainger turn him into a laughing stock.

His reverie was interrupted by the doorbell.

'DCI Weaver,' the man on his doorstep introduced himself, 'and this is DS Morgan. We'd like a word, Mr Radcliffe.'

Radcliffe stood back to let them in. 'God Almighty. I thought I'd done with you lot. What do you want now? Brian,' he yelled, 'we've got two more for coffee.'

He led them into the smaller of the two living rooms and waved them into chairs, noting that Weaver sprawled in his and the woman perched, with her notebook poised, on the edge of the sofa.

'I heard you were mugged, Charlie,' Weaver began.

'Yeah, not safe to walk the streets now. But then, if you lot did your job, instead of harassing honest businessmen, we'd all sleep safer,' Radcliffe replied.

'More bobbies on the beat. That it?'

'It'd be a start.'

Henshaw came in with the coffee and set the tray on the table close to Charlie. He sat down next to the woman on one of Charlie's oversized sofas. Watching, Charlie was amused to see her shift a fraction away from the big man. She kept her eyes fixed firmly on her boss as if that might distract attention.

'Anything taken?' Weaver asked.

'Taken?'

'In the mugging. What was taken?'

'Oh,' Radcliffe shrugged. 'Nothing. They were interrupted.'

'Lucky that.' He gestured towards Henshaw. 'I didn't think they let you out alone, Charlie. What was your escort service doing while you were getting beaten up?'

The colour rose to Charlie Radcliffe's face, but he held his tongue, refusing to rise to Weaver's jibes.

'Mr Radcliffe should be resting,' Brian Henshaw said. 'So if you've nothing else to ask, it might be best for you to go now.'

'You his doctor now, as well, Brian?' Weaver dug in his pocket and threw an evidence bag onto the table. Inside was an ATM card, Colin's name clearly visible. 'You like to tell me what that was doing in your office?'

Radcliffe made a show of picking up the bag and examining the contents. 'I found it in the street,' he said. 'I was going to hand it in tomorrow, when the bank opened.'

'Very public spirited of you.' Rose Morgan commented.

'One likes to help out.'

'Does one?' Weaver asked. 'Then maybe you can help with this. He removed from his pocket several pages of printed paper and laid them on the table.

'What's this?' Radcliffe wanted to know.

'Hoping you'd tell us. Oh, don't worry, Charlie, that copy's for you. Study it at your leisure and give me a call when you're ready.'

Charlie Radcliffe made a show of looking at the documents and then casting them aside. 'I know nothing about this,' he said. 'Now, perhaps you could tell me when I get my stuff back. Your lot took my computers and my CCTV tapes, so Brian here tells me. I've got a business to run.'

'And we're sorry for any inconvenience caused.' Weaver got up, ready to go. 'I'll let you know when we're done.'

'Did you want to make a statement about the mugging?' Rose asked.

Radcliffe scowled at her. 'I didn't get a look at his face,' he said.

'You think we rattled him?' Rose Morgan asked when they got to the car.

'I bloody hope so. Trouble is, he knows we can't use what we've got. It was illegally

194

obtained, as it stands it's inadmissible.'

'And there's nothing on the office computer.'

Weaver sighed. 'There's bugger all on the office computer. His assistant, what's her name. Sandra...'

'Porter,' Rose supplied.

'Porter, reckoned it crashed and they'd had the hard drive replaced.'

'Nice coincidence.'

'Don't believe in coincidence. Thing is, they didn't have much time between Colin alerting them with his little prank and our lads going in last night, so they must have shifted. Sandra said they got one of their employees to change it. We got the details on him yet?'

'Morantz is dealing.'

'Good.'

'The printout,' Rose ventured. 'Someone mentioned money laundering?'

Weaver nodded. 'That's what John figures and for once I'm in agreement. My ... our guess is that Radcliffe was keeping his own record of transactions. He'd be creaming it off the top anyway. Service charges, I suppose he'd call it. But I can't think his clients would be too happy to know Radcliffe was keeping details of how much money they were putting through and, if our guess is right, keeping a record of the source.'

'The source. You mean the crime that

generated it?'

'Uh uhn.'

'Would he have that info?'

'He's been in business since before you were a gleam in your daddy's eye. It wouldn't take much guesswork on his part. Radcliffe keeps his ear to the ground, watches as the trends change and it looks like he deals with the, shall we say, currency exchange for some surprisingly influential names, so he's got a lot more info than should safely be in anyone's hands. At least, that's the way his clients are going to see it.'

'So Charlie Radcliffe could be in deep shit.'

'If it gets out. Yes.'

'But why keep these records. He must have known the dangers attached. You get into the laundry business, your key word is discretion, I'd have thought.'

'No, I'd have said your key words were selective blindness. My guess is, Charlie Radcliffe was about to embark on a little high level blackmail. Threaten to tell the left hand what the right is doing if they didn't give him a bigger cut. Maybe a share in business. We've not done a full analysis so far, but some of the names on that list, well, to say they're business rivals is putting it mildly.'

'So, how come Radcliffe deals with both sides? Don't they know.'

'Probably not. Radcliffe has controlling

interest in three other casinos and I doubt his clients come in person to do business. Like I said, discretion and selective blindness, meanwhile, Radcliffe gets ready to play both ends against the middle.'

'Sounds like a good way to get yourself killed.'

Weaver nodded. 'As I say, Radcliffe's been around a long time. His knowledge and expertise is useful. Might make him worth not killing, especially if he could convince both sides that they could cut the nose off the opposition. But, you're right. It's a risky game.'

'Why do it now?'

'I don't know. The new legislation will mean he has to tighten up his act. His business will be audited regularly and that might mean cutbacks in his profit margins, though I doubt the effects will be long term, to be truthful. There's still too many loopholes to exploit. But, maybe it's rattled him enough to take a risk. Maybe he's planning for his retirement.'

Rose Morgan nodded thoughtfully. 'You going to see DI Moore, now?' she asked.

Weaver nodded, pulling up in his regular parking space to let Rose out. 'Chase up Morantz. If he's got anything, get hold of me at the hospital.'

'Will do. Give DI Moore my best.'

'Your best what?' Weaver asked.

21

John had tried to sleep during most of the morning, his rest disturbed by hourly observations, offers of the bed pan and the various rituals of hospital life. All of which seemed to generate noise.

When Weaver arrived he was playing with his lunch. It had already gone cold, which did nothing to add to the appeal of some sort of meat in gravy and pureed vegetables.

'Apparently, I wasn't here to order yesterday, so I've got what was left over,' he told Weaver, noting his expression of disgust. 'And before you ask, yes, it does taste as bad as it looks.'

He gave up trying to eat and dropped his fork onto the plate, wincing as it clattered loudly against crockery and tray.

'Well?'

Weaver took a floppy disk from his pocket and shoved it into the drawer of John's bedside cabinet. 'It's a copy,' he said. 'I've been to see Charlie Radcliffe. Left him studying a printout of what was on the disk. It'll give him something to think about at any rate.'

'He's back home?' John asked.

Weaver nodded. 'Looks a bloody mess.

Our boy did a fair job.'

Our boy, John noted. Colin seemed to have graduated from being a superfluous use of skin.

'We ran the names through the police national computer,' Weaver continued. 'Here,' he handed John a list of names and details. 'Some reading matter to be going on with.'

John scanned the list and whistled softly.

'Quite. Our guess is he was hoping to play one off against the other. Didn't you once have dealings with Billy James?'

John lay the papers down on the bed-clothes and leaned back into the pillows. 'I grew up on his patch,' he said. 'I've not been back since my dad passed on.'

Weaver nodded curtly. 'He's supposed to be legit these days.'

'On some level, I think he always was,' John confirmed. 'Last I heard he was Coun-sellor James, campaigning for the working man and family values.'

Weaver snorted. 'How long are they keeping you in?'

'Why? We that short of manpower?'

'Many a true word. I spoke to the doctor, he reckons you were lucky. The bullet should have shattered your scapula. You'd have been laid up for weeks, he reckons.'

'You sound disappointed.'

Weaver considered. 'It wouldn't hurt to

take some time out,' he said. 'Think about it.'

'Already have. I'll take sick leave … when they put Radcliffe away.'

'Thought you'd say that. Tried moving yet, have you?'

'Your point being?'

'According to the doc, you'll have enough of a time going to the toilet on your own, never mind chasing Radcliffe. Give yourself a break … if you pardon the pun.' He stood, made for the door. 'I'll have someone drop by later, keep you up to speed,' he promised. From Weaver that was almost compassionate.

'Thanks,' John told him. He watched his boss leave, wincing again as the door slammed shut and settled himself for an afternoon of boredom similar to the morning he had already spent.

Colin arrived at Staithes in the early evening. From Leeds, he'd hitched, zig-zagging across country for the best part of the day and finally getting a lift that went where he wanted to be.

The lorry driver pointed out the side road, then left him standing on the high escarpment, windblown and freezing.

'So much for the bloody moors,' Colin moaned.

It was almost five and the dark was already closing in. A line of brightness still lit the horizon where he guessed the sea must be, but that was fading, clouds thickening even as he watched. The main road was busy with what he supposed must pass for rush hour traffic headed towards Middlesbrough and he stood on the verge, waiting for a break so he could run across.

Colin was cold and hungry and tired, and very much aware of being alone.

The side road leading down to Staithes was unlit and high hedged. Colin found it hard to judge the distance he had walked. Eventually he rounded a bend and came upon the little town. Never had streetlights looked so welcome or so beautiful.

The lorry driver had told him there was no proper vehicle access. Cars usually had to park at the top of the hill and visitors continue on foot, either down what passed for the main street, or, as Colin soon found, follow a series of narrow alleys that staggered down the cliff side towards the sea.

Feeling his way as much as seeing, Colin took the pathway leading from the car park. There was a wall on one side of him, a sheer drop into a succession of back gardens and then allotments on the other. Then the pathway dropped between the houses, in places it became so narrow and so tight, he wondered if he were traipsing through someone's garden.

How to find the boarding house?

There was no one about to ask. Lighted

201

buildings surrounded him, crowding the alleyway in a manner that was at once comforting and claustrophobic. Even coming here in the half dark, Colin could see that it was a pretty place, but that did nothing to comfort him. It was not somewhere you could get out of in a hurry. He imagined himself being chased back up the steep and seemingly treacherous paths and began to consider that this small town was in the nature of a picturesque rat trap and that he'd walked openly and voluntarily right into the most lethal heart of it.

Suddenly, the vista opened up in front of him and Colin found himself standing on the small quay, the sea almost at his feet. Looking around, hearing a burst of noise emitted from a briefly open door, Colin realised that there were two pubs.

People.

Aware that he must look travel stained and completely shattered, Colin slipped quietly into the closest and moments later, armed with directions, he was making his way back up one of the little alleyways towards the Matthews boarding house and rehearsing what he might say once he'd got there.

It was six fifteen when he knocked upon the door and Jan Matthews opened it. Inside it was light and warm and the scent of food made him feel sick with hunger. All of Colin's carefully prepared speeches failed him and he stared eagerly into Jan Matthews's friendly face.

'John Moore sent me,' he managed.

To his relief, she smiled at him and beckoned him inside.

'From John's description I'd say you must be Colin,' she said. 'He called us from the hospital. Come along in, I've cooked extra, just in case. We've been expecting you most of the afternoon.'

22

Sandra and Brian Henshaw arrived back at Radcliffe's bringing with them a takeaway and a couple of bottles of wine.

'No sign of her,' Sandra reported as she dished food onto plates. She frowned. 'I'm not sure this is still hot, Charlie. Stick it in the microwave, just to be sure.'

'Anyone know where she might be?'

Sandra shook her head. 'We talked to the neighbours and went looking for her at Ian's school.'

'Not very subtle,' Radcliffe chided.

'Oh, don't you worry, I did most of the talking,' Sandra reassured him. 'I told anyone that asked we were worried about her 'cause she'd got upset at work and had to go home

203

and I'd heard there'd been a death in the family. Most didn't ask. You know how it is in these high rises. People wouldn't notice if their neighbours took a dive off the balcony. There was a woman at the school reckoned her son and Ian were best friends and that her son was due to go round and play tonight. They arranged it yesterday so...

'Either she did a flit on impulse, or she's cleverer than we gave her credit for,' Henshaw concluded.

Charlie Radcliffe shoved the first of the plates in the microwave and paused to examine the label on the wine Brian was opening. 'Hardy's,' he approved. 'Though I don't think I've tried this one. So, what's your next move, San?'

'I've got her mam's address,' Sandra told him. 'I thought I'd go round tomorrow morning. I'll go on my own though. I think this one needs a woman's touch.'

'You find anything in the flat?'

Brian shook his head. 'She might have taken clothes and stuff with her, but it was hard to tell. If she did, then they're travelling light, most of her clothes are still there.'

'Even personal things,' Sandra agreed. 'She might have taken odd bits, but there's a little box with jewellery in on her dressing table – nothing expensive, mind, but one or two nice bits – and her makeup and hairbrush were still on the bathroom shelf. I got some useful numbers from the book she kept by the phone – don't worry, I left it where it was – but we messed the place up a bit.'

'Oh?' Radcliffe was intrigued.

'Well, we had a talk and we figured we could turn this our way. Get the Mam to go round. Place is trashed. No sign of Julie or the boy. She panics, informs the police and local press and Brian thought we could well, drop Grainger's name into the conversation. You know, how she'd said she was seeing someone new and how he'd been having a few problems lately, what with his ex wife being murdered and, according to our source, he was the first person the Old Bill dragged in for questioning.'

Radcliffe had begun to smile and the smile broadened as he thought about it. He kissed Sandra. 'You are the best,' he told her. 'We make the police and the press do our legwork for us and all free, gratis and for nothing.'

'And we've still got whatever other information comes our way,' Sandra affirmed. She raised her glass. 'To Rose Morgan,' she said.

The aforesaid Rose Morgan put the key into her front door and leaned against it. The wood was swollen from the rain and even after she'd unlocked it didn't really want to budge.

The hallway carried the scent of fresh coffee from the kitchen. Phil was already home. For a moment, she felt a pang of disappointment. It had been a heavy day and she'd planned on running a hot bath and relaxing alone for an hour before he arrived.

'Coffee?'

'Thanks. I've just got a call to make.'

She stood in the hallway, getting the number she needed from her mobile phone and then dialling on the landline.

'Trouble with your phone?' Phil asked, setting her coffee down on the hall table.

She shook her head. 'Battery's low. I don't want it fading on me mid conversation.'

'Give it here, I'll plug it into the charger. You really should...'

'I know.' She waved him into silence as her call was answered and Weaver, sounding even grumpier than usual, barked his name.

'Sorry, Guv, I've been trying to reach you all afternoon, but you've either been switched off, in meetings or engaged.'

'It's been one of those days. Anything on this hard drive?'

'No, not yet. Morantz went round to his digs, but apparently he's away on some field trip or other. Won't be back for a couple of days and there's no phone contact.'

'Where the hell is he? Outer Mongolia?'

'No Guv, just Scotland. Morantz is still trying to track him down.'

Phil wandered back into the hall, coffee in hand. He leaned against the door frame, watching her. She turned away suddenly irritated. 'Any more news on...'

'He's been in touch,' Weaver told her. 'John has our other witness stashed with friends and Colin's joined her.'

'They safe?'

'I think so. It's a little place on the Yorkshire coast, just North of Whitby, I believe.'

'Oh, I used to go there on holiday when I was a little kid. Wild coastline.'

'Nice for you. So if I send you and Morantz to get them back I can rely on you not to get lost.'

'Maybe. I was only eight the last time we went.'

'Not much use then. Ok, I'll see you at morning briefing.'

'Ok, Guv. Night.'

She replaced the receiver and leaned wearily against the wall.'

'Take off your wet coat and drink your coffee,' Phil, said. 'Want me to run a bath?'

'Yes. Thanks.'

'Where were you when you were only eight?'

'What? Oh, Whitby, that way on. I might have to drive up, collect a witness.'

'That's a bit off your patch, isn't it?'

Rose shrugged. Picked up her coffee. 'You're home early.'

He nodded. 'We finished the job ahead of time. I hear your lot raided Radcliffe's place last night?'

Rose frowned. 'You know I can't talk about that.' He gestured placatingly, almost spilling his coffee in the process. 'I know. I'm just saying, that's all. Any idea how long it'll be closed?'

Her eyes narrowed. 'I'm going to run a bath,' she said.'

'I was going to do that for you.'

'I can run my own. I thought you'd given up on the gambling. You promised me, Phil.'

'I have! What have I done to make you think otherwise?'

'Then what's it matter when Radcliffe's place reopens?' He sighed and went back into the kitchen. 'If that's the way you feel.'

It was. Rose continued up the stairs. She was soaking in the tub when she heard the front door close. She leaned forward and added more hot water, a few drops of perfumed oil, not sure if she was glad or sorry he had gone away.

23

Friday had been a quiet day. John had asked the nurse to get him a card for the pre pay television in his room and dipped in and out of the programmes, finally discovering an old episode of *The Streets of San Francisco*, late in the afternoon. He watched with amusement and, it had to be admitted, a fair amount of enjoyment, reliving the times he had watched this as a kid. It had been late night fare then. He'd had to have special permission to sit up.

Times changed.

From six o'clock he was checking the door, expecting a visit from Weaver and flicking channels, hoping to find some news. He watched with limited interest as the latest casualties on the West Bank were detailed, discovered that his mortgage rate would stay the same that month – courtesy of the Bank of England – and that trains had been hit by delays yet again. Repairs and bad weather, the reporter said.

'Probably too many leaves clogging the line,' he muttered irritably. He leaned back against the pillows as the newsreader announced the changeover to the local section, wishing that Weaver or Morgan – or anyone – would arrive. It had come home to him with quite brutal force, just how few friends he had outside of the job. He had no family to speak of – a sister in Canada he'd not contacted since the previous New Year and cousins he never saw. In general he had led a solitary existence ever since leaving home, his career choice cutting him off from many of those who'd shared the years of childhood and adolescence.

His reverie was broken as the local presenter listed the headlines for the day. Suddenly John was all attention.

The lead story was the disappearance of Julie Wise and her ten year old son, Ian. Julie, the announcer said, had failed to turn up for work. Her employer had been worried because her absence and failure to phone in was out of character and because they knew she'd been having unspecified personal problems, so, unable to raise her they'd contacted her family. Later, relatives had discovered that her flat on the Bishops-wood Estate had been broken into and Julie and her son nowhere to be found.

Cue cut to weeping mother and frantic sister. 'She'd never go away without telling us. Not just take off like that. She knows how we'd worry.'

'Something's happened to her. I just know something's happened.'

Cut back to reporter on scene preparing to give background. 'Mr Radcliffe, I believe that Julie Wise works as a croupier at your casino?'

Charlie Radcliffe nodded. His face was a mess, John thought absently. 'She's a good girl. Works hard for us and she's an excellent mother. Whoever broke into her flat trashed the place thoroughly. I've seen the damage. I just hope ... just hope she's safe and well somewhere.'

The camera moved in, focusing on the sincerity on Charlie Radcliffe's face. 'Julie, wherever you are, whatever's happened, we can all sort it out between us. Nothing's so bad you have to run away from it. For your mum's sake, please, give someone a ring. She's worried herself sick here.'

Out of the corner of his eye John saw Weaver walking down the ward towards his room. His face was hard, set in a scowl and he carried a rolled up newspaper in his hand, looking as though he was waiting to swipe someone with it.

'You've seen it then?' Weaver demanded, coming through the door.

John nodded.

'It gets worse.' He threw the newspaper at John and slumped down in the chair beside the bed.

Brady Timms had handled the story factually. Been careful to stress that Julie was a grown woman who didn't have to tell her mum every time she went somewhere and that there was nothing to link the break in to her departure, but the inference was still there, hidden between the cautious wording.

There was worse, as Weaver had said. Allegations had been made, the paper said, about Radcliffe's casino – Radcliffe, he reminded his readers, being the concerned employer of attractive Julie aged thirty-two. Police had raided his business and his home on the day Julie was believed to have dis-appeared. 'Mr Radcliffe himself having been a victim, apparently, of a mugging that same night.'

But what really troubled John was that it mentioned Colin. '"Sources suggest that..."' He raised a questioning eyebrow. 'Sources?' Weaver shrugged. '"...suggest that Julie Wise had recently begun a relationship with Colin Grainger of 29 Malling Road, Hillford, who was also an employee of Mr Radcliffe and who, neighbours confirm, has likewise been absent from home for several days. This association with Miss Wise was believed by friends..."' 'Friends?' John asked. Again the shrug. '"...by friends, to have been the first relationship Mr Grainger had entered into since his divorce three years ago. By another tragic coincidence, Mr Grainger's ex wife was Detective Sergeant Moira Barker, who was found beaten to death in an alleyway off Preen Road two weeks ago today. It's under-stood that she had reverted to her maiden name after the divorce."'

John tossed the paper back at Weaver. 'Great,' he said. 'Just bloody great.'

'We've arranged for a statement from the press office to be released tomorrow,' Weaver told him. 'Maybe something more direct, if the Super deems it necessary.' He picked up the paper again, looked at it, then tossed it back onto the bed.

'To be fair, Brady got onto the press office before he released this,' Weaver continued. 'Apparently he'd been talking to a colleague on one of the satellite news channels. Radcliffe was shooting his mouth off after the television interview and they plan to run the story as soon as, so there was no point in telling him to hold off.'

'Brady's handled it as best he can,' John agreed.

'But if we could have kept it quiet for now, it would have given us a few hours grace to organise ourselves,' Weaver said. 'As it was, it was in the public domain before everyone who should have been informed, our end, had been briefed. I had Superintendent Cauldwell on the blower, narked as hell that the story broke without him being informed.'

'How *did* he find out?'

'His wife showed him the evening paper.'

Wearily, Weaver wiped his hands across his face and then stared at them as though they might hold answers. 'He's suggested I'm not up to the job,' he went on quietly. 'I fought tooth and nail to be officer in charge on Moira's murder and, as Cauldwell pointed out, we've got bugger all to show for it except another body and a young woman missing with her son. Oh and an officer shot in his own home. You noticed you didn't appear on the news, I take it?'

'I noticed,' John said. 'What's the story,

should anyone ask what I'm doing here?'

Weaver's look was withering. 'You're off sick,' he said. 'Rose and Morantz know and, before you say anything, I'm aware I can't keep the lid on this for long, but do you really want Brady Timms and his ilk camping outside the hospital waiting for you?'

'Brady Timms doesn't camp,' John commented. 'He'd send one of his trainees to keep look out, then arrive in his Jag when he got the word.'

Weaver glared, then seemed to sag under the weight of his problems. John had never seen him look so despairing or so tired.

'Did you tell Cauldwell about the disk?'

Weaver shook his head, 'Not yet. I tried to get to see him today, but he was off at some conference or other. I'm on my way round now. You'd better get on to Colin and Julie, tell them what's kicked off. Make sure they stay put and I'll get Cauldwell to arrange a safe house. I don't think a B&B in Staithes is going to be the best place for our two star witnesses. He stood up and John saw that his hands were clenched as though he fought to keep something inside. 'John, this is off the record and I never said it, but I want this bastard nailed. For what he did to one of my officers and what he did to that girl, Alice. You saw the state ... of both of them. I owe them. We owe them and I want Radcliffe nailed, any way you bloody can.'

He left without saying goodbye and John was left to ponder. He wasn't shocked at Weaver's last comments, but he knew, or thought he knew the man well enough that he'd be in denial of them by the following morning. Weaver was under tremendous pressure. So much that it needed a release if he were not to burst from it. John, on the other hand, he really did feel that way. He wanted Radcliffe to pay, maybe even wanted Radcliffe dead, with such a passion that he no longer considered the rights and wrongs of getting justice. Should the opportunity for revenge present itself, John had no doubt that he would take it. He shifted awkwardly against the pillows and laughed silently at his own protestations, knowing that Radcliffe would have to oblige him by holding very still.

He could, now, make it across the corridor to the toilet, but he needed painkillers and about an hour's worth of recovery time after.

He thought of Weaver's other parting comment. He agreed that Colin and Julie and especially Ian – the innocent in all of this – deserved and required protection. But star witnesses to what? Julie had seen Moira at the casino on the night of her death. When it came down to it, that was all. Colin had stolen info that, in the wrong hands, could have major repercussions and not just for Radcliffe. If their guess was right and

Radcliffe had been planning to play all sides against the middle while creaming off the best profit he could, then if any one of the main players found out, it would be the end for Radcliffe and that ... that would leave a vacuum that someone would move to fill. Someone perhaps a whole lot worse than Charlie Radcliffe. John toyed with the idea of releasing the information anyway and taking the consequences. Once out in the public domain, it would be like a snowball down the mountain, taking on its own momentum and leaving Radcliffe and his clients fighting over what was truth and what was lies. It was tempting, but John knew it would finish him as a police officer and he wasn't sure he knew how to be anything else. To say nothing of the effects on those unwittingly caught up in the fall out.

John was aware that law enforcement was so often just making the best of a bad job. You did the best you could to solve the major ones. Played social worker to the domestics – and some seventy per cent of call outs were to deal with domestic problems – and you kept the lid on organised crime. John knew as well, the harder you pressed down on the lid, the more got forced out from underneath. Sometimes, it was tacitly agreed, it was best to leave the likes of Charlie Radcliffe alone. He at least acted as a buffer between rivals and, John supposed, he could be seen as a sort of neutral country, carrying out the banking and the laundering for whoever came along without fear or favour. It wasn't ideal. It wasn't good or even acceptable, but at least you had some idea of who was doing what and where they were doing it and were likely to be informed, by the status quo, of any new talent trying to muscle in.

Though, John reflected, no one had any idea of the scale of Charlie Radcliffe's operation until now or of the network of connections he had formed.

Colin had discovered something, brought it to the surface and forced anyone who saw it to take notice and a part of John, the part that had grown up with the likes of Billy James and, indeed, John's own cherished and much lamented father, cursed him for exposing something that was just too dangerous to know.

The other part of him – the part that had chosen law enforcement and which had taken this particular moral stance – knew that the Charlie Radcliffe's of the world had also to be controlled and not just by the criminals whose system they supported and who supported them. John had long since learned that the world existed only in shades of grey. There were few absolutes at either end of the spectrum.

He needed to let Colin know what was going on before it hit the nationals. Wearily, he pressed the call button and asked the nurse to bring him the pay phone.

He'd talk to Colin, he decided and then he'd call a taxi, get himself out of here. He wasn't even sure he could make it down the stairs without assistance, but he was sure as hell going to give it a try. He'd spent the best part of two days lying here like a lump and, frankly, John could take no more of it.

Weaver was right – even though the DCI would change his mind when his calm returned – they had to get out there and do something. And John had decided, job or no job, he didn't care if what he did was within the law or without it.

24

John was awoken the following morning by a hammering on his door. It took him a moment to figure out that he was at home and had fallen asleep in an easy chair in the front room.

Awkwardly, he got out of the chair, gasping with the sudden pain that breached his right side, travelling down from the shoulder. With difficulty, he held back the nausea that followed. Making it to the door, John opened it to find Weaver and Rose

Morgan standing on his doorstep.

John stood aside to let them in. A draft of chill air followed them and he realized that he was stiff with cold himself. The heating hadn't been on in the house for several days and he'd not had the energy to bother with it last night. He'd come in through the back, unable to open the front door, and discovered that some thoughtful soul had put a new bolt on the door for him, the Yale lock being ruined when his colleagues had broken it to get to him. After that, he'd settled in the chair for a few moments, still in his coat, intending to get himself up to bed. He must have passed out or fallen asleep.

'I've bought you milk and bread,' Rose told him. 'I'll make a brew, shall I?'

'Thanks.' He managed a smile. Weaver glowered but said nothing.

John managed to shrug out of his coat and made it to the downstairs cloakroom, discovering once again how difficult it is to do things with a left hand when you were usually profoundly right dominant.

Rose was seeing to the tea when he returned to the kitchen.

'What the hell do you think you're playing at?' Weaver demanded.

'I discharged myself.'

'And for what? Look at you. Can you even dress yourself?'

The nurse had helped him, John admitted.

219

She'd finally taken pity on him after watching him struggle for the best part of an hour, but she'd let him know exactly what she thought of him into the bargain. The taxi driver had been only too eager to see him into the house. He'd kept watching John in the rear view as though expecting him to faint or throw up or bleed over the seats. There were moments when John had felt about to do all three.

'You've got blood on your shirt and bandages,' Rose observed.

'You look a mess,' Weaver confirmed. 'And it's bloody freezing in here, don't you go in for heating?'

John told him how to switch it on. He was shivering now he'd removed his coat and Rose grabbed a sweater from the drying rack in the utility room and helped him into it. 'You should get that dressing changed,' she advised. 'Is anyone coming in to see you?'

John shook his head. He didn't know. His right arm was strapped firmly across his chest. Padding and more bandage blocked the exit wound. It felt stiff and sticky. John guessed it had bled and dried and now bled again. He had to admit, at least to himself, that this may not have been the wisest move.

Weaver sighed heavily. 'I'll get welfare to arrange something,' he said. 'I doubt your doctor's going to be too sympathetic with you. Seeing as you walked out. Anyone you can stay with?'

John thought about it and shook his head. With Moira gone, there was no one.

'Well, if you'd stayed put, you'd have had the news by now.'

'News?'

'Colin and Julie have done a flit. Your friends at the B&B have been trying to get hold of you at the hospital. They tried your home phone. Fortunately, you've still got it set to divert and they got through to Rose here.'

'Oh God! When did they leave? Did they say where they were going?'

Weaver shook his head: Rose was busy getting mugs out of the cupboard. 'Where do you keep your sugar?'

'Top left. That's it.'

'No, no idea where they've gone. They left a note for the Matthews saying they were scared and that it was better no one knew where they were. Mrs Matthews said Julie was paranoid about one of our lot informing on them. Seems she was spooked once she'd found out they'd been able to get to Colin.'

'Chances are they had him followed,' John commented.

'So. She just figures she lost Radcliffe's lot once, she doesn't want them finding her again.'

'Lost them?'

'Jan Matthews said she gave them the slip

at the shopping centre. Stole a car and left hers behind.'

'God almighty.' John closed his eyes. 'She's sure she was followed?'

'Pretty sure and from her description of the men, one of them sounds like our sandy haired wannabe policeman. Same as saw Brady Timms.'

'We need to get someone up there to talk to Jan. Rose, you can drive me.'

'No way,' Weaver interrupted. 'You are on sick leave and you are staying put. You any idea where they might have gone?'

John shook his head. 'No,' he admitted. 'None. I don't know Colin, apart from what Moira told me about him and Julie ... I didn't even know she existed 'til a couple of days ago. What a frigging mess.'

'Drink your tea,' Rose told him. 'If we don't know, chances are no one else does either. And Colin might make contact.'

'Drink your tea!' Weaver mimicked. 'What are you? His bloody mother? At least it's starting to warm up in here,' he added. 'Right. Rose and Morantz have an appointment with Julie Wise's mother, then I've got a bloody press conference at noon. Cauldwell's idea of damage limitation.'

'What are they driving?' John asked. 'You say Julie stole a car?'

'And they left it at Staithes. Took Jan Matthews's car. We've got a trace out for the

222

number, but...'

John nodded. They could be anywhere by now and tracking the car meant someone in whatever location they happened to be in having checked the most recent bulletins and kept them to hand and then noticed the car. Jan, he remembered, drove a Ford, he thought an escort, but whatever, it was ordinary, anonymous. It wasn't even an unusual colour. Though, he thought miserably, it was probably the best lead they had unless Colin chose to contact him.

When Rose and Weaver had gone, John drank more tea and managed to make himself some toast, buttering it by wedging the crust under the edge of the butter dish to keep it still. Left handed, he was clumsy to the point of ineptness, but, hungry, he persevered, amazed at how good it tasted after two days of eating almost nothing.

Then, needing to be useful, he fired up his laptop and accessed his work emails. Three days worth, mainly junk, was opened with difficulty. Not good with a mouse at the best of times, he found it hard to manipulate with his left and the little roller ball on the lap top key board was even worse. He satisfied him-self that there was nothing urgent and that colleagues would soon be informed that he was out of action anyway. It had occurred to him that Colin might have tried to contact him this way. Maybe gone into an internet café or used the Matthews's computer before he and Julie had left. Given some clue as to where they might be headed and what John could do to help. But there was nothing. He even checked the junk mail, just in case Colin used some weird and wonderful online name, but once again he drew a blank. Looking at the clock, John saw that it was eleven fifteen. The press conference would go out live at twelve. That gave him just enough time at his snail's pace to make more tea and toast.

The armchair he had slept in looked so temptingly comfortable and he felt so weary that he almost gave up, gave in and told the world to sort it while he slept. Not bother him again until it was done. With a massive effort, he got to his feet and made his way to the kitchen. When he'd arrived home the night before, Crime Scene tape had still clung to his back door. Traces of silver grey powder from where the SOCO had searched for prints rubbed off on his clothes as he brushed against them. Small reference markers had been left on the floor from where they'd marked his fall and the angle of the shot. And there was the blood. Soaked into the laminate and marking it irrevocably. His blood. His mortality, staining the kitchen floor.

Angrily, he tugged a towel from the drawer

and dropped it over the offending mark dragging it roughly into position with his foot. Not gone, but at least he didn't have to look at it.

He was shaking again. Shivering, but this time not with the cold but the shocking reminder of how casually, how easily he could have died.

25

Lynn Wise lived three streets from her daughter, Julie, in the new development that had replaced some of the tower blocks on the Bishopswood estate. Julie's block had been scheduled for demolition the following year, Rose recalled.

Lynn's house was small. Two bedrooms – one for herself and one for Julie's younger sister on the first floor, together with a bathroom. A living room and dining kitchen made up the space downstairs. There was a small patch of lawn in front of the house and in the rear a pocket sized garden, also laid to lawn. Beyond the addition of a washing line, Rose doubted Lynn had done anything with it, except maybe give the lawn an occasional trim, since moving in.

The inside of the house was clean and

tidy, if a little brash. Lynn seemed to like vivid colours and the hall was a bright lime green. Rose's taste, being more muted, found it all a little hard to stomach, but Morantz won brownie points by telling Lynn Wise that they had exactly the same colour in his downstairs toilet at home.

The instant coffee was cheap, but no worse than the machine produced stuff they got at work and Lynn was at least eager to talk.

'So, you last saw Julie about ten days ago?' Rose confirmed.

Lynn nodded. 'She dropped some stuff in for Karen. Her sister. Didn't stop long, she was on her way to work.'

'Do you babysit for Ian?' Rose asked. She wasn't especially close to her own mother, but if she'd gone ten days without contact, there'd have been an inquisition.

'Well, I do from time to time, but Julie's always been the independent sort. Mind of her own, always has. She does things her way.' She sniffed as though disparaging Julie's way but not wanting to put her dismissal into words.

'So, did Julie phone you in the meantime?'

Lynn frowned. 'She might have,' she said. 'I don't remember.'

'And so, you wouldn't really have known if Julie went away a week ago. Longer even,' Morantz put in. 'You see, we got the impres-

226

sion from your statement to the television, that you were in frequent contact with your daughter. That you were worried because that contact suddenly stopped.'

Lynn stared daggers at him. 'You saying I was lying?'

'No,' Morantz said cautiously. 'But, Ms Wise, if Mr Radcliffe hadn't drawn your attention to your daughter's absence, how long do you think it would have been before you noticed she was gone?'

Lynn Wise opened her mouth and then closed it again.

'It's not always easy to keep in touch, is it, though,' Rose suggested. 'I don't see my parents nearly as often as I should.'

'No, it's not,' Lynn affirmed. 'You're not going to accuse me of being a neglectful mother. We just live our own lives, that's all. It doesn't mean I don't care.'

'No, I'm sure it doesn't,' Rose soothed.

Morantz raised an eyebrow but left her to it.

'Did she have friends she'd visit regularly? Did she go out much, apart from work, I mean?'

Lynn thought about it, then shrugged. 'She didn't say a lot,' she said. 'Ian's father was a right nutcase and we stopped talking so much then, I suppose. After he left, I don't think we got back in the habit. Look. She's a good kid, works hard and looks after

Ian and I don't want nothing to happen to her. Like Charlie Radcliffe said, someone trashed her place, but I've been round there and they didn't take the telly or the video or the bits of jewellery her Nan left her, so what was all that in aid of?'

She looked from Rose to Morantz, searching for an answer. When none was forthcoming, she sniffed again and picked her coffee off the table, hugging it to her as though it afforded her a security they did not. 'Then there's that Colin she's supposed to have picked up with. Sounds like another nutter if you ask me.'

'Did she mention Colin Grainger to you?'

Lynn shook her head. 'No, but she'd long since stopped asking my opinions on her boyfriends. She knew what answer she'd get.'

'You didn't approve of her relationships?'

'Like I said. Ian's dad was a psycho.'

'And since then? Anyone serious?'

Lynn pursed her lips in thought and then shook her head as though in revelation. 'You know, I don't think she'd really hooked up with anyone since then. Not now you mention it. She was a bit stand-offish, like, with men after that. I told her, that boy needs a dad and you won't get one acting like you're better than the lot of them.'

Morantz and Rose exchanged a glance. His mouth was twitching as though he held back laughter. Rose knew how he felt. It looked as though Julie would get it wrong in her mother's eyes no matter what she did. Lynn didn't seem to notice the contradiction of her own remarks.

'So,' Rose pursued. 'What about friends? What about places she might have said she wanted to visit?'

Lynn's laugh was savage. 'I can't see her getting on a plane for New York,' she said.

'New York?'

'Oh yes. Always talking about it like it was fairyland. I told her, keep your feet on the ground, girl.'

'Anywhere closer to home?' Rose asked hopefully, but Lynn was losing interest now. Her hand inching almost unconsciously towards the TV remote. The set had been playing silently in the corner since they had arrived and a hairdressing slot of some kind in the morning magazine seemed to have caught Lynn's interest.

'Ms Wise?' Rose tried again.

'What? Oh yeah, friends. I already gave a list to Charlie Radcliffe. He's been a brick, he has. A real gentleman.'

They left a few minutes later with a hastily scribbled list of Julie's known friends. They let themselves out, the volume on the television rising even before they were out of the door.

'Loving mother,' Morantz commented.

'Hmm. I don't think it's that she doesn't care, you know. Just that she hasn't got a bloody clue. You know what I'm wondering, though?'

'How much our gentlemanly Mr Radcliffe paid her for that act on the news last night.'

John sat in front of the television waiting for the news to begin. He'd carried his tea and yet more toast into the living room, one thing at a time and placed them on the tallest of the occasional tables that generally nested unused in the corner near the bay window. He'd dragged it over to his chair and been shocked at just how much pain he had in his unaffected arm and shoulder. He supposed it must radiate from the wounds on his right side. He was grateful that they'd at least given him a limited supply of painkillers when he left the hospital. Somehow, he didn't think that even max strength Ibuprofen would fix this and he wasn't even sure he had anything in the house in any case.

Chewing thoughtfully on his buttered toast, John glanced around at this familiar and yet unfamiliar room. He'd lived in this house for the past eight years and redecorated ... once. And then, not throughout. It had been one of their plans, his and Moira's that they'd take time off in the spring and, as Moira put it, sort him out. She'd already dragged him into the local DIY superstores to look at paint and paper. Suggested ways to 'dress' his windows and pulled back the carpet to inspect the quality of the boards; been thrilled to discover the original parquet hiding beneath the underlay.

He laid the toast back on the plate noticing that it was suddenly very hard to swallow. Already, Moira had got into the habit of spending a couple of nights a week with him and they both knew without having to say anything that before long she'd be moving in and they'd make their relationship known and official.

He wondered if Colin had understood that or if he still clung onto the hope of getting his ex wife back.

Moira had loved Colin. John found it hard to cope with the fact that she'd never stop loving him, not completely. Colin, she had tried to explain, was the one who'd been there at some of the happiest times of her life. She'd adored her time at university, relished the freedom, the opportunity to discover just who this young woman called Moira Barker really was and Colin Grainger had been a major part of that.

But, she had told him, that was past. It was a debt to an old and much cherished friend that made her check up on Colin, listen to Colin, take notice of Colin. Her future, she told him, was something else again and, over that final month or so, John had begun to take her at her word.

The fact that this other man, this man John had now taken on the charge to protect, had the same memories of Moira was a hard one to take. Colin would have held her while she slept. Would have woken beside her and watched her stretch, cat like and sensual in the early morning light. Would have heard her sharp retorts and her swift laughter and...

He blinked hard and forced himself to focus on the screen. The latest instalment of a revamp-your-home programme finished and the news began.

Absences in this case were as interesting as noting those present. Weaver was seated at a table in front of a crowd of journalists, from the look of them both local and national, the logos spelling out their affiliation, visible here and there on a microphone or a film camera.

Beside Weaver was Charlie Radcliffe. Of Julie's family, there was not a sign.

Rose was due to interview the mother, John recalled, but that would not have prevented her from taking part in the press call had she wished it. The notion of Charlie Radcliffe standing in loco parentis was slightly sickening.

A figure could be seen crouching in front of the blue draped table adjusting something connected to the microphones. Clearly, this was going out live and something wasn't quite right. The cameraman, as though seeking distraction, panned around the room while the local reporter made some comments about delays and hoping to bring the item in a moment.

The location was a sports hall. John caught sight of basketball hoops high on the walls and the sections of the floor not concealed by journalists had something marked out on it that looked like a netball court. Drop cloths had been set beneath the chairs to stop the feet from scratching, but John guessed there'd still be a worried caretaker standing guard, waiting for these invaders to depart.

A handful of men stood on the periphery of the group that seemed not to have anything to do. They glanced about them, restless and observant, watching the crowd. Watching Charlie Radcliffe. John studied them, recognising one as Brian Henshaw, manager of the Casino and Radcliffe's right hand man.

The technical difficulties seemed to be over now and the camera began to pan back towards the table at the end of the hall. Its track took it back past Henshaw and his group and John nearly jumped out of his chair. Stepping forward, just for a moment as though to see what was going on, was a sandy-haired man of about forty with a small but distinctive pock mark scar marring his cheek, and, as the camera caught him, he was glancing at his watch.

26

Weaver had begun by reading out an official statement. It was true, he stated, that Julie Wise and her son had left home, probably at some time on Wednesday evening. It was also true that there appeared to have been a disturbance or possible break in at Julie's home, but nothing seemed to have been taken and there was no reason to link the two incidents.

'Neither is there any reason to link the disappearance of Julie Wise to the apparent absence from home of Colin Grainger,' he added. 'It's known that Mr Grainger has been under considerable strain since the murder of his ex wife. It's known that they remained close friends even after the divorce.'

'Is he a suspect in the murder?'

The questioner had not identified himself and Weaver frowned. He replied anyway. 'No. Colin Grainger was never a suspect in the murder of Moira Barker.'

'Jo Brinks, Hillford FM. You say that, Chief Inspector, but isn't it true that he was taken in for questioning the morning Sergeant Barker's body was found?'

'Mr Grainger saw his ex wife the morning before her death. We questioned him as a matter of routine. But,' he held up a hand to stop further questions. 'What we're here for today concerns Miss Wise, not the murder of DS Barker.'

The flurry of questions began anyway, but they were interrupted by Charlie Radcliffe. 'I'm sure you can understand the concerns though, Inspector?' He raised his voice to be heard clearly over the audience and the questions died down. 'Two murders in a quiet little place like Hillford, then the disappearance of this young woman and her son and the possibility that she's gone missing with a young man known not to be of entirely sound mind.'

Weaver glowered at Radcliffe. 'Mr Radcliffe,' he said quietly. 'I have nothing on record about Mr Grainger's mental state, beyond the fact that he was grieving for a quite considerable loss and,' again the forbidding gesture with the hand 'I'd like to remind you that you are here purely as a representative for Miss Wise's family; at their request. I would ask that you restrict your comments to facts and leave the speculation to others.'

There was a faint ripple of laughter from the audience. Charlie Radcliffe leaned back in the chair and steepled his fingers. 'I'm merely asking,' he said in seeming innocence, 'if we should be worried, as citizens of Hillford, about this sudden rash of violence on our streets. I, myself was victim of a mugging on the night Julie disappeared and I believe one of your own officers was attacked in his own home that same evening.'

The frisson of interest in the room was palpable. Charlie Radcliffe had them eating out of the palm of his hand.

'Two murders,' Charlie Radcliffe repeated, 'both beautiful young women with everything to live for. Who knows what's happened to Julie Wise and her little boy. And, it seems, you can't even keep your own officers safe. It doesn't look good, Chief Inspector.'

Weaver stared at him for a moment, then turned back to his audience. 'If there are no further questions,' he said, 'a further statement will be issued later, as we have more news. Thank you for your time.' He got up and left the hall, the camera following him, then zipping back to where the excitement really was; to Charlie Radcliffe fielding questions from the audience.

The local news was out of time however and the reporter came back in slot, unable to keep the excitement out of her voice as she wound the item down and returned to the studio.

So much for damage limitation, Rose Morgan thought as she cradled her tea-cup in her hands, trying not to let them shake with the frustration of it all.

'He's got a point, you know,' Annie Sanders said as she stared at the television. 'First that policewoman, then our Alice, then this girl. What the hell's going on here, love?'

Rose shook her head. 'I just don't know, Annie,' she said truthfully. 'We've interviewed anyone at the camera club that had anything to do with Alice and there's still leads to explore. We will get to the bottom of it,' she promised.

Annie nodded. She'd aged in this past few days, Rose thought. First the loss of her child, then the loss of innocence that went with that. The shock of knowing that there was so much she'd been ignorant of. Rose wasn't sure which loss had hit Annie hardest. And the worst thing of all from Rose's point of view was knowing that ultimately she'd have to tell Annie just how utterly wasteful her daughter's death had been. Alice Sanders had died because her pictures just happened to be on a disk that just happened to fall into the wrong hands. Murders should never happen, Rose thought, but worst of all were the ones that had no reason. No motive, no sort of excuse.

'What he was saying about the other officer?' Annie asked. 'Mr Radcliffe said someone was attacked at home?'

Rose hesitated. The decision had been

made to keep under wraps that DI Moore had been shot. People were edgy enough and political pressure already unbearable. Once it got out that guns had come into the equation the pressure would become unbearable and panic escalate. Murder of any kind was enough to make public confidence nose dive, but in the present climate of hysteria concerning gun crime, the shooting of a police officer would be almost worse than the death of the two women in the public consciousness. Personally, Rose felt that the longer they kept it quiet, the worse it would look when the truth – or some version of it – finally did come out. But she wasn't the decision maker here. Except that, in a way, here and now with Annie asking her this question, she was.

'Something happened that's still under investigation, Annie, so I can't tell you much. An officer was injured, but he'll be fine.'

Annie nodded as though aware of the younger woman's predicament, but she wasn't about to let go. 'Was it anything to do with Alice?' she asked. 'Alice, or that other one?'

Rose found she couldn't tell her a straight lie. 'We don't know,' she said. 'Annie, right now, we just don't know.'

Annie's expression hardened. 'I'm not getting at you, love, you've been sensitive and kind and I appreciate that. But it seems

238

to me you lot don't know very much right now.'

John had watched the fiasco of a press call in a mood of increasing despair. Radcliffe had made Weaver look like a fool and an inept, ineffectual one at that and while John might occasionally quarrel with Weaver's methods and attitudes, he knew him to be a good copper and a thorough investigator.

Collectively, it made them look bad and that little hint about John's own injuries had been particularly troubling. Radcliffe was so bloody confident and, John had to admit, at this moment in time, he had a right to be. They were getting nowhere fast and, after all Charlie Radcliffe should know what happened to him; he'd been responsible for it. He was curious that no reference had been made to the raid on Radcliffe's club, but maybe that had happened after Weaver had left and the report ended. He would have to ask Rose or someone to bring him the local papers later and, if nothing appeared, have a chat to Brady Timms about balanced reporting.

He thought of Weaver's parting comments that night in the hospital. The previous evening, he reminded himself, that was all. It just *felt* like a hundred years ago. Thought of how Weaver had said it didn't matter any more if they played within the rules or not so long as they got a result. Weaver hadn't meant it. That wasn't his way. He'd given in to a moment's sheer frustration, that was all. John, on the other hand, was in the mood to take such declarations to heart.

He'd phoned in after the broadcast, left a message about Sandy-Haired Man for Weaver and suggested he get Brady Timms and his employees to look at the video tape. Now he was left with nothing much to do, no energy to do it anyway, and a lot of questions.

He checked his emails again, just in case there was something from Colin.

Nothing. And even his regular office mail had been diverted straight to Weaver. They'd agreed this would be for the best, but it still made him feel strange. Unwanted. Outside.

Irritably, he flicked through the television channels, looking for something worth watching, then he went through to the kitchen and put the kettle on again.

The paperwork that Weaver had left him was still in his coat and John fetched it while waiting for the kettle to boil, glanced back at the lists of names and transactions yet again.

The earliest date was May of this year, he noted. May 25th and three separate figures of £6000, £4000 and £385. Then underneath a second set of figures which, when John worked them out, came to an even twenty percent.

Radcliffe's cut?

The name attributed to these numbers, John didn't recognise. Ben Parks, whoever he was.

He glanced down the list. The other entries were similar in pattern. A name, three figures, sometimes with the reference word 'guest' beside the second. The third figure was always smaller and generally for an irregular amount, then the commission, if that's what it was, always for twenty percent and taken from the first two figures, never from the third.

A couple of times the word 'sundries' was attached to the third figure. Other times it was listed as 'miscellaneous'. John puzzled over it but could come to no conclusion. It was, he guessed, an amalgam of incidental expenses, sort of like petty cash, but John felt it would take someone better versed in fraud and company accounts and the like to make real sense of what it meant.

He wondered again what had possessed Charlie Radcliffe to make computer records of these accounts, but reminded himself that people still saw their computers as private property and therefore inviolable, despite the evidence to the contrary.

He made tea and then, while waiting for it to infuse, focused on the names and the information Weaver had obtained from the PNC.

Geographically, they represented quite a spread. Known criminals and a few dodgy businessmen from as far afield as Leeds and Manchester in the north and Swindon in the south. More than half, though, were local, or fairly so. A fifty mile radius, John would have said. Those he recognised included Danny Thompson, who fancied himself as a drug lord. Presently doing two years, though it was understood that his sons were keeping the business ticking along. It had taken a long time to get anything to stick on Danny Thompson; there'd always been a nice supply of hangers on to take the fall whenever the law had got too close. His present conviction was for GBH. For once there were witnesses willing to testify. The fact that they'd probably been paid to do so by a certain Preston Hayes, who'd been hoping to move in on Danny's patch, was something the courts either didn't know or hadn't cared about.

Then there was Preston Hayes himself. One conviction for employing underage girls in one of his strip joints, but otherwise his network of drugs and prostitution, on paper at least, ticked along without his interference or design. He was always elsewhere or legitimately engaged when anything went down.

And, of course, not forgetting our pillars of the community, John thought. The local magistrate, Christopher Vincent, who was listed for regular contributions totalling ... John added swiftly and whistled. Something like fifteen grand over the year and all paying twenty percent to the man with the plan. Radcliffe, however you looked at it, was minting it and this was aside from his legitimate customers, most of whom would rub shoulders with his more dubious clients and not know the difference.

Then, of course, there was Billy James.

He'd known *of* James all his life.

No, be clear about this. He'd *known* James all his life, only lost touch with the man when his career choice took him away from home ... and Billy.

James had been part of the landscape of John's childhood. He'd grown up on one of the rundown, half-forgotten council estates in Nottingham, not a stone's throw from the railway and sandwiched between that and the River Trent. There had seemed few ways out for the likes of John Moore, a young kid of average brightness, less than average finance and not a hell of a lot of motivation. Those ways of making money and changing lives that did exist often seemed to have James as gatekeeper.

He was angry that Billy James should have chosen his patch to launder his money, but he guessed it had been a deliberate choice. Billy would have enjoyed the joke. Enjoyed it, even had John never found it out. That was the way with Billy James. Self contained. He liked to have his skills admired, but could get by just fine with only himself in the know.

Billy James classed himself as a patriot, a supporter of his country and champion of the working classes. John had not thought about Billy's affiliations growing up. As a kid, Billy had been something of a hero. Anything needed doing in the community, Billy got it done. Any trouble on Billy's patch and the makers of that trouble either took it on advisement to depart peacefully, or they were evicted – often just as quietly in the dead of night. No one complained because Billy made the estate a peaceful place to live and he did his bit, made sure the kids had presents at Christmas and old ladies could go out at night without fear of being attacked for their bit of pension. James had been a frequent visitor to the family home, his visits always accompanied by a sense of occasion, however frequent they might be.

It had been years before John had questioned any of it. He'd nothing to compare his life to, nothing to tell him that this might not be normal.

In fact, in a crazy kind of way, it had been James who had inspired his choice of career – an irony he was sure Billy himself would have appreciated. The fact was, Billy made things better and John wanted to do the same.

John had joined the force and, the day after his passing out, been hauled up before his erstwhile mentor.

'I respect your dad,' Billy told him, 'good, solid working man, and your mam, God rest her, she was a good woman. Loyal,' he added, emphasising the word.

He eyed the young John Moore with … well, John recalled, not exactly distaste. More a kind of wondering curiosity, as though unable to reconcile these 'good people' with their product of a son.

'Well,' he said finally. 'You've made your choice, boy. Everyone's entitled to do that, but now I'm giving you a piece of advice. Father like, seeing as yours isn't in a fit state of health to give it to you. Put in for a transfer, boy. I'll make sure it goes smooth and does your career no harm.'

And that had been it. John had applied to be transferred and it had happened with almost undue haste. He found himself some sixty miles away from his boyhood home.

He'd been back at intervals to visit his dad – always making sure to give advance warning – and then, several years on, for his father's funeral. Home, to bury the man who'd barely recognised him in those final years. Home to a funeral organised by Billy James and attended by men John only knew from fat files and entries in the PNC.

Billy James was at the wake. A respectable

man in business suit and heavy, grey overcoat, welcomed as a familiar guest at the nursing home where John's dad had lived. A quality place that John alone would never have been able to afford.

'I saw your dad right in his last years,' Billy James told him.

'I know. I'm... grateful.'

James patted him on the shoulder. 'I know you are,' he said and just for a moment both men locked gaze and knew they spoke the truth.

'You'll be leaving then,' James told him.

'Tonight, when I've wrapped things up here.'

'I hear you're doing well for yourself. Inspector, isn't it now?'

John confirmed that it was. His promotion had just come through.

'Well, goodbye Inspector Moore. I doubt we'll meet again. I'll keep an eye on your dad's grave.'

John thanked him and Billy James left. He had wished, or at least, a part of him had wished, that he'd found out more, about what the bond had been between his dad and Billy. But the major part of him didn't want to know. Didn't want to spoil the memory of the gentle man, middle-aged even when John's mother had married him and who had become Dad.

John stared at the creased paper spread

out on the table in front of him, at the name he'd heard from time to time over the years, implicated obliquely in some action or other and now tied up in the almost legitimate world of the local politics of John's home town. Looking at Billy James's name he knew he had a way to get to Radcliffe. A way of bringing him down and, if he was honest with himself, of exacting the kind of brutal revenge it would take to truly repay the death of the woman he had loved.

27

Radcliffe and Sandra were enjoying a quiet drink at the end of what he felt was a successful day. True, the evening paper had put something of a dampener on things by making allusions to the police search on his home and Casino, but they'd had to stick to inferences and drawn no real conclusions, so Charlie wasn't too bothered by that. It was also true that he was no further on in the search for Colin and Julie. The information that they were in a small coastal town, just north of Whitby, narrowed his field of search somewhat, but was still pretty vague, but he'd had less to work with in the past and still got results, so he was only mildly fazed.

Julie's mother didn't seem to have a clue either, but Sandra was finding the aunt somewhat more help, particularly as there seemed to be a fair amount of rivalry between the two women in the 'I care most and I'm the better parent' stakes.

Neither woman had come up with the answers they wanted yet, but Radcliffe was a great believer that people generally know much more than they realise and all it takes is the right kind of prompts to bring that information to the surface. Sometimes it was the likes of Henshaw that best promoted these revelations; at others, when time was not such an essence and subtlety was the order of the day, then Sandra was the agent of choice.

'People don't run off into the unknown,' Radcliffe stated firmly. 'They go to places they know – or *think* they know – and I don't think Colin Grainger will be the one to take the lead here.'

'He might,' Sandra retorted. She was playing Devil's Advocate, a role Charlie valued. It kept him from being blinkered and narrow in his thinking.

'Oh, so he might. And where would he go?'

Sandra shrugged. 'There was bugger all at the flat,' she said. 'An address book with half a dozen names in it. The doormen at

Skunk's reckon he didn't socialise a whole lot. He seemed closest to Mark.'

'Mark?'

'Big black guy. No hair.'

'Oh yes, I know him.'

'They got on well, apparently. I've left Mickey having a nose around.'

'Mickey!' Radcliffe was amused. 'You've slipped up there, San. He's an adequate manager, but other than that, Mickey wouldn't know good information if it got up and bit him.'

Sandra sipped her drink, watching him over the rim of her glass. 'Don't get so cocky,' she said. 'Mickey's capable of putting the wind up and he reckons Mark's been shaky since Colin took off. I've got Brian down there tonight anyway. Put the pressure on a bit.'

'So,' Radcliffe continued. 'Where do you reckon he'd make for?'

'He went to University in Lincoln,' she said. 'Same as Moira Barker. That's where they met. Apart from that, I don't think he's set foot out of Hillford,' she admitted.

Radcliffe refreshed their drinks. 'Well,' he said. 'You keep working on the families for me. Keep up the concerned employer act and see what bubbles up to the top. You know,' he frowned, 'what I really don't get is why the stupid bitch came here that night.'

'I take it we're onto Sergeant Barker now?'

Radcliffe nodded. 'I mean, was the woman thick, or what?'

'Beats me. All I know is Brian saw her snooping around trying to get in through the fire escape. He brought her to me and I guess that's when Julie must have seen her. I don't know. Maybe she was trying to prove herself or something. Maybe she hoped to rattle you. I mean, she'd got what she saw as evidence of something, but I don't reckon she knew what and she knew she couldn't use it. I suppose she thought, coming here, she might be able to find something that'd stick.

'Could be she wasn't above a bit of blackmail. You didn't exactly give her the opportunity to explain herself.'

'You saw how she was, San, shooting her mouth off. She didn't give us a lot of options, did she? I thought I'd let Brian and his ginger friend sort it out.'

'Which they did, I suppose, after a fashion.'

Radcliffe shrugged. 'Her own stupid fault,' he asserted. 'You want to play with the big boys you have to learn to take the falls, so to speak. Damage limitation, that's what it was. Damage limitation.'

Sandra was about to tell him that she didn't think the damage had been particularly limited, but she was saved the trouble. There was a knock on the door and

Brian Henshaw strode in.

Radcliffe poured him a drink.

'Anything?'

'Well, something. I know what the link was with Alice Sanders.'

'Oh?'

'There wasn't one,' Brian told him. 'She had nothing to tell us which is why she told us nothing.' He seemed pleased about that, as though he'd been worried he'd lost his touch. 'Grainger downloaded pictures of her for Mark Harris, the doorman. Most likely her photos just happened to be on the disk when he added whatever it was Moira thought she'd got. It was nothing more than that.'

'Poor little bugger,' Sandra said.

'One less loose end, though.' Radcliffe sounded pleased. 'So, now there's just Colin and Julie to get rid of.'

'What about the investigation?' Sandra wanted to know.

'What about it? They've seized anything there was to seize and they'll find nothing. What can they prove? Any so called evidence that DS Moira Barker thought she had was inadmissible anyway and what reason would we have had for doing in someone like Alice Sanders? Like Brian said. Coincidence. Find those two and get rid and we're in the clear. The Old Bill can *know* anything they like, they can't prove it.'

'What about the boy?' Sandra asked.

Radcliffe reached over and patted her hand. 'Provided he doesn't get in the way, love, he'll be fine. And we'll make sure his gran's looked after if she takes him on. That do you?'

Sandra didn't look too pleased, but she nodded. 'It'll have to do,' she said, but there was an uncertainty in her voice, a lack of conviction that had never been there before.

Radcliffe made no further comment, but he glanced across at Brian Henshaw. 'This is not the time,' he said quietly, 'to be losing our nerve.' He left the comment hanging on the air for Sandra to make of what she would.

Julie turned left at the final roundabout out of Bridgewater. From here, if she remembered rightly, there was a short stretch of dual carriageway and then several miles of speed traps and winding roads. She'd never driven this route in the dark before and seemed to remember that the turn off in the village they were headed for was tough to see even in daytime, half hidden by the bend in the road as it wound up the hill.

She waited until she'd settled on the dual carriageway and then reached across to shake Colin awake. Ian was well away. She could see him in the rear-view slumped sideways and held in place only by the seatbelt. She and Colin had shared the driving and boy, had it been some trip, diagonally across the length of the country from darkest Yorkshire to deepest Somerset. She felt as though she could sleep forever.

'Col, wake up. I need you.'

'Uh? What? Are we there yet?'

She almost laughed. That had been Ian's refrain through most of the day.

'Nearly, but this is a bloody awful road if you don't know it. The dual carriageway runs out in about another mile and it's all bends and overhanging trees and then the turnoff we want is hard to spot. I could do with another pair of eyes.'

Colin shrugged and stretched as best he could trying to get his body moving and his brain into gear. 'Where the hell are we?'

'Just through Bridgewater. Kilve is about ... I don't know, another ten miles.'

'OK, what am I looking out for?'

'Nothing. Yet. I just wanted you awake for when I do need you.'

It was eleven thirty according to the clock on the dash. They'd taken a circuitous route, avoiding motorways with their CCTV systems and A roads with their speed cameras, just in case. Breakfast had been a sandwich eaten in a lay by and lunch, they had risked a pub restaurant, having put a good distance, they hoped, between themselves and anyone searching for them. Even so, it had been a hurried and anxious affair.

They'd also risked a supermarket, the Safeway in Glastonbury. Purchased groceries enough to keep them going for several days and eaten in the little café in the superstore. Colin had scanned the papers. Nothing obvious. Yet.

Colin gazed out through the windscreen. The road twisted through hills. The landscape seemed to climb, most of the time, off to his left. On the right, where the hedge was lower and the trees thinned, it fell towards the sea. Where the headlights hit the bends, he could make out fields and they passed through villages, silent and sleepy, lights on in houses and the occasional pub still open. The headlights caught a sign off to Colin's left. The Castle of Comfort, it announced. He stared at the strange little building; squat and crenellated, tucked in under the forested hillside.

'Not much further,' Julie told him, 'so keep an eye out. Our turn is not far after the Kilve village sign. There's a shop on the corner. We turn down Church Lane immediately before that.'

Before? That was helpful.

He kept watch, peering into the dark. The sky was clear, studded with stars, and the road seemed slick beneath the tyres as though ice had formed after the earlier rain. The illusion was so strong that they were the only people in the world awake and travelling that it was almost vertiginous. Colin shuddered, anticipating the cold.

They passed the village sign and Julie slowed. Even so they almost missed it and she took the right hand, almost right-angled bend far too close to the high stone wall bounding the garden behind the shop. There were two streetlights and then nothing but dim lit, heavily curtained windows as they passed houses closed up for the night against the dark and the world's intrusion.

'There's the duck pond,' Julie said, 'and look, the church and the abbey ruins. We're here. She turned abruptly into a parking space beside a cottage, bringing the car to a halt beside a porch which jutted from the side. Then she cut the engine and slumped wearily in the seat.

'Ian, wake up, we've arrived,' Colin reached between the seats and shook the boy gently awake. Ian moaned in response, unwilling to move.

'Now what?'

'We hope they still leave the key where they used to.'

Colin didn't dare ask what would happen if they hadn't. Julie got out of the car and fumbled around beside the porch. Moments later he could see her grinning as she returned, key in hand, triumphant. He watched as she undid the porch door, then went in after her. The inner door was locked.

'We need something to prise it,' she whispered. 'It's not strong and I think there's only the one lock. Try the boot of the car, there might be a tool kit or something.'

Reluctantly, Colin took the car key and retreated from the porch. It was so quiet here, he felt as though every sound was magnified. The boot of the car creaked when he opened it and he found himself peering into the dark, frozen with terror, convinced that someone would hear that Radcliffe and all his cohorts were just waiting to descend upon them.

Jan Matthews had left a small tool kit in the car. He opened it, rummaged for a flat blade screwdriver and then returned to Julie.

'Here. This do?'

She took it from him and jammed it between the door and frame just above the lock. It gave with a crack and splinter of wood that had them both staring out into the lane, waiting for the alarm.

Nothing. Julie pushed the door. 'Get Ian and let's get inside,' she whispered. 'I'll go round the back and switch the cylinder on.'

'Cylinder?'

'For the gas. There's no mains here.'

'Oh.' He went to the car for Ian. The boy had fallen asleep again. By the time he'd woken him, Julie was back. She hustled him inside and then helped Colin fetch the groceries. They locked the car, then locked the porch door and closed the inner one, Colin wedging the handle with a chair, just like in the movies. He saw Julie watching him, but she said nothing. She left the kitchen and he heard her fumbling about in a cupboard. 'Electric,' she said, switching on the lights. 'Close the curtains.' She pointed through to another room off the kitchen. 'I think there's a fire in there too. The heating will take a while to make a difference.'

He did as he was told, dragging curtains across windows and figuring out how to use the electric fire.

'Now what?' he asked her as she came through rubbing her arms, still wrapped up in her coat.

She shrugged. 'Hadn't thought that far. We got here, now, I guess we just sit it out, hope for the best.'

'I've got to get hold of John.'

'What can he do? He's bound to be still in the hospital.'

'Probably,' he conceded. He looked around the room, hoping for inspiration. There was at least a phone. The walls looked thick, the windows set deep with wide windowsills. A sofa, a bookcase a couple of chairs, the atmosphere chill and slightly damp. Julie reckoned this place was hardly used this time of year. He wished she'd been able to tell him never.

'I'm going to put the kettle on,' she said. 'You want some tea?'

Tea, the great British panacea. 'Best get Ian into bed,' he said. 'He's all in. I'll look after the kettle.'

She nodded and left him to it. He heard her talking softly to her son as she led him up the stairs. Colin went back through to the kitchen, busied himself with filling the kettle and rinsing out the teapot and mugs. He felt more utterly lost and completely bereft than he had felt since this whole business had begun. While they had focused on getting here, he felt there had been some purpose, something to be doing and in planning their convoluted route, something to keep his mind from thinking. Now, they were here and no feeling of safety or security came with their destination.

Julie came back to the kitchen. She seated herself at the round table and looked up at him. 'I've put him in the back room,' she said. 'You take the double and I'll sleep in the other single room. I've told Ian that's where I'll be.'

'All right.' He poured the tea, looked at the shopping and figured he ought to put anything perishable away.

'You'll need to switch the fridge on,' she told him, pointing to the socket.

'Oh, yeah. Julie...'

'Don't. Please Colin. I'm not up to it

tonight. I just want to drink my tea and go to bed. If a dozen Radcliffes came and broke down the door, I think I'm too far gone to care. I'm too knackered to be scared tonight. If it's all the same to you, I'll get back to the blind terror in the morning when I've got the energy for it.'

She smiled and he smiled back, sat down opposite. 'OK,' he said. 'We'll put it all on hold. Freeze frame.'

He reached across the table and took her hand. 'Selfish, I know,' he said, 'especially as I wouldn't want Ian to be hurt, not for anything in the world, but I'm glad you're here. I don't want to be alone.'

28

Ten o'clock on the Saturday morning saw Brady Timms, Chrissie, his PA, and Tom Clarke, the office junior with Weaver watching the raw footage of the press call. They'd managed to acquire not only that shot by the local news, but also a second recording, taken from a slightly different angle, courtesy of a cable channel. And there was a little extra footage, showing events after Weaver himself had left.

They'd been told to look for anyone they

recognised and Weaver had set up two separate TVs and VCRs at opposite ends of the briefing room. Brady was occupied with one while Tom Clarke and Chrissie studied the other.

Timms was in no doubt about what he was seeing. 'Oi, Chrissie!' His shout echoed down the length of the room. 'Come here and look at this.'

Weaver sighed. 'She's supposed to make up her own mind, Mr Timms.'

'And she can. All I want her to do is look.'

Rose came in with a stack of messages. Weaver motioned her to put them on the desk. 'Sightings,' she told him. 'All pretty random. They got anything?'

'Mr Timms thinks he has.'

Chrissie seemed equally excited. 'That's him,' she said. 'That's our phoney policeman. Take a look, Tom, but I know that's him.'

Weaver rolled his eyes. He knew his set-up wasn't exactly scientific or double blind, but he'd kind of hoped to have separate confirmations. He'd attempted to have all three in separately, but Timms had intervened, saying that no one wanted to waste a Saturday and Weaver had taken the path of least resistance. He wandered over to the VCR now. They'd stopped the film and had it on pause. The sandy-haired man John had noted flickered slightly as the tape buzzed against the heads.

'You're sure. All three of you?'

'Absolutely.' Chrissie said. 'Look, I was with him in the other office for a good fifteen minutes until Brady could see him. I gave him coffee and we chatted. He was cool all right and yes, I know that's him.'

Weaver nodded, satisfied. He turned back to Rose Morgan, intending to tell her to give John Moore a call. Her face seemed drained of all colour as she stared at the semi-frozen picture on the screen.

'You all right?'

She nodded and left the room. Weaver followed her.

'What?' he demanded.

'I know him,' she said. 'He calls himself Joe Crowther. He's a friend of Phil's.'

29

By contrast with Rose, Colin, Julie and Ian had enjoyed a peaceful day. They had been exhausted and no one had woken until well after ten. Colin was first to come round, waking with a start and then enduring the disorientation that came with waking in a strange room.

His first instinct was to leap out of bed, fear of Radcliffe's men hiding in dark corners momentarily overwhelming. He forced himself to calm and lay, staring at the cracked white ceiling, listening to the silence.

He'd rarely been in a place so quiet. The cottage walls were thick and the lane was used, so Julie told him, only by residents and people wanting to get to the beach. Only, she said, it wasn't a beach. It was rocky and wild and she thought ... what had she said? So beautiful it almost hurt to look at it.

It was, Colin considered, a pretty cool thing to say. The sort of thing Moira might have said, though she'd have said it about a picture or a film, or a book. Something of that sort. Moira was never much of one for nature. He smiled wryly. This was, so far as he could recall, the first time he'd ever compared his Moira unfavourably with anyone.

The cottage was set back from the lane and Julie had moved the car late the night before, driving it carefully around the back, while Colin held a torch so she didn't hit the walls or the gas cylinders or any of the dozen or so obstacles she might have done. He wasn't sure he'd been much help, he'd spent more time peering behind him into the dark, worrying in case someone should hear, the sound of the engine, so very loud in the stillness of the star studded night.

'No one's going to take any notice of us,' Julie told him impatiently, weariness losing her the last vestige of patience with Colin.

'They'll just assume Josie's made a winter letting. She does sometimes. And with the car round the back no one's going to see the reg number.'

He knew she was right. They were hundreds of miles away from both home and Staithes. No one knew where they were and Josie, the owner of the cottage, didn't live in Hillford. It was unlikely anyone would think of looking for them here. Colin had forced the remaining unease from his mind and gone to bed. He'd not expected to sleep but had done within minutes, he reckoned, and now it was a new day and he could not help but feel more hopeful.

A small window in the bedroom looked down onto the side garden and gave a view of just a few yards of lane. The sun was shining, sky blue. Time to get on.

He had washed and was making breakfast when Julie emerged. 'I've woken Ian,' she said. 'I could smell the bacon.'

Colin grinned. 'I was going to bring you breakfast in bed,' he told her. 'Will Ian eat any of this?'

She shook her head. 'I doubt it. He's a toast and cereal man. We'll just have to finish it all.'

She looked very pretty this morning, he thought. Her hair still a little tousled from bed and her eyes sleepy, but bright with anticipation. A faint flush touching her cheeks. She'd pulled on a pair of jogging bottoms and a sweatshirt and her feet were bare. She looked very young and, he thought with a pang, terribly vulnerable.

'I thought we could see the beach,' he said. 'Maybe go for a walk or something. I think we could all do with the fresh air. I feel like I've been cooped up forever.'

She nodded. 'Good idea. I'm stiff from sitting still so long yesterday. Ian's never been here. He's going to love it.'

He filled their plates. 'God, I think I've cooked enough for an army,' and passed hers over then poured orange juice and tea, glancing at the supplies they'd brought with them and working out how long they'd last. He was already thinking what to do next and, if Julie didn't object to it, had a plan for tomorrow. He figured the big supermarket in Glastonbury would be open Sundays and thought it safer to use that than the local shop or even the larger shops they'd seen in Bridgewater.

'When were you last here?' he asked, watching with satisfaction as Julie plunged enthusiastically into her breakfast.

'Years ago,' she said between mouthfuls. 'I was pregnant with Ian and going through a bad time with his dad.' She rolled her eyes. 'Not that there were many times that weren't bad. I was what, seventeen, I guess. Scared and confused.' She laughed. 'Maybe that's why it seemed like a good place. Coming here when you're scared and confused, I mean. The family had put the pressure on to … well, to terminate. But I couldn't. It just felt wrong and Josie, my auntie's friend, she said I could come here for a few days if I wanted. Get away from it all.'

'You've never come back?'

She shrugged. 'We've not had a lot in the way of holidays, me and Ian. For a long time I didn't have a car and when I finally got the Fiesta, well, to be quite honest, I wasn't sure we'd make it back even if it got us here.'

He nodded. 'It's so quiet. I couldn't believe it this morning. The only time I heard anything was when a tractor went down the lane and the windows rattled.'

'Good, isn't it,' she grinned. Then, 'Ah, the march of the zombies' as Ian made his entrance and flopped down on the nearest chair.

He revived a bit over breakfast, the juice and cereal livening him up enough to demand some toast and ask plaintively why they'd not saved him any bacon.

'You don't like bacon.'

'I might have done this morning,' he contradicted with ten-year-old logic. 'This isn't like at home.'

Colin washed pots while they got themselves ready and mid-day saw them making their way down the lane, past the ruined

Abbey and towards the shoreline. She was right, Colin decided as they crossed the near empty car park and then climbed the stile. It was amazingly lovely.

A fierce wind blew across from Wales, the coastline visible on so clear a day. The wind beat the sea into a frenzy and the sound of waves crashing and breaking against the rocks some distance out was exhilarating. The path to the shore rounded a deep pool of clear water where the stream running parallel to the lane reached its final destination. The outlet from the pool disappeared beneath a boulder strewn bank, before emerging, spring like, where the bank dropped away onto the rocks. There was little in the way of sand. Instead chains of rockpools settled between walls of upturned strata that some great upheaval had once ripped from the high cliffs and turned upon their sides.

'It's a fossil beach,' Julie told him. 'Look carefully and you'll see ammonites in the rocks.'

'Wow,' he heard Ian say. Then, 'Mum,' pleadingly.

Colin looked in puzzlement at the boy, but Julie understood.

'Go on,' she said and Ian ran, leaping from rock to rock, down towards the sea.

'Will he be all right?'

'He'll be fine. He won't go out of sight, but he loves the water and I've told him about Kilve so often...' Her voice trailed off. 'I thought I'd be bringing him here to celebrate,' she said. 'You know, life's looking up for us, we can afford to take a holiday, with a decent car that'll cope with all the hills.'

'And instead...' Colin didn't bother to finish.

'And instead,' she confirmed, 'we're running away from a mad man that kills people who happen to get in his way.'

Colin took his mobile from his pocket and switched it on. There was a signal here, but it wasn't good and his battery was low.

'I tried from the cottage,' she said. 'Nothing unless you hang out of the back bedroom window. We could try the cliff-top later.'

He nodded.

'But John Moore's not likely to be out of hospital. There's not going to be much he can do for us. Try the hospital from the phone in the cottage I suppose. Or do you think they'll be able to trace us? Bugger,' she added. 'This wind!' She rooted in the pocket of her coat, sorting through what looked like a year's worth of bus tickets and till receipts before she found the hair band she was looking for. She scooped the curls back from her face and tied them in place. 'How easy is it to trace a phone? Can they find us if we use the mobiles? I heard somewhere they can tell what transmitter the phone goes through or something.'

Colin thought about it. 'I think we're safe calling the hospital,' he said. 'It'll have to go through the switchboard and then the ward extension. Land lines are mostly digital now, so it can take seconds rather than minutes to trace a call, but they'd have to be waiting for us. I think. I'm not sure if they can back track afterwards, but if it's a direct line they can tell what number we're calling from and, I suppose, get the address dead easily from that.'

'Could they tap John's phone?'

'Who, Radcliffe or the police?'

'Either. I still think it's not safe. Moira was convinced there was someone working for Radcliffe. She used to tell me not to talk to anyone but her. The only reason I contacted John was because she said he was OK.'

Colin nodded. 'I talked to John about that. He didn't seem to think it was a problem, but I wouldn't want to risk it, really. They can triangulate a mobile, if it's switched on. Some mobiles announce themselves to the network whether they're switched on or not.'

'What do you mean?'

'Well, if you've got a mobile, every time it passes a different transmitter, it tells the system where it is, so that messages can be re-routed via the closest or most powerful transmitters. Sometimes, if you've got a mobile in the car and the radio's on, you can hear it. It interferes with the radio signal. Just for a half second or so.'

'I didn't know that. But you said some can even do it if they're switched off.'

He nodded. 'Some newer phones have a default setting in their protocol. I mean, when they're set up in the factory, there's a switch, if you like, that's set to 'on', even when the power's off. It uses the back-up battery.' He grinned, 'It's like carrying a bug around with you. A phone like that can be pinpointed within yards. So can a lot of the others but only if they're switched on and they can triangulate with three different transmitters.'

'Why would they want to do that? Can our phones do it? I mean, I've got mine switched off, but...'

Colin shook his head. 'Ours are both getting on a bit,' he said. 'They're not up-to-date enough or sophisticated enough to do that. But the reason's simple, really. If a supplier always knows where a phone is, it can route the signal the best and fastest way. And you can actually buy the software that makes it easier to track your phone. There's a couple of companies marketing it as a safety feature. You know, always know where your kids are.'

'Sounds like they're making money off

people's paranoia,' Julie said. Then she shrugged. 'Mind you, Ian's not old enough to be much out of sight. I don't know how I'll feel when he's older. Probably want him tagged and tied to a long string.'

Colin laughed. They stood quietly together watching as the boy jumped from rock to rock in the shallows, leaping back every now and then, when a wave got that bit too close. 'He's going to ruin his shoes, and soak his trousers,' Julie said, but, hearing the boys whoops of delight, seeing him savouring the freedom and sheer ordinariness of the moment in a life that had become so far from ordinary, neither of them had the heart to worry about it or call him back.

By late that afternoon, it had been decided that Rose should take a few days leave and her boyfriend, Phil, had been brought in to answer a few questions. His alleged friend, Joe Crowther possessed a handful of other names, including the one he had used for the benefit of Brady Timms. He had a record for assault and armed robbery, but had gone quiet since his last five year stretch inside. He'd served half his term, been paroled and was, so far as the probation service was concerned, working as a salesman at a local car auction warehouse and keeping his nose clean. It was interesting, Weaver noted, that Brian Henshaw's brother, Dave, managed the place on behalf of a consortium that included Charlie Radcliffe.

'Got a finger in every bloody pie,' Weaver noted bitterly. A warrant was out for Joe Crowther's arrest and Phil was in interview room two. After spending several hours energetically denying all knowledge of the man, he had finally admitted that he'd been passing on odd bits of gossip, as he called it. Phil had gambling debts. Radcliffe had given him a way of paying them off. He didn't see he had any choice but to agree.

Rose was now at a loose end and the last place she wanted to be was home. Alone.

John took his time getting to the door, but was clearly pleased to see her. His expression changed, however when he registered hers.

'What's wrong?'

'I think I've done something stupid.'

'Oh?'

She took a deep breath and told him about Joe Crowther, alias DC Sandford alias an old friend of her boyfriend, Phil.

'What if I said something?' she asked. 'What if I've told Phil something important and he's passed it on?'

'Do you think you have? Do you discuss your work with Phil?'

She shook her head vehemently. 'No, but he asks and sometimes, if I've had a bad day, I know I've had a rant about things. Little things mainly, but how do I know if what

I've said ... I don't know, put someone in danger. Jeopardised the inquiry some way?'

John regarded the young woman with a mix of sympathy and irritation. It was hard, he knew, to do what they did, see what they saw every day and not take it home.

'What does Weaver say?'

Rose shrugged. 'He's been well ... really nice actually, but we both know what might have happened. If I've given information to Radcliffe, what then?'

He wanted to tell her it would be all right, but couldn't. He knew, from his own experience of intelligence gathering, just how useful odd snippets of random inform-ation could be when you fixed them into a known matrix. What leaps of intuition they could lead to. He liked Rose Morgan, thought she was good at her job, but she was young and inexperienced and, in a job where it was hard to maintain relationships even on the most superficial level, would have been eager to hang on to this young man. He'd heard her chatting about Phil, knew she'd congratulated herself on having someone who could put up with the erratic hours and be so nice about it when she had to cancel a date. Of course she'd have talked about work. She'd have been careful and circumspect, but not careful enough, now it turned out that Phil had been deliberately using her. And Radcliffe, via Joe Crowther, deliberately using him.

'Weaver's right,' he said. 'You need some distance. He could have suspended you pending investigation, you know that, don't you?'

She nodded.

'But he hasn't, so take the leave and get away for a bit.'

'Where would I go? I can't. I have to stick around.'

John nodded. 'OK,' he said. 'You can drive me somewhere.' He regretted the words the moment they were out. 'No,' he corrected. 'I can't ask you to do that.'

'Do what? When?'

He'd been thinking about this all day, decided to act upon his idea of involving Billy James, getting even with Radcliffe. It occurred to him though, that in asking Rose he was using her much as her lover had done. He told her so.

'What are you planning?'

'Asking a favour, I suppose. Selling our friend Radcliffe down the river.' He smiled weakly. 'Truthfully, I'm probably delirious and should be locked up somewhere until I come to my senses. I need a driver, Rose, but that's all. If I tell you more, you'll be in deep shit and not just with Weaver.'

She nodded slowly. 'I'll drive you,' she said. 'After all, how much worse could this get?'

'Oh, a fair bit, I'd say.'

Rose grimaced. 'You must have a good reason for doing whatever it is you're doing,' she said. She stood up clutching at her bag. Straightened her shoulders with a funny little jerk. 'Right,' she told him. 'You want me to drive, you'd better tell me where and we ought to go now, before I get sensible on you and change my mind. Give me your keys. If we're going anywhere, we'll take your car.'

They drove through the night streets of John's old home town, Rose following his directions, crossing the river and then leaving the main drag for the quieter roads and side routes to the estate he'd known in childhood.

'So,' she said finally, when it seemed their destination must be in sight. 'I take it we're visiting Mr William James.'

John stared at her.

'I'm not stupid, Guv. There are rumours galore about you before you joined the force. How you were a bad boy mixed up with ... well, you pick it, someone reckons you did it.'

John stared some more. 'I didn't realise I was that exciting,' he said. 'But, Morgan, don't call him William. It pisses him off. His dad was William and the two didn't see eye to eye.'

'Ok, I won't.'

'In fact, don't call him anything. I think you should stay in the car.'

'What, you mean, guard the hub caps?' She grinned at him. 'Or don't hub caps go missing on Billy James's patch?'

'Not outside his house, they don't. Turn down here. On your left.'

Rose did as she was told. The sixties built council estate was behind them a street later, giving way to older, terraced housing. At the end of the road were a cluster of larger, more prominent buildings and it was in front of one of these that John told Rose to pull in.

'Houses for the workers over there.' He pointed to the flat front terraces. 'For the managers and overseers here.'

'Nice to know there was equality. You really want me to stay here?'

John shrugged. Mistake. He grunted in pain.

'Come off it, Guv. You won't even get out of the car without my help,' she told him, reminding him how awkward it had been to get him in and settled.

The door to the James' house was opened on the second knock.

'It's late,' the man told them. 'Mr James is about to go to bed.'

John glanced at his watch. It was ten thirty

five. 'Please,' he said. 'Tell Mr James that John Moore would like to see him. It's important. Give him these.'

He fumbled for the papers in his coat pocket, Rose finally having to help. Gave them to the man guarding the door. The man, tall and square, with hands that looked capable of pinch gripping a football, didn't look at the documents, but motioned them inside and then into a front room. 'I'll ask,' he said. 'Stay here.'

'You been here before?' Rose asked. She was whispering. It was that kind of room.

'Once,' John told her. 'Before my father died.' It hadn't changed. He had waited in this room then. Ron, John's stepfather, had gone into the home twelve years before his death. John had been about twenty-one at the time. His dad had already been sick, forgetful, sometimes confused. The first stages of Altzheimer's showing themselves. In one of his more lucid moments he had pulled a large wooden deed box from the depths of the cupboard in the hall. John had seen it from time to time, but had no idea of what it had contained. It was his mother's and, therefore, private.

From the box, his father took a bundle of papers. 'Insurance,' he said. 'We've already paid for the funeral. My will, a few other bits. Take them to Billy. That way, when I'm gone everything will be sorted and you'll

276

have no need to bother.'

John hadn't argued. He'd already applied for the force, taken his entrance exams. His dad wasn't happy, though he'd not tried to stop him. It had caused a rift though, unchallenged and uncrossable and this removal from John's future life of those final responsibilities confirmed that distance in a way that hurt profoundly. He'd come here that day, sat in this room, with its formal wing backed chairs and walls filled with leather books and old orange Penguin paperbacks. The fire had been lit and had burned low in the grate. There was even an aspidistra in an ugly green jardiniere standing in the window. The whole looking exactly what it was. A front parlour, kept for guests who wouldn't be staying long, and frozen in some seemingly ancient time.

Aspidistra was still there – he wondered if it was the same one. Heavy drapes still hung at the windows. Books, dust free but untouched, finished off the walls. Only the fire had changed, the open hearth replaced by gas.

The door opened and the guardian came back inside. 'Mr James will see you,' he said. 'The young lady can stay here and I'll see she gets refreshments.'

John glanced at Rose. She was staring open mouthed. It all seemed so fictional. So out of time. The man indicated the fire. 'If you're cold,' he said to Rose. 'It's the switch on the side.' To John, 'I'll show you the way.'

Billy James was waiting in a room upstairs. It had been converted into office space, occupied by a large desk, complete with computer and several more leather chairs. More books on shelves occupied one wall. These looked well thumbed, meant to be read rather than act as interior design. On the wall opposite hung three watercolours. Originals, John noted. They were landscapes. Somewhere mountainous and wild. Billy James sat beside the fire in a wing backed chair similar to the ones downstairs. He was in pyjamas and a deep red dressing gown and held a drink in his hand. The other, he extended to shake John's then drew back as he took note of the strapped up arm.

'I could shake your left,' said James, 'but I always regard that as a little crass. Would you like a drink? Painkillers, perhaps? Though I find that brandy is an effective analgesic.'

John shook his head. He'd taken his day's quota of tablets and was contemplating starting on the next. Alcohol was not permitted and anyway, he needed as clear a head as he could muster.

'I heard you'd been hurt,' James said. 'And I heard about the woman. You were very close.'

'I wanted to marry her,' John said. 'I should have asked. I didn't. I'll have to live with that.'

James nodded. 'Regrets like that are almost the hardest,' he said. 'There was a young woman once, when I was a lad of sixteen or so. She was twenty, but the difference didn't seem to matter. I wanted her like I've wanted no woman since, but my mother got wind of it and that was that. I heard she married a sailor, had five kids and a miserable life. I regretted that.'

John wasn't sure where this was leading.

'I had him killed, the husband. He deserved it. She never knew, of course, but I like to think I did the right thing.'

He paused, just for a beat. 'Is that what you'd like done, John Moore. *Inspector* Moore?'

John froze. He hadn't known where the conversation would lead, but he'd not expected that. All things considered, maybe he should have done. 'It's a tempting thought,' he said quietly. 'No doubt it would solve some of my problems, but I don't think I could say yes with a clear conscience.'

Billy James smiled. 'What then?' he asked. He indicated the papers John had given him. They were lying on his desk, in a tray marked pending. Pending what, John wondered, ill at ease.

'Mr Radcliffe runs a profitable business,' he commented. 'He also has more power and information than is good for one man to have. One man like Charlie Radcliffe at any rate.' James paused as though considering. 'He's getting greedy, Inspector Moore and that's not good. When a man is turning a decent profit and running his business well, he should be satisfied, don't you think?'

'I wouldn't know. Never having been in that position.'

'How did you come by the information?'

'How valuable is it?'

James raised an eyebrow. 'Valuable?'

'To you, to your rivals. To Radcliffe. You said he had power. How much?'

James got up and fetched himself another drink. He half filled a second tumbler with Dry Ginger, topped it with ice and brought it back to John. 'As a child, you loved this,' he said and just for an instant his eyes softened as though remembering something precious. 'You reckoned it looked like a grown up drink'

John took it from him and sipped. The ice rattled against his teeth and the crisp tang of the ginger was pleasant on his tongue. 'I'd forgotten,' he said. Strange, he thought, how some things... How some things evoke such strong emotions and such vivid memories. Billy James and his father sitting in the tiny living room while his mother knitted or read. John watching the TV in the corner, with the sound turned down low so it didn't interrupt the menfolk. His chair pulled close so he could hear – one ear open for what his dad was saying. Mysterious things. Exciting in their sheer incomprehensibility. Ginger beer poured into a tumbler, taken from the bottle Billy brought along with the whisky. The only time his dad drank it.

'In itself, not valuable at all,' Billy James told him. 'But put together with other things, with what I know of Radcliffe's dealings, it tells me a great deal, John. Now, how did you get this information and, perhaps more important, what is it you want from me?'

For the next hour, John filled Billy James in on Colin and Moira and Alice Sanders and the mess this had become. Billy listened with barely a word, simply raising a finger and indicating that John should back up a little when he didn't understand. And when he'd done, John sat back wearily in his chair while the fire – still real in this room – crackled in the hearth and James sipped his drink and thought and then, when John gave in to weariness and slept, leaned forward to take the glass gently from his hand.

It was another hour before he woke and then it was to the sound of voices, James and two others talking softly on the other side of the room.

He moved, groaned with the pain that shot through his arm and side and James looked across at him.

'I've had some sandwiches made for the young lady,' he said. 'She took a fancy to one of my old Penguins, so said she was welcome to it. She's an educated girl.'

'Penguins?' For an instant a bizarre black and white image came to mind. Rose Morgan packing a large seabird into the boot of his car.

'The orange paperbacks on the shelf downstairs,' James said patiently. 'We had a chat about them. Some are first editions apparently. I must get them catalogued, but I had a duplicate of H.G Wells's *The Time Machine,* so I said she could take it.'

'You've talked to Rose?' He sounded drowsy still, brain clouded and stupid.

'Of course. John, she's a guest in my house. I had to welcome her.'

'She shouldn't be here.'

James waved an impatient hand. 'And she never was. I understand that. She did a favour for a friend, no reason she should get into trouble for it. Now.' Suddenly very businesslike. 'Are you hungry?'

'No, I don't think so. Thank you.'

'Right, then you should be on your way. Go home, get some rest. As soon as we know where Colin Grainger and the girl are hiding, I'll send someone to get you.'

'You think you can find them?'

The look Billy James gave him was that of a teacher for a child that is being deliberately

282

stupid. 'You came to me so I could find them. You've given me a business advantage. I find Colin and I consider us even. Does that suit?'

Dumbly, John nodded.

James indicated one of his men. John recognised the guardian who'd kept the door. 'Martyn here will take a look at your shoulder before you leave. Rose tells me you've not had proper care since leaving the hospital. Bullet wounds can be troublesome to heal, John, but Martyn is something of an expert in that regard. He'll look after you and I'll see you again soon.'

A half hour later they were driving away from Billy James' house, back through the silent early morning streets and onto the main road. His shoulder felt more comfortable than it had in days and the painkillers Martyn had given him had kicked in almost too fast. John was too grateful to ask what they might be. He only knew he had about four day's supply.

'He's an unusual man,' Rose said, finally breaking the silence.

'That's one word for him. Under no illusions though, Rose, he's a bloody dangerous man.'

She glanced sideways at him with an expression he wasn't sure how to read. 'Takes one to know one,' she said.

He smiled weakly. 'Look,' he said. 'It goes

without saying that you were never there. That the meeting never took place.'

'What did you say to him? What's he going to do?'

John shook his head. 'That never happened either,' he said.

30

When they arrived home there was a message on the answerphone. It was brief and had been left just after they'd gone out the evening before. It was from Colin.

'Phoned the hospital,' it said. 'You should have stayed there. But I'll be sending you an email, tomorrow.'

'An email?' Rose questioned. 'He must be somewhere with a computer.'

'Maybe,' John frowned. 'Unless he uses a what d'you call 'em. Cyber café.'

'Isn't that dangerous? I mean, he might be spotted.' John thought about it. 'If he's risking that, he must be a long way from here,' he said. 'I don't think there's been much of a splash nationally yet. He's lucky, it's the weekend and the Sundays are unlikely to run with it. The story would have broken too late, and I doubt they'd see it as important enough to bother with yet. I've not seen the nationals for Saturday yet, have you?'

Rose shook her head. 'God, but I'm tired.' She hesitated. 'Do you think they'll have let Phil go? He might have gone home, I mean. I don't feel ready to face him yet.'

'There's a spare room upstairs. You'll have to make the bed, but there's spare sheets and stuff in the airing cupboard and I can lend you a t-shirt or something.'

She smiled. 'Thanks. I know it's maybe not … you know.'

'I think your reputation's safe,' he said, indicating his right arm. 'Look, get yourself to bed and get some sleep. I don't know about you, but I've had it.'

'Do you think they'll have let him go?'

'Phil? I don't know. We'll get onto Weaver first thing. If it's any consolation, I don't believe you'll have given them anything significant.'

'You're lying,' she told him. 'But thanks, anyway. I appreciate the thought.'

Weaver arrived before they were awake and banged on the door until the neighbours were looking out of their bedroom windows.

John stumbled to open the door. 'What's the noise? Don't you know it's bloody Sunday?'

'Thought I'd bring breakfast. Rose can help me cook.'

'Rose? You been watching me or something?'

Weaver chuckled to himself. 'I knew she'd
have to come and tell you herself. Knew she
wouldn't want to go home, just in case.
Deduction, my dear Holmes. Anyway, her
car's parked next to yours.'

'Oh, the power of deduction. Let me get
some clothes on then. Oh and you might
like to play my answerphone messages,
there's one from Colin.'

Weaver was in the kitchen when they both
came back downstairs. 'How come you
didn't call that in last night?'

'Because I wasn't here.' John told him. 'He
managed to pick a time we were out. I
needed some air.'

Weaver looked sceptical. 'Email.' He said,
'do you actually check yours then?'

John ignored the jibe. It was a complaint
of Weaver's that he failed to respond to
office memos. 'So,' he said. 'What's
happening with Rose's boyfriend?'

'Rose's *ex* boyfriend,' she retorted quickly.

Weaver shot Rose a look. 'I'm going to
have to let him go,' he said. 'We'll have kept
him for his twenty-four and I don't have
reason to apply for an extension.'

She nodded, but she didn't look pleased.

'From what we can gather, he's been
passing tit bits on to Crowther for about the

past six months.'

'Six months?' Rose was horrified.

'You know he has problems with gambling.'

'Had,' Rose insisted. 'He promised me he'd stopped. This was, what, three, four months back.' She sighed. 'Stupid,' she said. 'He had no intention of stopping, did he?'

Weaver shrugged. 'I wouldn't know. About five months ago he dropped something like three thousand at Radcliffe's place. Then tried to win it back and lost another two.'

Rose was aghast. 'Where did he get money like that from? He earns sweet F.A. compared to that.'

'It was his money,' Weaver told her. 'His grandad died and left him some cash. Something like ten grand. It was gone inside a few weeks.'

She sat down, hard. 'He told me about the funeral. Said the old man had nothing much and he hoped he'd get a keepsake or two. Damn him, I even tried to take time off to go to the service with him.'

Weaver tried, and failed, to look sympathetic. 'This Joe Crowther was an old school friend. They'd kept in touch and Crowther had just got out on parole. Radcliffe set you up as a way of your boyfriend discharging his debts, but it wouldn't have stopped there. Crowther reckons you weren't feeding them enough of anything and they were blaming Phil. It's only a matter of time before Radcliffe would have had him doing something else and before he knew it he'd be caught and hog-tied, and the threat of violence if he didn't go along was one Phil took very seriously indeed. Crowther told him that if he tried to do a runner, he'd turn up dead somewhere and it wouldn't be quick or painless. We've no reason to believe he was bluffing and neither did Phil. He's asked for police protection, by the way.'

'Think he needs it?' John wanted to know. Weaver shrugged. 'He can want,' he said. 'Doesn't mean we've got the manpower to give and anyway, I don't think Radcliffe will make any move at the moment. This one ties directly to him. Phil goes missing or turns up with a bullet in the back and Radcliffe knows we'd be camping on his doorstep, though, to be frank, I don't suppose we'd cause him more than passing inconvenience. It's Crowther's word alone that Radcliffe had this arrangement. No money changed hands and there's no record of how much Phil went down for. We can trace the money from probate to his bank account, after that, he might as well have lifted the nearest drain and chucked it down.'

'But, what was it, five grand, Guv, surely...'

Weaver shook his head. 'All small individual transactions over a period of about three, four weeks. It's peanuts in an establishment like Radcliffe's.'

'Rose, think. Is there anything you remember him asking about specifically?'

She shook her head. 'I've done bugger all *but* think,' she said. 'He was always so ... nice. You know what it's like. You come home having seen scum all day and you want to know there's something nice and clean and ... ordinary in the world. I love my job, but it gets to you.' She looked desperately from one man to the other. 'It gets to you and lately ... I liked Moira a lot. She was good to me when I was in uniform and then, when I started working in CID, she showed me the ropes. Made sure I didn't take too much flack. It's still tough being a woman and a newby into the bargain.'

Weaver nodded. 'Was he interested in the investigation?'

Rose considered. 'He'd see things in the newspaper and he'd ask if I was involved. If they'd got the facts right. I'd tell him I couldn't say and he'd say well, that just showed it was right then. That sort of thing. It was like he was playing a game and I was too damned stupid to notice what he was really after.'

She got up from the table and began to poke at the bacon sizzling under the grill. 'I think this is done,' she said, her voice was thick with tears.

'You want to cook the eggs?'

She nodded, not turning or trusting

289

herself to speak.

For a while there was silence in the room broken only by the sound of eggs frying and the ticking of the kitchen clock. Funny, John thought, he'd never thought about it ticking. It must be the hands moving.

'Where *did* you go last night?' Weaver asked suddenly. 'I called round, late, wanted to tell you how things were going and to talk to Rose. You were out then and I had someone do a drive-by around two thirty. They saw you coming back.'

'Spying on me?' John asked.

'Checking on you. Don't want anything else happening. Anyway, Brady tells me there's a rumour going round that you've been shot. He thinks the nationals are bound to pick up on that, along with everything else that's happening in this nice little town of ours.'

'Funny thing, rumours. They come up with the most unlikely stories.'

Weaver held his gaze for a long time. 'We've had enough secrets, John. We're on the same side, remember?'

John sighed. 'Superintendent Cauldwell won't like it,' he said. 'It'll be bad for his blood pressure.'

'Then we'll tell him later. I don't want a superior officer put at risk. Now, spill.'

'I went to see Billy James,' he said, noting the hardening expression in Weaver's eyes.

Rose set food on the table, red eyed and silent as John described his visit with the old man.

'Your food will go cold,' Weaver told him starting on his own. They ate in silence while Weaver absorbed what he'd just heard.

'Can he be trusted?' he asked finally.

John shrugged. 'I don't know,' he said. 'Truth is, I don't really know.'

31

Cafe Galatea was on the High Street in Glastonbury. It was more than a cyber café, serving vegetarian food in addition to internet access and doubling as a gallery for local artists.

'Do they serve chips?' Ian wanted to know.

'Um, they do potato wedges, with dips. You'll like that,' his mother told him.

Ian wrinkled his nose, then shrugged. 'OK,' he said. He looked across to where Colin was logged on and typing rapidly. 'Is he sending it to that policeman?'

Julie nodded, glancing round to see if anyone had heard. The café was fairly empty this time on a Sunday. She'd been surprised to find many of the shops were closed, even those dedicated to the tourist trade. It seemed that for all its fame this was, after all, a traditional old town.

'Colin says he can use a special email they can't trace,' Ian leaned forward confidentially. 'You make up a name. Anything you like. Then send it to this special site and after anyone reads it the email just deletes itself. He knows a lot, doesn't he, Mum?'

Julie smiled at her son. 'About some things, yes.'

He poked at his milkshake with the end of his straw.

'Is that alright?'

He nodded. 'It isn't as thick as the ones we get at home, but it's OK. Do you like him?'

'Do you?'

Ian nodded. 'Yeah. I hope you two stay friends when we get home.'

If we get home, Julie thought, but she just smiled again and then looked across at Colin. He'd paused now, seemed to be considering something. She turned back to her son.

'You missing your friends?'

He nodded. 'You think we can go back soon?'

'I hope so.'

'It seems like we've been away forever.'

'I know.' It was less than a week since she'd met John Moore in the pavilion, but Ian was right. It did feel like forever. She wondered if she'd ever feel safe again. If going back home was in fact even an option. How could anything make it right?

Colin came over to the table and sat down next to Ian.

'You want to order?'

'Finished?' Julie asked.

He nodded. 'He should call me tomorrow. I don't know how long the email will take to reach him or when he'll check his mail, so I didn't say today. I just hope the battery's got enough charge. I've kept the phone switched off, but you never know.'

'Will he come and get us?' Ian wanted to know.

'I don't know. He'll be able to tell us what's happening, at least.' He hesitated for a moment then said, 'I've told him I'll find a way of putting what I've got on the internet if he doesn't sort it soon. We can't go on like this. I'll send the stick drive to the tabloids if I have to.'

'What good will that do?'

'Radcliffe can't shut everyone up.'

Julie looked at her son, wondering if they should be discussing this in front of him. 'It's all right, Mum,' Ian said, seeming as usual to read her thoughts. 'I agree with Colin,' he added stoutly. 'Can you do it from here?'

'No. I need a UBS connection. It's not like an ordinary floppy disk. I might be able to persuade them to let me upload a floppy, but I'm not sure about being able to transfer from the stick drive here.'

'Then, what's the point in threatening?' Julie wanted to know.

'John won't know that and anyway, it's not an empty threat. I could find a way. There are people I could call on if I had to that would let me use their system. I just don't want anyone else knowing where we are if I can help it. And, like I say, there's always the papers.' He straightened up, wriggling his shoulders, easing the tension. 'Tell you what,' he said, brightening suddenly. 'Let's have lunch then make like tourists for the rest of the day. See the sights, climb the Tor, commune with King Arthur.'

Ian giggled. 'What?'

'You don't know about King Arthur?'

'Sure I do. What's a Tor?'

Colin pretended to be shocked. 'Where were you educated, child?'

'It's a big hill,' Julie told him. 'A very special hill.'

'Why?' Ian was asking. Then he stopped and studied both of the adults. They were staring at each other across the table. Staring and smiling. Ian looked pleased. He picked up the menu and pretended to study it intently, looking at his mum out of the tail of his eye. Despite everything she looked almost happy. In that moment Ian knew that it would, somehow, be all right.

John had checked his emails twice that morning. There had been nothing. The third time he looked was a little after midday. One new message: kingcole@recidivist.com. It had to be Colin.

'Anything?' Rose asked.

'Looks like it.' He opened the mail and read the brief message. Colin said they were all safe but money was running low and he didn't think they could stay in hiding much longer. He wanted to know what to do, but in the meantime he'd reached his own conclusion. '"Publish and be damned" as they say. Once it's out there, Radcliffe can't stop everyone from knowing. And if I tie him to Moira, he'll be like a worm on a hook. He can't hide from everyone. If I can't get it on the net, I'll go to the press. I mean it, John, you lot have been acting like you have no hands and no brain. Publicity's what you need and I figure something like the *News of the World* will be able to protect us far better than you lot. Call me tomorrow at twelve thirty and tell me what you plan to do."'

'He could be right,' Rose said. 'We've done a bloody awful job. Let him try it his way.'

'If he and Julie had stayed put we might have stood some chance of protecting them,' John said with considerable heat. His anger directed as much at himself as Colin.

He disconnected the modem, plugged the

phone line back in and dialled.

'Who are you calling?'

'Weaver. See if he has any bright ideas. And then, Billy James, tell him he's got to move and move fast before this gets away from all of us. For what it's worth, I don't think that Colin going public would slow Radcliffe. He's got the bit between his teeth now and this is personal.'

32

At ten o'clock on the Monday morning, Charlie Radcliffe had a surprise visit … from Billy James. James had been to the casino, of course, but Radcliffe had spoken to him only on the level of a regular client. Their other business was always carried out by a third party. James had certainly never visited him at home.

He left one man in the car and a second standing in the hall, seated himself in Radcliffe's front living room and waited for his host to speak.

'To what do I owe…?' Radcliffe asked. 'It's always a pleasure of course, but I thought you didn't go for the personal touch.'

'Only when the matter is personal,' Billy James told him. 'I understand you've got some business worries. Police raids, a disappearing employee. Is there anything I should be worried about, Mr Radcliffe?'

Charlie Radcliffe shook his head. James rattled him maybe more than anyone else. He'd been on the scene when Radcliffe was just a kid in short pants and had a reputation then for efficiency and for doing things according to a code of Billy James' own making. 'The police have to seem to be doing something,' he said smoothly. 'Some allegations were made apparently. A client who thought he'd lost too often and then the missing girl. Boyfriend trouble, I expect. Flighty, these young people.'

James said nothing. He waited as though expecting more. Charlie Radcliffe found himself mentally adding up the cost of the older man's overcoat, his shoes – Gucci, if he wasn't mistaken – even his bloody walking stick with its silver handle and inlaid stem.

'There's really nothing for you to be concerned about. We'll be having a grand reopening in a few days time. I hope that this slight hiatus won't have inconvenienced you too much.'

'You're a bad liar, Radcliffe,' James said. 'I hear on the grapevine that someone got hold of information. Client lists, throughput of funds. I thought you were big on confidentiality, Charlie. To find that my trust has been broken and the efficiency of my transactions compromised is something I find unacceptable. I may have to take my business elsewhere and I'm sure if it gets out that Charlie Radcliffe leaks like a sieve, keeps confidential information lying around where any Tom, Dick or Harry can find it – confidential information, which, truth to tell he had no right to be keeping anywhere...' He paused, clucked his tongue reprovingly. 'It won't look good, Charlie, and some of your clients are, I hear, a lot less gentlemanly in their dealings than I believe in being.'

Radcliffe took a deep breath and released it slowly. 'It's in hand,' he said quietly. 'We know who's responsible and we're doing all we can to track him down.'

'I'm glad to hear it, but I also hear that you've been chasing this perpetrator since Wednesday last? Sloppy work, Charlie. Very lax. You had him in your office and you let him get away from you, is that the size of it?' He leaned forward, studying Charlie Radcliffe's face. The bruising was diminishing, but it was still easy to see the scars that Colin had left behind. 'He nearly had your eye, Charlie.'

He straightened, then stood, the stick held lightly in his hand, more for show than for support. Billy James would not see seventy again, but his fitness and posture was of a man a couple of decades younger.

'You've got until Wednesday, Charlie, to

solve this one. That's a week, in case you've lost count of the days. And Charlie, make sure this is clean. No ripples, no waves or I won't be the only one with an interest.'

When Rose returned home, Phil was waiting for her.

'Hi,' he said.

'What are you doing here?'

'I live here, remember.'

'No. No you don't. This is *my* home. You might be in the habit of staying here, but you've no right if I say you've got to go.' She took a deep breath. 'I want your key and I want you out.'

'Rosie, love,' he reached a hand towards her. Supplicant with soft brown eyes. Pleading brown eyes. 'I'm sorry. I don't know what to say to tell you how sorry. But I had no option.'

'Didn't you?' She slapped the hand away. Tried to ignore the pained look that crossed his face. 'I don't want to know, Phil. I trusted you and you used me. Give me one good reason why I should listen to one more word.'

He backed off, stood with his hands thrust deep into his pockets, staring at the floor. 'I can't give you a single one,' he said. 'You've got every right to feel the way you do. I can't say anything that would justify what I did to you.'

Different tack. Transfer of guilt to the innocent party. Rose hesitated, just for an instant. He felt the uncertainty and looked up at her a brief gleam of hope in the melting umber of his eyes.

Rose saw and closed her own. 'No,' she told him. 'No more. I won't listen to any of it. Give me my key and get out of my house. And Phil. Don't even think of coming back.'

'I love you, Rosie. God, are you going to throw everything away? We had it good, you know that. You might be blazing, right now, and who can blame you, but are you going to throw away all the good times because of one mistake?'

He was right. She was blazing now. She turned on him, fists clenched and held close to her sides as if afraid she might strike out. The fury evident in the tension of her body, the expression of something close to hatred on her face finally gave him pause. He stepped back, uncertain of his ground.

'You think I could forgive this? You think you can come here and talk me round. You betrayed me, Phil, you may well have ruined my career. You've certainly ruined my chances of having a relationship for Christ knows how long. You think I'll be able to settle down and believe in anyone after this? Give me my key and get the hell out!'

She'd never raised her voice at him before. Rarely indulged in bad language even at work, where it was so acceptable as to be commonplace, though she seemed to be on the verge of it. Raised not to cuss, Rose saved expletives for the time and occasion that really warranted them and now seemed such a time. She could see that he was already shocked. That she'd undermined his fond held belief that he could start again and make his little faux pas all right. Could he ever have thought that? Or did he lie to himself as well?

Slowly, he reached into his pocket and withdrew his keys. He took hers from the ring and dropped it to the floor, then stalked out with not even a backward glance. She watched him go, realising, belatedly as he opened the front door, that he had a bag packed and sitting ready in the hall.

'Bastard,' she muttered as the door slammed behind him and she slid the bolt home, just to be sure. He had planned for either eventuality. Stay or go. She leaned against the locked door and glanced around, wondering if his own possessions were all he'd taken with him.

33

While Radcliffe was undergoing his uncomfortable interview with Billy James, his men were still out looking for Colin. North, as per information received.

Before his arrest, Phil had told them he believed Rose would be collecting both Julie and Colin from some place on the coast, north of Whitby. It was vague, but Radcliffe had decided to ignore the main resort and send his people out into the smaller towns and villages, concentrating on those directly on the coast. Phil had said he had the impression she was talking about a B&B, though, he'd warned, it could have nothing to do with Colin at all.

Radcliffe, short of anywhere else to start, decided it was as good a place as any.

He'd assigned a half dozen of his people, armed now with copies of the local paper – carrying Julie's picture – and a snapshot of Colin he'd taken from his flat. It showed him arm in arm with Moira and looked to be a couple of years old – Colin's hair was shorter now. But the likeness was a good one and Radcliffe had it copied. His people had worked their way up the coast, showing the pictures in local pubs, chatting to the landlady's at the various B&Bs, taking advantage of the fact that this was off season and many places were effectively running on empty.

Many of those interviewed assumed they were police. Others that they were journalists, following up on a lead and nothing was said to disabuse them of that notion. The mention of Ian helped. A missing child, with or without his mother, was always a sympathetic draw. But so far, they had come up empty-handed.

It was an onerous task and one guaranteed to attract attention. Once or twice they had been approached by members of the local constabulary, wanting to know what the hell they were doing. Julie had, in this process, acquired a cousin along with a concerned friend. Radcliffe had been credited with financing the trip – wonderful, caring employer – and their reasons for searching here? Julie loved the place. Came to Yorkshire on holiday as a kid and never forgot it.

The fact that the locals had been primed to watch out for Radcliffe's lot had so far gone undetected. It had been decided that, given the range of their search and the fact that they went from boarding house to pub often in the same street, it would have seemed odd had someone not called it in and their motives been questioned.

Radcliffe, until the visit from Billy James, had been quite pleased with the way things were going.

That Monday morning, two of the team had been dispatched to examine the residents of Port Mulgrave and the other two had headed up to Staithes.

Lunchtime found them in the pub right on the quayside. They bought beer and ordered hunch, ate it at the bar, chatting with the landlord and then, laying the photographs and newspaper on the bar, asked the inevitable question.

'You get many visitors this time of the year?'

'No, it's a bit wild for the tourists. You think it's wet now, you should see it when the wind gets up. You can't see a hand in front when you're crossing the open, there–' he indicated the paved area outside and the beach beyond.

'So, you'd recall seeing either of these two?'

The landlord looked and grinned. 'I'd remember her,' he said. He read the headlines. 'Missing, is she? You relatives?'

'Cousin,' one said. 'The family think she may have headed this way.'

The landlord shrugged. 'No. Like I say, I'd remember her.'

'I seen him though,' the youngster collecting glasses informed them.

'Oh,' this from his boss. 'When?'

He shook his head. 'Not sure, few nights ago. Stuck his head round the door and asked for the Matthews's place. I recall him on account of his hair. It's the same colour as our Brian's.'

The landlord looked again and nodded. 'It is quite similar, I'll give you that.'

Before it could disintegrate into a discussion on the exact shade of ginger hair, Priestly, Radcliffe's man, asked, 'Matthews's place?'

'Yes, it's a B&B. You sure he asked for the Matthews?'

The boy nodded, took his glasses behind the bar and disappeared into a back room.

'The Matthews' is called Sea Spray,' the landlord said. 'It's back up the hill a ways. Just let me serve this customer and I'll give you some directions. You'll not find it otherwise.'

He took his time, or so it seemed, pulling pints for the two newcomers, chatting about the weather expected that afternoon, then he returned to the men armed with a pen and paper. A few minutes later they were gone, complete with a set of instructions that would get them to the Matthews's place through the twists and turns of narrow paths heading back towards the road.

There was a quicker way, but, the landlord thought, why should he oblige. His son, the glass collector emerged from the back room a moment later.

'You call Jan?'

'I did and that Sergeant.'

'Good. Cousin my arse. It'll take them a good ten minutes to get there the way I've set out. And now,' he said as another customer came into the bar, shaking himself free of the pouring rain. 'What can I do for you this lovely day?'

In Kilve the day was bright and clear, though a dark band of cloud gathered on the horizon and hid the coast of Wales from view. Rain and gale force winds were promised for later and, so the forecast said, likely to continue through the night and on into the following day. Colin was high on the clifftop, standing in the mud on the coastal path that in places wove dangerously close to the cliff edge. On the other side of him was an open field, ploughed over but not yet planted. Beyond that, more fields and the line of trees marking the main road.

They'd walked up here on the first day, Julie not happy about the proximity of the path to the edge of the eroded cliff. It was possible to see where the line of the path had been in years gone by. In places it now led out into empty space and Colin and Ian had teased her, threatening to follow the wrong line, practising cartoon cliff falls, legs pedalling the air as they jumped up and down mimicking the way Roadrunner or Wily Coyote might try to avoid hitting the ground.

A little further along from where Colin stood was a reminder that this had once been a lookout post, guarding against invasion. The remnant of a concrete pill box left from World War Two clung to the now crumbling cliff. They had hoped, seeing it from the beach, to get a closer look, but Julie had vetoed it and on closer inspection, Colin had to concede that she was right. It might once have been tens of yards inland, on a safe foundation, maybe even with gun emplacements facing out to sea. Now, it was a bare two feet from the edge and, from the look of it, another winter storm might rip what remained of its foundations from out beneath it and send it to join the fossils of an even earlier time on the rocks below.

Colin switched his mobile on, staring at the display as it took its time registering with the network. Battery power was very low. His charger was among the things he'd had to abandon the night Radcliffe had come for him.

It rang, dead on time. John was nothing if not punctual.

'I got your email. Colin, where the hell are you?'

'Can't tell you that. Sorry. When can we

come home?'

John hesitated. 'I don't know. Look, tell me where you are and I'll send someone for you. I'll come myself. We've got a safe house arranged 'til this blows over.'

'Blows over? I didn't know murders did that. You mean until you lock that bastard away?'

'Colin, it's in hand. I promise you, we'll nail Radcliffe.'

'I'm not sure, John. Julie's still convinced there's someone working for him among your lot. She said Moira was worried about someone's boyfriend?'

He felt John hesitate.

'She's right, isn't she. You know about it?'

'There was a problem,' John conceded, 'but the leak is plugged now, it's...'

'Where there's one, there might be another.' He sounded scared, tried to get a grip. 'You told me, John. Told me you thought everything was hunky dory, now you're telling me that we were right. There was an insider.' Until now, he'd only half believed it. To hear John Moore confirm their worries was a hammer blow. He'd been willing John to say, It's all right now, Radcliffe's in custody, you can come back home.

Colin made up his mind. 'I've told you what I'm going to do,' he said. 'If this is all out in the open then he can't do anything. I'm sorry, John, but I've got Ian to think of.

And Julie.' His phone was starting to beep at him, the signal fading. 'I'll be in touch,' he said and rang off. He stood for a moment, staring at the mobile as though it could talk to him, tell him what to do. Then he felt in his pocket for the package containing his stick drive. They'd found an envelope in one of the kitchen drawers. Stamps, Julie told him, could be had from the village shop. He worried that he might be recognised. That someone might ask questions; a visitor so late in the year. The envelope was already addressed and Colin hoped that someone would actually look at the contents before consigning it to the bin. He'd taken precautions against the editor being as much of a compute illiterate as John Moore and written instructions for use, wrapped them around the drive. All they'd need was a USB connection. Surely anyone with a computer would understand that?

He wished, fervently, that he'd brought this whole episode into the public domain earlier, maybe gone to the local paper or the television, even. Would it have helped? Colin didn't know. Would anyone actually see the significance of what he had? Colin didn't know that either though he'd included in his note details of Moira's death, how he'd come by the pictures of Alice and what had subsequently happened to her. That, surely would give everything some provenance?

And the fact that Julie had seen Moira at the casino the night she died, a fact that had led Radcliffe to chase her across half the country, surely that would count for something.

Resolutely, Colin began to walk back toward the cottage. He'd stop off and tell Julie what he had decided to do, then post the thing before he changed his mind.

'Well?' John turned to the others crowding into his living room. The call had been recorded and the expert was fiddling with the tape, trying to balance the sound. He tuned out the voice until it was almost a whisper and they listened to the sounds behind the obvious.

'Best I can do here,' he said. 'I'll take it and get it processed properly.'

'Sea birds?' John said.

'Sea birds, wind. Not a hell of a lot else.'

Weaver was standing across the room talking on his own mobile.

'Anything?' John asked him.

'They're trying to triangulate, but it might take some time. I'll have a location in about an hour, they reckon. They think they can get it down to about a half mile.'

'Better than nothing I suppose.' John was not inclined to be generous. 'You heard what he said?'

'And I can't blame him. Maybe Radcliffe's the one we ought to have in protective

310

custody. Once his clients know he's been a careless little double dealer they'll come looking. And frankly, I don't relish the shit hitting the fan on my shift.'

John jumped as the phone rang again. Hopeful, he snatched it up. It was Jan Matthews. They'd just had a call from the son of the pub landlord. Two men asking questions. They've been directed to the B&B.

As if on cue, Weaver's mobile rang. The local police telling him they were in position. John passed the message on.

'Jan, just be careful,' he told her. 'Call me after.'

'I will. I've got to go, there's someone at the door. Probably them.'

She rang off. At least, John comforted himself, something was coming together.

'Can I help you?' Jan Matthews smiled at the two men outside her door. They were dressed for the miserable weather in jeans and warm coats, comfortable boots. They looked like walkers, she thought, except few people bothered walking the coast path in this weather.

'We're looking for a friend,' one of them said. 'He's here with his girlfriend and her little boy, but we've forgotten the name of the boarding house they're staying in?'

'Well, it won't be here. We've no guests at the moment.'

'Oh,' he sounded disappointed. 'Well, we might have misunderstood. Maybe they were here and they've gone. They said at the pub that our friend had been in. This is him.'

Jan looked obediently at the picture of Colin. The rain was heavier now and hard drops fell and ran against the glossy paper.

'Sorry. He isn't here.'

'Maybe we could come in and talk about it?'

'Nothing to talk about,' said Jan. 'He isn't here.' She began to close the door and the second man, who'd been silent until now, pushed against it, forcing it open. 'Hey,' Jan protested.

'You don't understand,' he told her. 'We know our friend was here. Now are you going to let us in nicely, or what.'

'I call that threatening behaviour,' a voice behind them announced.

Jan allowed her breath to escape.

'What the–?'

One of the men lifted his hands in a gesture of submission. 'Nothing meant,' he began, but the second had pushed Jan aside. He burst into the house, a uniformed officer in pursuit, a second shouting on the radio for someone else to intercept. Jan heard her kitchen door and then the back door slamming open with a crack of splintering wood. Her little bit of a yard backed onto the path heading back up to the car park. He'd have to climb but after that it was an easy run, but also a relatively easy intercept.

'Jumpy, your friend,' the plain clothes officer commented. 'I think we'll wait for him in the car.' He handed the now quick-cuffed man over to another officer. 'You alright, Mrs Matthews?'

'I'm fine, you get off. I'll go and see what damage he's done to my door.'

He nodded, smiling at her. 'You do that. Bill us for the damage. We'll pass it on to our friends down south.'

Jan laughed, though she noted, the laugh was a little shaky. When she'd agreed to do a favour for her friend John, she hadn't expected anything like this. Rehearsing how she was going to wind him up about it, Jan went to put the lock on her back door and then get John on the phone.

34

Weaver collected Morantz and they went to tell Radcliffe about the Staithes arrests. He knew they couldn't hold the men for long. The threatening behaviour charge might stick, but he doubted it would get past the Crown Prosecution Service, if indeed it got that far. It was doubtful they'd accept that it was in the public interest to prosecute. After all, there's no law against asking questions and the prompt arrest had prevented it from going any further.

Weaver doubted they'd have done anything more than try to put the wind up Jan Matthews. They knew Colin had been there. All they'd want to do most likely was to satisfy themselves that their quarry had fled the field and see if Jan had an idea of where they might have gone.

There was nothing she could tell them even if she had a mind to.

Brian Henshaw was at Radcliffe's place. Weaver noted that Radcliffe's bruises had faded to a dirty yellow and though the cuts still looked red and angry, they were scabbed over and healing well. Weaver wondered if there were any legal way of opening them again.

'What do you want now?'

'Is that a nice welcome? What's been rattling your cage, Charlie?'

Radcliffe regarded him with narrow eyes. 'Make it quick, whatever it is. Brian and I were discussing business.'

'I don't imagine it's too good at the moment, is it?' Weaver inquired. 'Must be losing revenue, having to shut up shop over the weekend.'

'My lawyer will be getting in touch.'

'I look forward to it.'

'We came to tell you a bit of news,' Morantz announced, sitting down opposite Charlie and stretching his legs comfortably. 'Two associates of yours. Messrs Priest and Johnson. Got a bit above themselves, they did, and our colleagues in North Yorkshire are having a little chat.'

'I don't know what you're talking about.'

'Don't you? Well, Mr Johnson was trying to phone you when we caught up with him. Even got your number on fast dial. I'd say that means you're pretty important to him, wouldn't you?'

'I'd say so,' Weaver affirmed. 'Only person I've got on fast dial is my dear old mum.'

'Surprised you've got a mother,' Radcliffe sneered. It didn't quite come off. 'OK, so I asked them to have a look for Julie on behalf of her folks. Look on it as additional manpower. You lot are always screaming you're understaffed. No law against it. What you holding them on anyway?'

'Threatening behaviour,' Weaver told him. 'Not a nice man, your Mr Johnson.'

'Hard to get the staff. Is that all? You can go now if it is.'

'When we're ready, Charlie,' Weaver told him. 'You see, me and Morantz, we got talking in the car coming over here and we started wondering. Why did your Mr Johnson try to run away if all he and his colleague

315

were doing was asking questions?'

'How the hell should I know?'

'You employed him. Presumably you know what makes him tick?'

'You see,' Morantz picked up, 'what we thought is, your Mr Johnson and maybe your Mr Priest, they were giving the impression they were something that they're not. Friend of Miss Wise, maybe or even...'

'Horror of horrors, Guv...'

'Police officers. And impersonating a police officer is a serious offence, Charlie. I'm sure you're aware of that after that little fiasco with Joe Crowther.'

'Joe Crowther's nothing to do with me. My brother was daft enough to give him a job, that's all.'

'That's not what Mr Crowther says. He reckons you were using him to extract information from a Mr Phil Jones.'

'But you already know all this, don't you?' Morantz asked. 'Oh, you might be interested to know, we've applied for an extension on Mr Crowther. We'd like to keep him with us a bit longer. Ask him a few more questions.'

'And our colleagues up north will be having a pleasant chat to your other little helpers,' Weaver added. 'We'll be sure to let you know the outcome. On both counts.'

'Do that,' Radcliffe said. 'I look forward to you coming up with a great fat zero. Now, if you'd like to find yourselves out. The door's through there.'

'I think he wants us to go,' Weaver said. 'And not even the offer of refreshments.'

Morantz heaved himself out of the deep armchair and stretched. 'Better get on then,' he said. 'Nice seeing you again, Charlie. Don't think of going anywhere, will you?'

Radcliffe ignored them. He waited until the front door had closed and Brian Henshaw checked on their departure before he spoke.

'Prats,' he said. 'I've got nothing but bloody idiots working for me.' He glanced at Brian and puffed out his cheeks, then sighed deeply 'No offence. I sometimes think you and San are the only effective people I've got.'

'And we're expendable,' Henshaw commented quietly.

Radcliffe looked at him, his gaze sceptical and slightly accusing. 'Just so long as you both remember that,' he said.

Two calls came through as they were driving away. The first was from the mobile phone company. 'We've narrowed it to the North Somerset coastline, somewhere west of Bridgewater,' he was told. 'We're working on it, but there's a problem in that neck of the woods.'

'Oh?'

'The network's controlled by three different companies. We're all co-operating, but depending on where exactly he was when he received that call, it could have been routed a couple of different ways. There's all hills and hollows down there, it's not easy to get a signal in some places, so we figure he must have been up high. Our best guess is on the cliffs somewhere between Hinckley Point and Lynmouth, but that's quite a stretch. Like I say, we're working on it.'

'Thanks,' Weaver told him. 'Get back to me as soon as.'

'Useful?' Morantz wanted to know.

'Somerset. Somewhere near Bridgewater, they reckon. It's a start.'

Morantz nodded. 'Long way from Yorkshire.'

'At least he had *some* sense. Or Julie did.' He frowned. 'But why there? It's not the kind of place you'd choose at random. There's got to be a reason.'

'And if there's a reason there's a chance Radcliffe will figure it out.'

Weaver nodded. 'Just hope we're ahead of him,' he said.

The second call was about Sam Warner. His parents had rung in to say he was back from the field trip and come round to get his washing done. They'd talked to him and he'd reluctantly admitted that he'd kept the hard drive from Radcliffe's computer.

Sam Warner looked nervously at the two policemen and Weaver tried to be reassuring. 'We're not here to accuse you of anything,' he said. 'But your employer's in deep trouble and, basically, we want to make sure he stays there.'

Sam looked confused. He thought he was the one up to his neck in it.

'I don't want to get Mr Radcliffe into trouble,' he protested. 'He's been all right. I like the work and he pays well. He just asked me to do some bits of work for him and paid me double time. It was a weekend you see.'

'What kind of work, Sam?'

Sam hesitated and then, his father sitting across the table, prompting with a look, he explained about the messages Sandra said she'd got on her machine and how he'd fixed them up with a firewall and anti virus stuff. 'Then Mr Radcliffe said the machine had failed and someone told him it was the hard drive.' He shrugged. 'I offered to try and fix it for him, but he said, just replace it. Gave me the money and asked me to go and get what he needed, then I took the old one out and fitted the new one. He said to get rid of the old one, but well...'

'You wanted to keep it? See if it really was knackered or if you could use it?'

'No! No. Oh, it crossed my mind. I mean, they don't often fail catastrophically, like he

319

thought it had. I thought it was someone trying it on, you know, trying to get him to spend money he needn't have spent. I don't like seeing people getting ripped off, that's all.'

'If Sam says that's how it was, then it was,' his father supported.

'I'm not doubting you,' Weaver told him. 'Sam, why did you keep it and does Radcliffe know you have?'

He shrugged. 'I shouldn't think so. He told me to bin it. The dustmen were due the following morning, so he'd think it was gone, I guess. I had the packaging from the new drive and all that stuff to put in and he saw me do that. I guess he'd have thought I put the drive in as well.' He looked momentarily embarrassed. 'I had this idea, see. Thought if I fixed the disk, maybe recovered the data, he'd be pleased. There's always stuff to do on the technical side. Sandra – Mrs Porter was always asking me. I thought, if I did a good job, they'd take me on as sort of technical support as well as the other work I do.'

'Where's the disk now?'

'Upstairs. I live in halls at Uni, but I keep most of my stuff here, and I've still got my room.'

'Can you show me? Sam, have you had a look at it yet?'

He shook his head. 'No, I was off on the

field trip the following day. I didn't have time. I was planning to do it today and then Mum told me you'd been here and wanted to know about it. I can set it up in my machine for you to see, if you like?'

Weaver nodded. 'Do that,' he said.

Sam removed his own hard drive, put the new one in a cassette and slid it home. A few key strokes later and he was frowning in puzzlement. 'There's nothing wrong with it. Look, all the files intact, everything.'

'And you're sure this is Radcliffe's disk?'

'Of course. Look, there's a file with his name on it and there's Sandra's correspondence file.'

'Sam, would you be willing to testify in court? Only that you took the disk and that it definitely belonged to Mr Radcliffe.'

He shook his head doubtfully. 'That would make me a thief.'

'In law,' Moratz told him, 'it's stealing only if your purpose is to permanently deprive. That wasn't your intent, was it Sam? You were intending a good deed.'

He nodded. 'I'm still not sure about this. Look, you said Mr Radcliffe was in trouble. What kind of trouble?'

Weaver hesitated, then he said, 'the shit will hit the rotating thing soon enough. You recall a couple of weeks back a police Sergeant was found murdered?'

Sam nodded.

'We know Radcliffe was responsible, Sam. You might just have helped us prove it.'

Things had looked bleak for Charlie Radcliffe. He'd discussed events at length with Brian Henshaw, but they failed to coalesce into a solution.

Then Sandra came home and put a different spin on the day.

'I know where they are.'

'What? How?'

'You got a road map?'

It took her a few minutes to find what she was looking for. A tiny spot on the coastline. 'There,' she said triumphantly.

'Kilve? What the hell's that?'

'It's a village. God's sake, Charlie, don't be so obtuse. Julie's aunt's friend had a grandmother. She lived there. After she died and Julie's aunt's friend inherited, she kept it on as a holiday place. She lets it out from time to time, just to keep up with maintenance and expenses and such, but mostly she just keeps it for friends and family and she let Julie stay there once.'

'So?'

'So, she was always talking about going back sometime. Taking the kid with her. Look, it's out of the way and there's no one in it this time of year. Have you got any better ideas?' She looked from one man to

322

the other. 'Have your goons up in Yorkshire come up with anything?'

Radcliffe snorted contemptuously. 'Two of them got bloody arrested and Colin and Julie have definitely gone.'

'How did you find out about this?' Brian asked. 'If her mum thinks she went there, how come she hasn't told the police?'

'I told you before, the mam's a dead loss, but the auntie, we've become good pals. She's a nice woman. Anyway, it didn't come up when we were talking about Julie. Not directly anyway. We were talking about holidays and how neither of us liked it too quiet. When she mentioned this Kilve and then that Julie had been there, it all kind of clicked. She doesn't know what she's told me, Brian. You needn't worry on that score. They're all convinced she's gone north, seeing as we've spent so much time telling them about sightings and such up there.'

Radcliffe nodded. 'May as well give it a go,' he said. 'It's the best we've got.'

'You going to tell Billy James about this?' Brian asked.

'Billy James? Why should you tell him?' Sandra wanted to know.

'He paid me a visit this morning. In person.'

Sandra winced and then looked worried. 'That's bad, Charlie.'

'Bloody hell, woman. I don't need you

telling me that.'

He took a deep breath and apologised. 'Not been the best of days.'

'Well,' she shrugged, not feeling that he had been complimentary enough on her discovery. 'Maybe what I found will turn it around for us.'

'Maybe,' Radcliffe nodded. 'And as far as James is concerned, when we can tell him we've cleaned up our own mess, then I'll be in touch. Not before then. Now, clear off, the pair of you. I've got some calls to make.'

Brian Henshaw frowned and seemed about to protest, then thought better of it and stalked out. Sandra took a little longer to obey. She stood at the door and looked back at her boss, her expression confused and slightly hurt as though she was suddenly observing a stranger and didn't like what she could see.

35

John was not sure what time it was. He'd had trouble sleeping and the last time he'd looked at the clock it had been one in the morning. He didn't think he'd slept for long.

What had woken him was a faint sound from downstairs. A scraping, maybe, though now he strained to hear, there was nothing.

Awkwardly, he sat up and looked around, groping for the water and painkillers on the bedside table. He took two, drank a few swallows of water and then froze. His bedroom door was slowly opening.

John tried to examine his options. There was nothing in reach that he could use as a weapon and he didn't give much for his chances anyway. His right arm strapped tightly against his body, he didn't move so fast right now.

A shadow slipped through the door first. The landing window was just opposite John's bedroom door and it was un-curtained with a streetlight just outside. The shadow was followed by a tall, heavily built man, whose outline John felt was vaguely familiar.

'Oh,' it said. 'You're awake.'

'I am now. Martyn?' Yes, definitely Martyn, the doorkeeper at James's place. The man who'd re-dressed his arm. 'What the hell are you doing here?'

'Things are moving,' he said. 'OK if I switch on the light? Billy sent me to fetch you.'

The light flicked on half blinding John. Martyn blinked once, but otherwise seemed unaffected. He was dressed in black, John noted. Sweater, jeans, dark trainers. Black gloves and a hood stuck through his belt. He saw John looking and grinned. 'He said I should be discreet.'

John almost laughed. Felt he was verging on the edge of hysteria. 'What's happening?' he asked.

'We had word that Radcliffe was about to move. Mr James thought we should tag along. You need help getting dressed?'

John began to wriggle out of his pyjamas. He pointed to the clothes he'd discarded. Some on the chair others fallen on the floor. 'You know we tracked them to the West Country?'

Martyn nodded. 'Radcliffe's narrowed it further. Little place on the coast.'

'I should call Weaver.'

Martyn shook his head. 'Billy says you can call your boss after. He doesn't want to be falling over outsiders.'

'Outsiders?' Did that mean John was an insider? He wasn't sure how that made him feel.

Martyn was remarkably efficient when it came to helping him dress. He wondered how many times the man had helped in similar tasks, dealing with the walking wounded. James was known for his dislike of guns, but that didn't mean he was against their ... how had he once put it? Appropriate use. John tried to place where and when he'd heard Billy say that, and to whom, but the memory, half woken, wouldn't stretch and rouse sufficiently for him to claim it.

He pocketed his wallet and the bottle of painkillers – you want more of those, I've another bottle in the car – allowed Martyn to tie his shoes – I have an armed killer tying my shoe laces – and switched off the light before following him downstairs.

The lock on the front door had been replaced the day before and they went out quietly. 'You come in this way?'

'Sure. Easy.'

John winced. He felt like asking the other man if he knew how much the new lock had cost and how many assurances of safety he'd been given. He didn't bother. Martyn, he figured, would probably know down to the last penny. He made a wry mental note to ask the big guy for his recommendations when this was over. Maybe get him round to fix it up.

The car was black, with tinted windows. A Rover, John thought, though in the dark he wasn't certain. He was ushered into the back seat, made comfortable before Martyn got in beside the driver. The engine was already running, but purring so softly it barely disturbed the peace of the sleeping cul-de-sac. He wondered if he should tell them that Weaver would come looking should he not be at home in the morning. That he should insist on letting his boss know what the hell was going on, but, somehow, he didn't think they'd care. He was Billy James's guest in this little operation and, wherever and what- ever the outcome, he was, quite literally, along for the ride.

36

Seven o'clock on a November morning and a storm was raging, buffeting the heavy car. The car park, a hundred or so yards from the beach, was in a slight dip and surrounded by trees, though they failed to act as much of a windbreak and the gale funnelled down the two openings that led from the car park along marked paths down to the beach. The rain had ceased for a brief while, but that was little compensation. Rain still blew from saturated trees and splatted against the windscreen. Twigs and even quite substantial branches rained down upon them and Charlie Radcliffe was sick of counting the cost of his ruined paintwork.

Countryside? You could bloody keep it.

The faint sound of an engine attracted him and he lowered his window – the only way he could see more than a hand's breadth anywhere, and peered through the murk as the two other cars pulled up close by. He could just make out the silhouettes of figures inside. He'd sat here for the best part of an hour with only Brian and the wind and some crap on the radio for company, the music losing its battle against the attack of debris and the howling of the gale. A wet gust blew against his face and he pressed the button, rolled the window closed, grateful that in this model the heater was independent of the engine. Now they were all here, he could get on with things. Charlie Radcliffe was not a man noted for his patience.

A few hundred yards further up the lane, on the grass in front of the ruined abbey, two other cars pulled in and cut their lights and engines. A fence and high hedge separated them from Radcliffe and his men.

'What now?' John wanted to know

'We wait for instructions from Mr James,' the driver told him.

'You feeling all right?' Martyn wanted to know. He had made the same inquiry a dozen times on their journey down. Such concern for his well being was not something John was used to. It made him oddly uneasy.

'Where's Billy? Is he in the other car?'

'Just sit tight,' Martyn told him. He opened his door and slid out.

'Where's he going?'

The driver shrugged. 'Find out what's going on I suppose. I only drive the car.'

Reluctantly, John sat back and prepared to

wait. He wasn't even sure where this cottage was, or where they were in relation to it. 'Someone ought to go and warn them,' John said urgently.

'I think the plan is you'll be the one to do that, once we know exactly where they are and we won't know that until Radcliffe makes a move. In the meantime, you running around like a lemming would be as much use as pissing on a fire right now, so sit still until we get the all clear.'

John closed his eyes and shifted position, trying to ease his shoulder. Pain seemed to lock his ribs and made it difficult to breathe. He fumbled in his pocket for the tablets. It had been four hours or so since the last, hadn't it?

'Here,' the driver opened the glove box and passed him a bottle of water.

'Thanks.'

'Welcome, we're short of nothing we've got.'

John stared at him in the rear-view. That was something his mother used to say. He'd not heard it in years. Somehow, it fitted with the driver's use of mixed metaphors. He turned to stare out at the darkness, hoping for a glimpse of light that might herald a bright dawn, but there was only the grey of slowly lifting dark and then the rain began to fall again.

At seven fifteen Julie came downstairs. She wasn't used to sleeping in and neither was Ian. As she'd come out of her room, she'd heard him chatting to Colin and wondered if he minded being shanghaied so early in the morning. Yesterday had been the same, she'd taken them tea, finding Ian perched on the end of the bed with his feet under the quilt describing every blow and turn of the game he was playing to a half awake Colin. They'd continued to chat through breakfast, discussing the various merits of games and consoles and promising themselves the chance to 'thrash' one another on two player games when they got back home.

Ian had been amazing, she thought.

So accepting and so mature. But she was desperate for it all to be over.

The landing light was on a dimmer, low, it acted as a nightlight for anyone going to the bathroom. The kitchen light was at the foot of the stairs. She'd just reached to put it on when she saw them, or rather sensed a fractional movement that told her they were there; someone hiding in the doorway to the living room, another standing behind the wall that separated the kitchen from the stairs. They moved as she reached for the light and Julie only just had the time to scream.

She heard movement from upstairs, Colin's shout and Ian yelling 'Mum'.

'Run,' she managed as the first man

331

grabbed her arm. He held a gun and it was pointing at her head. In that moment, Julie was convinced that she was going to die and, that being a certainty, all that mattered was that Colin protect her son.

'Run!' she yelled. 'Get him out of here.' The man's hand shot out and the fist holding the gun made contact with her face. She stumbled, kept upright only by the fierce grip he had on her upper arm. The pain in her face was unreal. That he'd broken her nose, registered somewhere in her brain before he hit out again. Her legs went from under her that time as the butt of the gun caught her temple and Julie went down. Dimly, as consciousness left, she heard the sharp retort as a shot was fired.

'Mum!' Ian was screaming hysterically. He leapt from the bed, reaching for the door. Colin hurled himself across and grabbed the child. Colin's jeans were on the floor at the foot of the bed and he pulled them on, trying to keep Ian from fleeing. 'We've got to get out of here. Get help.'

'But Mum!'

'I know.' He wrenched the door open. Sounds of struggle rose to them from below. Julie's sharp cry of pain.

'Mum!' then the sound of the shot froze them in their tracks. Ian stared at him and Colin stared back, suddenly unmanned.

The boy started towards the stairs and Colin recovered himself enough to pull him back. 'That way!'

He pushed the struggling child back towards his own room. It was at the back of the cottage and the kitchen extension would give them the one chance they had to get out.

Ian was fighting him. Colin, suddenly aware that seconds counted as they never had before in his life, grabbed him round the waist and half carried, half dragged him back into the other bedroom. A second shot. Ian wailed and Colin heard himself cry out. He grabbed the window catch and lifted Ian onto the window.

'She wanted me to get you out,' he told him. 'I'm going to do what she wanted Ian. Now go, let yourself down, then across the garden and run like hell.'

'What about you?'

Colin glanced back through the bedroom door. Only seconds had passed since the second shot. It just felt like an eternity. But now, he was sure he could hear footsteps on the stair.

'Don't leave me. Please.'

'Don't leave me as well.' The words were implicit in the boy's cries. Colin pushed him. 'Go. I'm coming after. Now go.'

Ian clambered out through the narrow window and dropped onto the roof below.

Colin followed, squeezing through. He lowered the boy down and had the satisfaction of seeing him take to his heels before he turned to let himself down too, stretching his arms fully before letting go and praying he would land all right.

The kitchen blinds were still drawn. He could see nothing through the window. As he ran, hoping the rain and the dark would swallow him, he heard a shout coming from the upstairs room, the words torn away by the gusting wind. The rain that beat upon his face and bare arms was bitterly cold.

Neither of them had anything on their feet. He slid in the mud and his soles were scraped and bruised by every root and stone. He barely recognised the pain.

Fear and darkness had separated them. Up ahead, he caught a movement, a small figure climbing over the garden fence and then fleeing into the trees beyond. Colin followed. The mounting death toll sounding in his mind like a listing of the damned. Moira, Alice and now Julie too.

The cold tightened his chest, making it impossible to cry, sobs crushed from him before they reached his throat. The rain soaked his face and only the heat, brief and quickly chilled, told him it was matched by tears.

'Ian!' He managed to shout the boy's name but the sound was killed by the roaring of the wind. 'Ian!' But there was no sign. Looking back, he could see the cottage lights through the trees. He was through them now, facing an open field and beyond that, the cliff top.

'Where would he go? Where? Ian!' He realised it in an instant. The only thing offering even the remotest shelter was the pill box on the headland. 'God, no. Ian, it isn't safe. God, no.' Perhaps safety was a relative thing.

He tried to get his bearings, the rising land telling him that the cliff was ahead. Rising land and fierceness of wind, blowing into him, straight off the winter sea.

The car door opened and Martyn stuck his head inside. He reached beneath the seat and pulled a green First Aid kit out, from beneath together with what looked like packs of extra dressings.

'What the hell's going on?' John asked, impatient for news.

'They've lost Colin and the boy, took off over the fields somewhere. Stay put. We don't want you getting shot again.'

'What? What about Julie?' but Martyn was gone taking his kit with him.

John got out of the car. 'Which way?' But Martyn didn't hear.

John stared after him, torn between following and trying to track Colin and the boy. He was already soaked, the rain hard enough to punch through his clothes. He ducked back into the car and grabbed his jacket. Struggled into it as he stumbled across the grass and onto the lane. Looking left there was a sign pointing to the sea. Right, a lighted cottage set back from the lane. That had to be the cottage. So, where would they have gone? It dawned on him that he could, as the driver said, go running about like a lemming or he could go and ask someone who might know a little more than he did. The sudden increase of light told him of the opening door and he saw Martyn go inside. Shivering with cold and something even colder inside, John trotted after him.

Charlie Radcliffe was alone in the car when the tap came at the window. He wound it down and someone reached in, unlocked and then opened the door.

'What the hell–?'

'Good morning, Charlie. I thought a little walk might be in order.' It was Billy James.

Somehow, in spite of the filthy weather, and the fact that his shoes and the hems of his trousers were caked in mud, he looked as dapper as ever. He held a large umbrella over his expensive coat and he'd slipped a bright pink rose into his buttonhole.

'Walk?' Radcliffe looked as him as though he passed for mad. 'What the hell are you

336

doing here? I mean ... I told you we'd clear this up ourselves.'

'I know what you said,' Billy told him. 'But I like to ensure these things are done to a certain standard. Umbrella?' he offered. 'It's an excellent design, has these straps, you see, tied down to the handle so it can't be blown inside out. I believe it's an American model.'

Dumbly, Radcliffe took the proffered umbrella. It was only then that he noted the man who handed it to him was Brian.

They walked, in the early morning, Billy James stepping out as though on a pleasant stroll, seemingly oblivious of the driving rain. Deep puddles had collected on the rough path and Radcliffe found himself skipping around them trying to keep the worst of the wet out of his shoes. Billy James seemed to have no such concerns. His expensive leather was soaked by now, but he ignored any discomfort and kept up a stream of jovial and irrelevant conversation as he led the way. Behind them strode Brian Henshaw and another man that Radcliffe didn't know. Neither said a word.

'I believe this is called the Pill,' Billy said as they came to the deep pool formed by the outfall of the stream. 'Or that might be the rocks out there, I really can't be sure. I rather like this place though.' He jerked his umbrella towards the rising cliff. 'I thought we'd walk up there. I'm told that on a clear day you can see Wales across the water. Do you like Wales, Radcliffe?'

'I've never been. What is all this?'

'You could call it a takeover bid, I suppose,' Billy told him 'or, what's that term. A hostile takeover. That's it. You see, Charlie, I don't like the careless way you've been running things. When I do business, I expect my dealings to be confidential, not available to any busy-body with a modem.'

'We've fixed all that,' Radcliffe argued. 'It's sorted. Colin Grainger can't have got very far and we've dealt with the girl.'

'Ah, the girl. You know, Charlie, she was never really our concern. She was a threat to you, not to me and only that because you acted impulsively. That policewoman had nothing she could use. You could have warned her off and, chances are, she'd have slunk away with her tail between her legs, too embarrassed to report it. You see, Charlie, you don't use force where mis-information would do and the details that Colin Grainger found could have been dismissed, if you hadn't drawn such attention to yourself.'

'I did what I had to do.'

'You acted without reason or finesse,' James said sharply. 'Colin Grainger is not a worldly man. He had no thought of black-mail or extortion or of making any kind of

338

profit from what he knew. No, for the likes of you and I, that makes him a fool, but there it is. What I admire about Mr Grainger and what will cause me to take no further action against him, is his loyalty, both to the memory of his dead wife and to the young woman you also wanted dead. Conscience may be a luxury the likes of me and thee can't well afford, but that doesn't mean I don't get a certain pleasure from seeing it in others. And loyalty, well, Charlie, I'm sure you know the value of that?' He looked meaningfully at Brian Henshaw.

'Anyway,' he went on. 'I really don't have to explain myself. I've taken on your business as a going concern. I don't plan any redundancies.'

Billy James turned and began to walk slowly back down the hill.

'What the hell did he mean by that?' Charlie demanded, but even as he said it he thought he knew.

'Sorry, Mr Radcliffe,' Brian told him, 'but as you reminded me, we're all expendable. This is, what you might call, a token of that loyalty Mr James was on about.'

The gun was silenced, Billy James barely caught the sound of it above the howling of the wind.

Colin had been right in his guess, the boy had crawled into the pill box. He moaned in fear when Colin found him, then clung to him as though he were the only sane thing left in the universe.

It was bitterly cold. They shivered in wet clothes, not daring to move much, Colin remembering how close to the edge the building was.

Ian was bleeding from scratches on his arms and feet. Colin could feel the stickiness against his hands as he held him close.

'The barbed wire,' Ian told him, his voice shaky. 'I got stuck. Colin. I'm scared.'

'I know.' He cuddled the boy, not knowing what to say to him. At first, neither of them mentioned Julie; she lay between them like a dead weight. To talk about what might have happened to her was to give up hope. But then, as though the silence had got too much for Ian, the boy burst out in a fit of rage. 'I'm going to kill them one day. I'm going to kill Radcliffe, stab him with a knife or buy a gun and shoot him dead. I'm going to...'

'Shush,' Colin whispered. 'You're not Ian, never. You're not. No, you're not.'

But the boy was shaking now, with anger as much as with the cold and Colin knew the pain he must be feeling. He remembered his own rage that night in Radcliffe's office and how clean and good it had felt, just for that short time. Also, how unutterably tainted he had felt after. He closed his eyes and tried to control the trembling in every muscle of his body, praying for the dawn to come.

The cottage kitchen was flooded with light. All turned as John opened the door. A gun pointed in his direction was waved down.

There was a dead man on the floor.

Julie Wise sat at the table, distressed and confused. Martyn was talking to her and cleaning blood from her face.

'Where did they go?'

'We don't know,' Martyn told him, 'but Julie thinks they must have used the back extension to get down.' He gestured toward large torches on the table. 'Soon as I've fixed her up we're going out.'

'You see to Julie,' John told him. 'You,' to the man with the gun leaning against the kitchen counter, 'with me.'

Martyn's look was sceptical. 'You'll get fifty yards,' he said.

John was inclined to agree with him, but Julie's tears and sobs had grown more urgent. 'Find them for me. Please, find my son.'

Martyn glanced from Julie across to John and shrugged. He bent, picking the dropped weapon from the floor, held it out towards John.

'I can't hit a barn door left handed,' he protested.

'Billy says different. Unless you've for-

341

gotten everything your dad taught you?'

John was stunned.

'Please, John.' Julie's eyes were filled with tears.

'We don't know who's out there,' Martyn added.

John Moore took the gun and in doing so, took back a part of himself he'd long abandoned.

Outside, the rain had eased a little and the wind dropped. It wasn't a lot of difference, but anything was welcome. The man beside him, whose name he still did not know, scanned the landscape as though looking for a sign. The beams of the torches illuminated the almost horizontal rain.

'They'll have to have gone down there, through that bit of wood,' John guessed. The other nodded, set off at a pace that John knew he'd not match for long. At the fence he halted, kicked it hard. A controlled sidekick, John noted with some admiration. The fence fell, John followed him through and into the wood, then to the open field on the other side.

'Now where?'

'Get up higher, we may see something. It's bloody freezing out here,' he commented. 'Julie reckons they didn't have time to get dressed.'

'At least it's getting lighter.' The first inklings of what passed for sunrise were appearing through the steady rain, a lightening of the sky, no more than that, but anything would help. They set off at the best pace they could manage, John on the point of telling him to go on ahead, but fearing that if he found Colin and Ian first, they'd panic and try to run again.

Let them be all right. Let it be OK. The gun felt heavy in his pocket. A small automatic pistol the like of which he'd not handled in more years than he wished to contemplate.

Colin didn't know how long they had crouched there. He could see Ian, faintly now in the grey light that seeped through the opening. Ian had stopped shivering and was crouched beside him, silent and far too still. Colin knew that cold and shock were a lethal combination and the boy had endured far too much of both. They had to get out and get out now. There was a farm not far away. He remembered seeing the house across the fields on their cliff top walks. Now it was lighter, they should be able to see their way. If they could make it there away from Radcliffe's men, they may be able to call someone. John or the local police. He'd failed to protect Julie, that was all he could think of and now he must look after her son. What Radcliffe might do to him was secondary.

Gently, he shook the boy, then harder as he failed to respond. 'Ian, wake up and look at me. Ian, we've got to move. Wake up now.'

The boy stirred and opened his eyes. Colin was horrified at how blank they were. But he moved at Colin's prompting, stiffly, awkwardly, but he tried to do as Colin urged.

And then the moment when Colin just knew it was all over. Movements outside of the pill box, and voices, faint but excited and a shadow blocking the light seeping in from outside.

Colin coiled himself ready for one last strike. There were two of them, at least, and he knew it was hopeless. Ian couldn't make a run for it even if he gave him the opportunity.

Then, just as he almost gave in to utter despair a familiar voice spoke his name.

'Colin,' John said. 'Are you both in there?'

37

John was close to collapse when they got back to the cottage. He heard Julie's joy as she greeted her son, watched Colin, dripping and miserable, being drawn into their embrace. Then dropped painfully into a chair while Martyn and Julie fussed around, getting blankets and running baths. Julie's face was a mess. The bruising from her nose was spreading across her face and one eye and temple were black and swollen.

Colin kept staring at her as though he was looking at a ghost, Ian saying over and over again, 'We thought they'd shot you. Thought you were dead.'

The dead man's body was missing from the kitchen floor.

Billy James sat enthroned on a kitchen chair, his overcoat draped across the back and his ornate walking stick lying on the table top. He watched proceedings with interest but said nothing. Finally, when he was alone in the room with John he said, 'When Julie and Colin are gone, I'll send the cleaners in. I hate leaving a mess.'

'Radcliffe?'

'Will be found, but not here. I've yet to decide whom I'll inconvenience with that particular puzzle.'

'So. What now?'

'You go back to your lives. What happens after that is up to you.' He paused. 'I understand just how unsettling this will be though, so no doubt there'll be some reassessment as regards your possible futures.'

'Which means?'

'Whatever you want it to mean.'

'You can't hope to cover this up,' John told

him. 'Julie saw Moira on the night she died...'

'And Charlie Radcliffe has paid.'

'Colin still has the evidence. My boss will still investigate.'

'Which is as it should be. I understand, from a message he left on your answerphone, that they've recovered the hard drive Charlie had removed from his computer.' He noted John's shocked look and said, 'I had someone posted at your home in case anything needed passing on.

'I've weathered far worse storms, John. But you're wrong on one score. Julie told me that Colin posted his information to one of the tabloids. *The News of the World*. I believe. Their story should sell at a fair profit, I'd have thought.'

'You're happy with that?' John was incredulous.

'I've told Julie I'll make sure my lawyers get in touch. I think they'll need legal advice. Neither of them are terribly savvy when it comes to money, I don't think. Look, John, sometimes the best place to hide unpleasantness is in plain sight. That way everyone feels justified and moral for a while and then it's all forgotten. Once you try to bury things,' he shrugged, 'then you end up with people creating their own versions of events and, frankly, invention is often far worse than a few facts and has a far longer lifespan. Personally, I don't care what comes out. I've got adequate advisors and the figures Charlie Radcliffe recorded mean very little with nothing to back them up. I like to gamble and I sometimes play for high stakes. The rest is mere speculation.'

He stood up and donned his coat. 'I'll be taking over Charlie's business interests,' he said. 'The papers, it seems, were signed some time ago. Charlie must have been planning his retirement. A place in the sun. It's a pity he couldn't manage that.'

John didn't know want to say. 'All this was for nothing,' he said. 'Moira's death, Alice, the hell Julie and Colin and young Ian have been through. Wasted, all of it.'

Billy James regarded him with oddly compassionate eyes. 'Moira's death and that other young woman's murder should not have happened. Casualties of war, you might say, but no less painful for that and indeed, more painful because they were so avoidable. As for the others, I think it will turn out all right for them. Colin will make a good stepfather. Every bit as good as yours, if a little less, shall we say, conventional. I'm leaving Martyn to make sure you're all patched up, he can drive home in the second car.' He patted John's good shoulder. 'Get some rest,' he said, 'then, maybe consider a career change or at least another transfer.'

Julie came back into the kitchen and stood

shyly in the doorway. Billy James smiled across at her.

'Everything all right?'

She nodded. 'Thanks, yeah. They're getting warm and dried out and Martyn reckons they'll both be fine.'

Billy James looked satisfied. 'That's good,' he said. 'Perhaps when you're up to it, you could give Inspector Moore here a lift home.' He smiled, slightly sadly, John thought and then added quietly. 'I may be wrong, but I don't think he's going our way.'

Acknowledgements

Books don't just happen and the writer – though spending long hours in solitary confinement – usually has other people who help them in the creative process, even if it's only in the vital provision of tea and chocolate.

Thanks are due to Bob Tanner, my agent, a man who has built an entire language from the one phrase, 'I see.' Wish I could pack so much nuance into so small a space.

Martyn Carey, who replied to the email which began 'I've just shot someone and...' with such grace and good advice.

For Julian, thanks for the technical info and just for being there, and Peter for surreal conversations – I now know which way up to plant an elephant.

I promise them both that the Nick Drake CDs will go away for at least a week or two, seeing as I've had him on auto repeat for ... probably the length of the book.

Finally, welcome to baby Jessica and much love to Rachel and to Rick. Always.